What's the Use of Wondering?

"This is a beautifully done, sweet, sexy, romantic, true love tale! Highly recommended to bring a smile to your face!"

—*Divine Magazine*

"…a sweet coming of age/transitioning to adulthood story."

—Jessie G Books

There Has to Be a Reason

"…a beautifully written story. Very realistic. Definitely a book I would recommend to others."

—Gay Book Reviews

"…I really enjoyed this. I had never read this author before but will definitely read more of her work."

—Night Owl Reviews

The Boy Next Door

"The story was unique and not something I've read over and over, which is refreshing!"

—Alpha Book Club

"I was completely captivated by this book."

—Inked Rainbow Reads

By Kate McMurray

Blind Items
The Boy Next Door
Devin December
Four Corners
Kindling Fire with Snow
Out in the Field
The Stars that Tremble • The Silence of the Stars
A Walk in the Dark
What There Is
When the Planets Align

DREAMSPUN DESIRES
The Greek Tycoon's Green Card Groom

ELITE ATHLETES
Here Comes the Flood
Stick the Landing
Race for Redemption

THE RAINBOW LEAGUE
The Windup
Thrown a Curve
The Long Slide Home

WMU
There Has to Be a Reason
What's the Use of Wondering

Published by Dreamspinner Press
www.dreamspinnerpress.com

KATE McMURRAY

RACE *for* REDEMPTION

Published by
DREAMSPINNER PRESS

5032 Capital Circle SW, Suite 2, PMB# 279,
Tallahassee, FL 32305-7886 USA
www.dreamspinnerpress.com

Mass Market Paperback ISBN: 978-1-64108-220-4
Trade Paperback ISBN: 978-1-64405-348-5
Digital ISBN: 978-1-64405-347-8
Library of Congress Control Number: 2020937735
Mass Market Paperback published January 2021
v. 1.0

Printed in the United States of America

This paper meets the requirements of
ANSI/NISO Z39.48-1992 (Permanence of Paper).

KATE McMURRAY

RACE *for* REDEMPTION

CHAPTER ONE

Two years before the Olympics

JJ COULDN'T breathe.

He woke up the morning of the one-hundred-meter sprint World Championship feeling like someone had shoved wads of wet cotton balls up his nose.

That was really bad news.

Anything that might inhibit his breathing could be the difference between winning gold and being left out of the medals, but this wasn't a mere case of the sniffles. JJ sat up and felt it all hit him: feverish body aches, drippy nose, his throat feeling as if he'd swallowed a knife.

This was really, really bad news.

JJ had won six international races. He was in great condition and had been training his ass off all year. The thing he coveted most in the world was the title of World's Fastest Man, which was bestowed on the winner of the one-hundred-meter sprint each year. Yesterday he'd been gunning for the world record. Today he had had a cold.

After a long, hot shower, JJ assessed that yes, some virus had taken up residence in his body. He texted Marcus, his coach, then headed for the stadium. This fucking virus would probably keep him from the podium, but he'd hate himself if he didn't still try.

When JJ walked into the locker room at London Stadium, Franco Greer, a friend and one of the other Americans who had qualified for the gold medal final the day before, stood waiting near JJ's locker. "Marcus said you had a cold."

"Yeah, feels that way." And boy did it. His head felt so foggy, it was as if he were floating out of his body. All he really wanted to do was lie on the bench in front of his locker and sleep there for three days.

"I have some cold medicine. You want some?" Franco held out his hand; two white pills lay on his palm.

JJ reached for them and then withdrew his hand, thinking better of it. "This gonna get me in trouble with the drug testers?"

"Nah. These have that other decongestant in it—not the stimulant one. They don't work as well, but they're better than nothing, right?"

"Yeah." JJ hesitated before taking the pills from Franco, knowing it wasn't smart to take something if he didn't know what was in it. But Franco was his teammate and his friend. He'd never given JJ any reason not to trust him. And if JJ could put his cold on hold until after the race, he wanted to.

So he took the pills. He walked over to a refrigerator at the end of his row of lockers and grabbed a

Gatorade. He swallowed both pills. Then he found a massage table and lay on it while he waited for the medicine to kick in.

He could breathe again, mostly, by the time his race started an hour later. The gold medal final had three Americans, two Jamaicans—including the reigning world champion and world record holder—a teenager from Kenya, a white guy from the UK, and a Canadian sprinter who came in second in this race a lot. The Jamaican champion was thirty-two years old now and past his prime, and there were unsubstantiated doping rumors swirling around the team, so JJ felt like this race was his… if he was healthy.

All he could do was run his heart out.

He tied the laces on his neon green sneakers, then undid the laces and tied them again. He'd painted his nails the same color as the shoes, but now he was regretting that choice. Neon green wasn't really a color associated with luck, was it? Suddenly it looked just like snot, or was that the cold medicine talking? JJ suppressed a groan, and he felt tired and gross instead of flashy and ready to race.

"On your marks."

JJ got himself into the blocks, kissed the little gold pendant his mother gave him, and carefully placed his fingers behind the starting line.

"Get set."

At the gun, JJ leaped off the blocks and pumped his legs as hard as he could, running with everything he had. The other runners stayed very close, and really, any of these guys could run a hundred meters in less than ten seconds and therefore had a shot at this medal. JJ could see the yellow jerseys of the Jamaicans on either side of him and felt new determination to beat them. His lungs burned, his throat scratched, but he pushed through all that. Adrenaline coursed through him, powering him further, and the roar of the crowd motivated him too, and he felt a burst of energy.

He could do this… he could do this… he could do this.

His whole body screamed, his legs and his lungs straining from this burst of energy, less than ten seconds of pushing his body as far as it would go.

He ducked at the finish line, hoping to get his nose ahead before anyone else, but he realized suddenly that he had crossed the finish line alone, followed a beat later by the rest of the field.

He'd… won.

He'd won!

He looked up at the scoreboard and saw his name, Jason Jones Jr., and the time 9.84 seconds. Not a world record, but fast enough to win the World Championship, despite his cold. Marcus ran out onto the field and handed him an American flag, so JJ raised it, still feeling dazed. He'd done it. Holy shit, *he'd done it*! So much joy coursed through his veins that it needed an outlet, so he yelled at the sky. Marcus yelled too and slapped him on the back.

JJ was the fastest man alive.

And then he dropped onto the track, utterly spent.

Jones Caught Doping, Medal Rescinded

LONDON, ENGLAND, May 21—American sprinter Jason Jones Jr. has tested positive for a banned substance at the recent World Championship, according to World Athletics (formerly the IAAF), the governing

> body that oversees all track and field competitions worldwide.
>
> Jones was found to have taken a banned stimulant, according to officials from World Athletics and the World Anti-Doping Agency, who administered tests at the recent World Championship in London.
>
> As a result of the positive test and World Athletics' no-tolerance policy for doping, Mr. Jones has been suspended from World Athletics events for six months and was asked to return the gold medal he won in the one-hundred-meter sprint final. Jones has filed an appeal, and a hearing is scheduled on September 9….

JJ SAT in a blandly decorated reception area outside of a conference room, slowly losing his mind.

He'd tested positive for pseudoephedrine, which the World Anti-Doping Agency banned because it was a stimulant. The only place it could have come from was the cold pills Franco had given him. Had Franco known the cold medicine had pseudoephedrine? Was it sabotage or an accident? Either way, JJ was furious.

He'd won that race on the power of his own body, even with a pretty bad cold. Said cold had kept him in bed for a week after he got home from Worlds. He didn't take performance-enhancing drugs. He knew "I love the sport too much" was a cliché, but it was true for him. Running was among the purest of sports, just the human body powering itself down a racetrack. It didn't require much in the way of special equipment, and athletes didn't need to have been training since the womb to be good at it. Running was raw, close to nature, one of the oldest sports on earth. JJ respected that. Took pride in it.

He would never try to enhance his performance with anything illegal, and he was deeply offended anyone would think he did. And yet here he was, his heart pounding as he paced up and down the length of the small reception area, waiting to march into a room and try to explain all that to a panel of strangers.

Marcus stood on the other side of the room. "You have to calm down."

"Calm down? Are you fucking kidding me? My future in this sport is on the line. They took my medal away. But I'm supposed to be calm?"

"Yes. You can't go off half-cocked in front of this panel. You have to be calm and reasonable."

JJ swallowed. Unfortunately Marcus was right. Yelling would not accomplish what he needed to do here.

The silence rang in JJ's ears as he tried to get his breathing under control. There were several long, uncomfortable moments when JJ tried to keep a lid on his rage at the situation he found himself in.

And then Marcus muttered, "Of all the things to get caught taking."

JJ grunted. "I didn't know. I had a cold."

Marcus stood and crossed the room. He stood close to JJ and whisper-hissed, "You want to play around with this stuff, you have to come to me."

"I don't—"

"I could get you on a regimen, you know. None of this namby-pamby over-the-counter shit. I've got a doctor on staff who understands what these things do to the human body. If you want to try it, we should do it right."

JJ balked. He couldn't believe what he'd just heard. "Are you kidding me right now?"

"You want to win?"

"Not like that."

Marcus rolled his eyes. "Your competitors are all doping, you know. Everyone does. You won't be able to compete if you don't."

JJ shook his head. "Uh, hello? Do you not hear what I'm saying? I had a cold so I took a couple of cold pills. Only I didn't know they contained pseudoephedrine. I wasn't trying anything."

"Sure. That's a great line, kid. Say it exactly like that to the committee."

JJ growled in frustration. "I won a gold medal running on my own power. World Athletics wants to take it back. That's the whole fucking reason I'm here right now. Remember? I don't need your fucking regimen to win races."

Marcus backed up and looked JJ up and down. "How many races do you think your principled stance will win you?"

Before JJ could answer, Tom McCoy, JJ's lawyer, buzzed into the room. "Sorry I'm late. They start yet?"

JJ shot Marcus what he hoped was a disdainful look before stepping away.

A few moments later a woman with mousy brown hair and wearing a sensible pantsuit stuck her head into the waiting room. "Mr. Jones? We're ready for you now."

They convened in the conference room. The officials from World Athletics sat in a row on the opposite side of the table from JJ, who was flanked by Marcus and McCoy. They sat primly and listened as JJ explained about the virus and the cold pills of unknown origin. JJ broke out in a cold sweat as he spoke and his voice shook a little. "I just wanted to breathe during my race. I took what my teammate offered. I didn't know the pills had pseudoephedrine in them."

McCoy took over then, putting verbal pressure on the World Athletics panel to exonerate JJ. They went back and forth for what felt like an hour, mostly hurling legalese at each other. JJ struggled to follow it, but he tried to keep his mind from wandering, because whenever it did, he managed to convince himself this one stupid incident spelled the end of his career. The panel asked Marcus questions, and he denied any knowledge of the incident.

JJ turned over what Marcus had said in the waiting room. He knew plenty of other runners were doping. He liked to think the American team was clean, but one of his teammates had been suspended the previous season after testing positive for anabolic steroids. JJ knew also, because he talked to other athletes, that there was a whole black market of drugs out there, stuff the World Anti-Doping Agency didn't know existed yet. Athletes were using it during practice but quitting long enough before competition for everything to work its way out of their systems. JJ also knew that shit ended careers early and made men impotent and had a lot of weird side effects. But some guys didn't care as long as the drugs made them stronger or faster. The goal was to win. The cost was immaterial.

And yet JJ had gotten busted for taking a couple of cold pills.

"So, you're saying it was inadvertent use," one of the World Athletics officials asked JJ.

JJ knew *inadvertent use* was the official term for using a banned substance without meaning to do it, and it was something that often got athletes off the hook.

Not that JJ was trying to…. He sighed. "Yes. That's exactly what I'm saying."

But athletes had been suspended for lesser offenses. JJ fretted and checked back out of the conversation as McCoy gave what was probably an eloquent speech about how JJ believed in the beauty of running and only wanted to win the right way and that he never would have taken anything to put his medal in jeopardy.

When JJ checked back in again, one of the officials was arguing about the medal, saying that he didn't like the precedent it set to excuse JJ with no penalty if he wasn't denying taking a stimulant to begin with. JJ tried to keep his anger in check, but the more this guy talked, the angrier JJ felt.

"You really expect us to believe that you were stupid enough to take some unlabeled pills without knowing what they were?" said the official.

That was when JJ lost it.

He shot to his feet. "Fine. You want the medal? Yes, I'm that stupid. I trusted my teammate, and that was my mistake." It took everything in his body not to drop an f-bomb. He took a deep breath and tried to get a handle on his emotions. As calmly as he could, he said, "I'm sorry. I genuinely am. If I have to surrender the medal to end my suspension, then I'll do it. The medal is not important so long as I can run again and have an opportunity to win another."

"JJ…," said McCoy.

The members of the panel looked at each other. "We need to consult," said the woman in the mousy suit. "Please wait outside."

JJ resumed pacing in the reception area, mulling over whether Franco had intentionally torpedoed his whole career. He wouldn't look at Marcus, not now that he knew Marcus was willing to hook his athletes up with a drug regimen. How many of JJ's training partners were doping? And how was it only JJ got caught?

Now he knew he was losing it. He was a corkboard and a ball of red yarn away from going full conspiracy theorist.

The mousy lady appeared again. "You can come back."

Everyone filed back into the room. JJ sat and closed his eyes for a long moment, wondering if this was how criminals felt before a jury delivered a verdict.

The mousy woman said, "The commission has ruled that the evidence indicates the consumption of the pseudoephedrine was accidental. The ruling stands on the championship medal, but we agree to lift your suspension, Mr. Jones, if you agree to regular drug testing."

JJ let out a breath. It felt like the best outcome he could have hoped for. He mourned the loss of his medal—he'd fucking earned that medal—but getting back on track, literally, was what he wanted most.

Marcus and McCoy both started to speak, but JJ held up his hands. "I'm fine with that."

"It was an accident," McCoy said. "Surely you can consider restoring the medal."

"We take doping very seriously," said another official. "We want to send a clear message that we run a clean operation here. Track and field must remain untainted by allegations of doping. Do we understand each other?"

JJ wanted to get out of there. He understood the theater of all this. An aggressive approach to doping violations gave the appearance that track was clean, even though the World Anti-Doping Agency had a dozen countries on its watch list. Track was hardly free of cheaters.

"It's fine, really," JJ said. He felt resigned. Underneath everything, he was still angry as hell that he'd been put in this position to begin with, but as long as he could run, well, he'd just have to win other medals.

McCoy pursed his lips for a second but said, "If you're okay with the ruling, then I guess we're done here."

On the way out of the building, McCoy rattled on about how they should do a press conference in which JJ defended himself, and JJ responded with "Yeah, fine, whatever." But his suspicions of Franco were plaguing him now. *Had* Franco lied about the pills having pseudoephedrine? Had he known? Had he done it on purpose? How would JJ ever trust anyone again?

When they got outside, before he walked off, McCoy shook JJ's hand and said he'd be in touch.

"You want a ride back to the hotel or…," said Marcus, pulling his keys out of his pocket.

JJ stared at his coach for a long moment.

"Nah, I'll get a cab. And Marcus? You're fired."

Chapter Two

Summer Olympic Games
Madrid, Spain
Day 8

JJ WANTED to sleep through the rest of the flight, but Tamika Brown, his coach of about a year, was trying to get him to visualize his race. Like JJ, Tamika was black and a LA native, and JJ was grateful to have found her after he'd fired Marcus. She was a former gold-medal sprinter, sharp as a tack, and excelled at strategizing before big events. JJ just didn't see why it was necessary to strategize *right now*.

"I heard from a buddy of mine who's already in Spain that the brand-new track at the Olympic Stadium has got more bounce than the track at USC," said Tamika. "I've got us some practice time first thing tomorrow, but really early. We have to clear out before the races begin. Which is why we should have flown out earlier, by the way. Some of these runners have had the whole last week to get used to the track."

"I had to work," said JJ. Because yeah, once he'd been cleared of the doping charges, the endorsement money had started coming in again, but JJ didn't want to count on it. So he tended bar at a club in West Hollywood to pay the bills.

"There's a practice track under the stadium, but the conditions won't be exactly the same, and—"

"Tamika. It's fine. A race is a race."

"I realize that, but you'll be more confident if you get in some practice, and—"

"*Girl.*" JJ meant it as a warning. Tamika was an anxious flyer, and she was apparently projecting that onto JJ's races—not one of her more endearing qualities. This was a long-ass flight; it would be longer if she didn't calm the hell down.

"Sorry. I wish Grady were here. But he flew out a week ago. That hurdler he works with wanted to be in Madrid for the Opening Ceremony. So Grady decided to fly out with him."

JJ leaned back and closed his eyes. "The really tall white kid, right? What's his name? Barton?"

"Brandon. Yeah. Have you met him?"

"In passing. I don't think we've ever had a conversation that lasted longer than eight seconds."

The plane bobbed with turbulence. JJ kept his eyes closed, but Tamika sat close enough to him that he could feel her tense up. To distract her, he said, "I'm sorry for depriving you from your husband for a few days, but you could have flown out with him, you know."

"And miss training with you right before the Olympics?"

"I'm ready."

Tamika blew out a breath. "I know. I'm sorry. Maybe we should talk about something else."

JJ sighed heavily. He'd worked the night before and had come very close to taking home a young fellow who'd spent the night flirting with him and buying martinis. But he'd thought better of it because he had to fly today. Still, he'd gotten home around 3:00 a.m. and had slept a whole four hours before he had to get up to catch this very flight. He was exhausted and just wanted to sleep.

"I did talk to Grady a few days ago. He warned me that Madrid is crawling with anti-doping officials. You should expect to be tested frequently. And because of the… incident, they're going to want to do blood tests on you."

"It's fine," JJ said, although he resented that taking cold medicine had increased the amount of scrutiny on him. He'd been cleared of wrongdoing and had given up the medal anyway. What more did these people want?

"I know it's a pain."

"Good thing I'm not doping."

"Yeah. Grady said Marcus is also in Madrid."

JJ's eyes popped open. Why couldn't Tamika just let him sleep? "A few of his athletes made the US team."

"Between Marcus and the anti-doping brigade… it means there'll be a lot of distractions for you."

What JJ wanted to say was *You talking is distracting me*, but he said, "It's fine."

"I don't want anything to take away from your focus."

JJ closed his eyes again. "I just have to run fast."

"Come on, JJ. You know there's more to it than that."

"Mm-hmm."

JJ knew it was rude to ignore his coach, but he'd lost the ability to open his eyes again. He was too goddamned tired. Her voice grew increasingly distant. His brain switched to imagining getting blood tests whenever he walked into the Olympic Stadium, and then he drifted into some half-dream in which he was running from a man in a WADA T-shirt who wielded a giant syringe.

"JJ? You awake?"

"No."

Tamika sighed. "Fine. Sleep. I'll talk to you when we land."

FOR BRANDON, everything was a math problem.

Four hundred meters, or one trip around the track. Ten hurdles. An average of fourteen steps between each hurdle. Ideally Brandon would only step thirteen times between hurdles. An odd number of steps ensured that Brandon always started with the same lead leg. A perfect race was 153 steps, including the beginning and last sprint.

Each hurdle was thirty-six inches high. The first hurdle was forty-five meters from the start, and the hurdles were thirty-five meters apart.

Edwin Moses, arguably the best hurdler in history, ran 153-step races consistently, and Brandon aimed for that. In hurdles, technique mattered more than speed; stepping fewer times between hurdles automatically made the runner go faster, and hitting hurdles would slow the runner down.

He looked out at the track. It was the same maroon as the flag of the city of Madrid, and bright white stripes demarcated the lanes. Most of the Madrid Olympics imagery combined maroon, green, and blue, and a splashy mural ran along the short wall between the track and the stands. The city's coat of arms showed a black bear and a strawberry tree, which appeared in the mural, as did Francisco, the cartoonish bull mascot of the Madrid Games. It was a little cutesy for Brandon's taste, but the colors definitely popped.

Brandon became conscious of his coach, Grady, staring at him. Brandon blinked and turned his attention toward Grady, a bald, middle-aged black man who had been coaching champion athletes for two decades.

Grady held up his stopwatch. "You ready?"

Brandon looked back at the track and mentally pictured the number of steps he had to take.

"You really think you can engineer this?" asked Grady.

"I know I can."

Grady sighed. Brandon knew he could be odd at times. But he'd learned that applying his engineering and math skills to a race gave him an advantage. He'd intently studied video of the best hurdlers, counting their steps, emulating their techniques. Taking this kind of approach might have seemed odd to other runners, but if he won races, why did it matter?

"You ready?" Grady lifted his stopwatch.

Brandon got into the blocks. He tried to imagine the race environment, with runners on either side of him and the stands full of people. Other runners practiced around him; he could practice as much as he wanted for the next twenty minutes, as long as he stayed in Lane 5. Grady moved to stand just behind him. "Under forty-nine seconds," said Grady.

Brandon nodded and waited.

"Go!"

Brandon pushed off the blocks and ran like the devil himself was nipping at his heels. This wasn't a real race, so he counted his steps. He managed thirteen between most hurdles but did eleven between two. That didn't feel quite right. But once he got a groove going, it was easy. He rounded the last turn, leaped over his last hurdle, and made an all-out sprint toward Grady, who'd picked up the blocks and was jogging backward along Lane 5.

"51.08," Grady said as Brandon crossed the finish. "You're thinking too much."

"It's not the final," said Brandon.

"This is a fast track. You're not going to make the final unless you run the race in under forty-nine seconds. More like forty-seven is probably what it's going to take."

"I ran 47.10 at the Trials."

Grady rubbed his forehead. "I know." He glanced at his phone. "Oh, Tamika just landed."

"Do you need to go?"

"Nah. It will take her a little while to get her luggage and check into the hotel. And she flew in with JJ."

Brandon took the blocks back from Grady and set them back down behind the line. "JJ?"

"Yeah, that sprinter she's training. Have you not met him?"

"Not that I recall." Brandon fiddled with his setup because Grady had jostled something when he picked up the blocks.

"I guess you train on different days. He's the one who paints his nails before a race." At Brandon's shrug, Grady said, "Everyone says the kid is America's best hope to win the one-hundred meter. He's fast as lightning and he might just do it. But he's got a chip on his shoulder the size of a boulder."

Brandon tested the blocks. When he was satisfied he'd gotten them back to the way he liked them, he practiced popping off them. He tried to signal to Grady that he didn't care about this sprinter and was ready to run the race again. He opened his mouth to tell Grady he'd try not to think this time, but Grady was still looking at his phone.

"You know, you and JJ should meet. I bet you could learn a lot from each other."

Brandon kept himself from rolling his eyes. Now that he thought about it, he did recall this JJ. They'd been at the USC track, where Brandon trained, together a few times. JJ was a little older than Brandon's twenty-two. A few years, at least. He was more seasoned, at any rate. JJ was black and handsome and loud and cocky—at least that had been Brandon's first impression. He was one of those guys who was hot and he knew it. Brandon had dated someone like that freshman year. No, thank you.

"JJ trains hard, but he can have a short fuse."

Brandon glanced at Grady, who was somehow still talking while looking off into the distance.

"You're always so zen," Grady said. "Maybe that will rub off on him. And JJ is driven in a way you don't seem to be."

"I want to win," Brandon said.

"You used the same tone of voice some people use to order lunch. You just said, 'I want to win' the way I might say, 'I want a turkey sandwich.'"

So, okay, Brandon was not great about expressing his emotions. He knew this about himself; he'd never been demonstrative about his feelings. Most of the time he didn't really see the point. He *did* want to win, and he knew he could. He'd set an American record during the Trials. He was clearly doing something right. "Let me do it again. I won't count steps this time."

Grady raised an eyebrow. But he also picked up the stopwatch and said, "All right. Get in the blocks. Under forty-nine seconds this time."

Chapter Three

Day 9

Brandon roomed with a long jumper named Jamal he knew from USC. The USC track team had fielded quite a few athletes at these games, as well as a number of athletes like JJ, who used USC's state-of-the-art facilities to train. Brandon and Jamal had taken a few classes together, so Brandon felt okay rooming with him even though he wasn't super comfortable sharing a space with a guy he didn't know very well. Brandon wasn't comfortable sharing space with anyone; there was a reason he'd moved into his own apartment as soon as USC had let him leave the dorms.

So far things with Jamal had worked out, but Brandon woke up Sunday morning—the first official day of the track and field competition—to the sound of feminine giggles.

He cracked open one eye and saw that at least everyone was fully clothed. Jamal sat on his bed with a woman Brandon recognized as the middle-distance runner Jamal had been flirting with all week. With a grunt, Brandon sat up.

"Morning, sleepyhead," said Jamal.

"What time is it?"

"Six. Shara and I are going to breakfast before we have to be at the track. You have practice today?"

Brandon rubbed his eyes. "Of course."

"We'll go," said the woman. "See you later, Brandon."

Brandon waited until her giggles disappeared down the hall before he lugged himself out of bed. He knew where this was going. It would only be a matter of time before Jamal asked to have the room to himself for a bit. Some athletes had superstitions about sex and their sports, but Jamal didn't seem to be one of them.

Brandon wasn't either—he thought most superstition silly and irrational—but it wasn't like men were beating his door down.

After a shower, he swung by the cafeteria and grabbed some breakfast on the go before hopping on the shuttle bus to the stadium. He mulled over his morning. Shara being in his room bothered him. He didn't know her, and he didn't like strangers in his space. He understood intellectually that Jamal was trustworthy, and Shara probably was too, but he'd felt unsafe. Didn't Shara have a room they could go giggle and make out in?

He finished the breakfast burrito the chef in the cafeteria had made for him: egg whites, mushrooms, tomatoes, cheese, whole wheat wrap—all things allowed by the diet Grady had him on. Brandon missed not having every element of his life spelled out the way it had been since he'd started training for the Olympics. He liked a routine, sure, but sometimes he just wanted some extra bacon at breakfast.

So he already felt irritated by the time he'd changed and met Grady at the track. It was still so early that the air was dewy with what would become oppressive humidity once the sun rose higher. It wasn't too bad, though. Not as hot as it would be during race day. Which begged the question: Why did he have to be here so early? He understood that track events would be starting in a few hours and this track would be unavailable, but he'd gotten in plenty of practice on it. He could do his daily training on the practice track under the stadium. There weren't even hurdles set up on the main track, so he clearly wouldn't be doing practice runs.

Grady and Tamika were huddled together at the side of the track, looking like they were having the sort of intimate conversation one should not barge in on. Brandon hung back for a moment. He looked around and spotted JJ jogging around the track. It was definitely JJ; Brandon remembered him now.

JJ was a little short for a sprinter, but he was wiry and strong. He kept his hair cropped close and was currently sporting a scruffy beard. A gold chain around his neck glinted in the sunlight and stood out against his dark brown skin. He wore an old USA jersey and a pair of very short shorts as well as hot pink sneakers. As he jogged closer, Brandon saw that JJ had glittery black nail polish on his nails.

JJ waved as he jogged past Brandon.

A jolt went through Brandon. His face heated, and something fluttered in his stomach. JJ was attractive, obviously, but Brandon didn't often react this viscerally to good-looking men who casually jogged by him.

He shook his head, then took a deep breath and walked over toward Grady, who spotted him and took a step away from Tamika. Grady smiled. "So you *do* know JJ."

"Barely."

Tamika smiled. "Nice to see you, Brandon."

"Likewise."

Making small talk wasn't a particular strong suit of Brandon's either. He really wanted to get rolling with his warm-up, but he figured he should wait for Grady to give him instructions.

"Tamika and I were talking," said Grady. "I think you and JJ would do well to train together a little today."

Brandon rolled his eyes and started stretching, because he didn't have time to stand around chatting. "Why? We don't run in the same events."

"No, but each of you has something the other lacks."

Right. The drive. Brandon was plenty driven, he just didn't see what purpose being enthusiastic about it served. He had emotions, but he was not demonstrative about them, and he was generally pretty introverted and awkward. What did he even add to this equation? Was he supposed to calm JJ down? Brandon had no idea how to do that. Running and math, that was what Brandon knew. Besides, he liked working alone. If he'd wanted teammates, he would have played soccer. So if Grady expected him and JJ to become best friends and training partners suddenly, he was delusional.

"Two laps," Grady said, an unreadable expression on his face. "We'll talk more when you finish."

JJ DEFINITELY recognized Grady's hurdler now. White kid, twenty-one or twenty-two if he was a day, tall and thin, dark hair, cheeks that were always flushed, heavy-looking glasses. JJ watched Brandon jog around the track and noted the little strap that went around the back of his head to keep the glasses on his face.

So, Brandon was cute in a long, lanky way, even with the glasses.

JJ filed that away for later.

Brandon finished his lap and jogged up to where JJ stood with Tamika and Grady. He wondered if this suggestion to make JJ and Brandon training partners for a few days was some scheme their coaches, who were married to each other, had cooked up as a pretense to spend more time together after a week apart. He crossed his arms and waited for an explanation.

"Sprint drills," Tamika said. "We've got Lanes 7 and 8."

JJ glanced at Brandon, who returned his gaze with a skeptically raised eyebrow.

"So… no explanation, no discussion, just, 'we're training together, do sprint drills'?" asked JJ.

"You can run a hundred meters in less than ten seconds," said Grady. "Let's see if Brandon can too."

"Er…," Brandon said.

"Just do it," said Tamika.

JJ didn't really understand what was going on, but he took his starting block from Tamika and set it up in Lane 7, behind the start line for the one-hundred. Brandon set up a block right beside him. Grady had a stopwatch in his hand and held it up. So JJ got himself in the blocks. He adjusted his feet a couple of times but kept an eye on Brandon, who carefully placed his fingers behind the starting line.

"Ready!" Tamika shouted.

JJ rose up in the blocks.

"Go!"

JJ took off. Brandon kept pace with him for the first forty meters or so, but then he started to fall behind. JJ wasn't surprised by that; JJ was one of the best one-hundred-meter runners in the world and Brandon was a hurdler. He didn't have to all-out sprint in the same way. It was like they spoke the same language but had very different vocabulary sets.

But then, when JJ was about ten meters from the finish, he spotted Brandon in his peripheral vision again. JJ turned on the heat and ran for the end as hard as he could. He crossed the finish line ahead of Brandon, but not by a lot.

JJ and Brandon both stood panting and bent over a few meters from the end of the line. JJ jogged off to the side because another set of sprinters ran toward them down the tracks.

"No drive," Brandon wheezed.

"Huh?"

"Grady thinks I don't have the drive to win," Brandon said between pants. "That'll show him."

Grady jogged over then. "All right. JJ, you could have turned it up a little higher. I know you weren't putting a hundred into that. 9.88. Very good. Brandon, 10.2."

"Look at you," JJ said. "Faster than Jesse Owens."

Brandon tilted his head.

JJ smiled. "Jesse Owens ran the hundred in 10.3 seconds at the 1936 Olympics. That's sort of the standard we all measure ourselves against. Your time is not bad for a white guy."

Brandon took a deep breath and rubbed some sweat off his forehead. "All right."

Brandon knew as well as JJ did that the reason recent generations of sprinters had destroyed that particular record had a lot to do with the material used to make tracks and the kinds of grip modern running shoes offered. Owens had run on a much more slippery dirt track and required more control to keep from sliding all over. JJ suspected that if Owens had run on a modern track, he'd have outrun Usain Bolt.

"So what Brandon needs is a real challenger," said JJ.

"I'll have those during the actual races," said Brandon.

Tamika walked over and hooked her arm around Grady's. "And?"

Grady told her the times. She frowned. "Still a little slow."

JJ rolled his eyes. "I just ran a hundred meters in less than ten seconds and she thinks it's slow."

Grady glanced at Tamika, then looked between Brandon and JJ. "Neither of you is running to your potential yet. Maybe the competition itself will get you to kick into fourth gear, but in the meantime, I think we should focus on the psychological factors of these races. Both of you run fast. That's not enough at this level."

"I've done this dance before," JJ said, feeling a little resentful that Grady was telling him how to be. This was JJ's second Olympics. He'd made the one-hundred-meter final four years ago but finished in fourth, just out of the medals. However, the Jamaican runners who had completely dominated this event for the past decade had all retired, so it was a brand-new field. JJ had won a handful of World Cup medals since the

Incident two years ago and intended to win a medal here. He was saving fourth gear, as Grady put it, for the final.

Tamika pulled Grady out of earshot. They conferred with each other for a moment.

Brandon rocked on his heels. "Do you think they talk about us when they're at home at night?"

JJ chuckled. "Probably. Right now Tamika is probably reminding Grady that I don't like being told what to do by people who are not my coach, and even then…."

"They're just trying to help."

"Don't take their side. 'Go faster' is terrible coaching advice."

"I agree, but maybe it's possible for us to… push ourselves more. My practice times yesterday were all below what would have even made the finals at the last World Championship."

JJ crossed his arms. "I'm still getting used to the track," he muttered, although that wasn't strictly true. Because yeah, this was running fast, but there was some strategy to it too. He'd have to think about opponents, about when to turn on the gas and when to hold off, about how hard to push off his blocks, about how much time he needed to get acclimated to this stadium.

Grady and Tamika nodded together. They gave each other a quick peck and then walked back toward them, both looking determined, as though they'd decided something.

"Let's do it again," Tamika said, gesturing at Grady holding up the stopwatch. "Two hundred meters this time."

CHAPTER FOUR

BY THE time the day of training ended on the underground practice track, while the first race heats began in the stadium proper, Brandon's legs were so wobbly, it felt like his bones had melted. He wanted to go back to his room and sleep for three days.

He changed back into his street clothes in the locker room. As he tied his sneakers, JJ walked over.

"So, do you think there's anything to this theory that we'd be good influences on each other, or is it a pretense for Grady and Tamika to spend time together while they're in Madrid?"

Brandon shrugged. He had no idea. Although after running with JJ so much, Brandon had posted a personal best time on the hurdles. He couldn't figure out how the competition had factored into his hurdles equation. Likely, he was just worked up, a lot of adrenaline in his system pushing him forward. He'd broken through to some new level of exhaustion, so perhaps there was some endorphin-related euphoria powering him through his last few practice runs.

He tugged on his shoelaces. "If it helps us, does it matter?" Because JJ had posted some excellent times too.

"Guess not."

JJ hovered, so Brandon looked up at him from his seat on a bench. JJ stood in a well-worn USATF T-shirt and baggy gray sweatpants and had a backpack slung over his shoulder. In other words, he was ready to leave the stadium. Did he want something?

JJ leaned back against the lockers across from where Brandon sat. Brandon tried to give him a covert once-over. JJ had an athlete's body, naturally tight and powerful. Strong, but built for speed. Brandon had long been fascinated by the shapes of athletes' bodies. Swimmers, divers, gymnasts—they tended to have specific body types that seemed tailor-made for their sports. But runners sometimes came in different shapes and sizes. Sprinters could be stretched out and tall or more muscular and compact, and both types seemed able to break the ten-second barrier with enough practice and training. Brandon found that being tall helped him at the hurdles because he didn't have to push off as hard as some of his shorter competitors to get himself over the hurdle, but it wasn't a guarantee of anything.

JJ was somewhere in the middle of the pack in terms of height and musculature. Not beefy, the way a couple of the other American sprinters were. Brandon liked that, liked the lines of his body, liked that he was friendly and not intimidating.

He had a handsome face too. He could have used a shave, but his eyes were a striking light brown and he had long eyelashes, smooth skin, a square jaw. There was no denying that JJ was a very attractive man, which made Brandon's nerves spike. He could hold his own in a conversation, but he sometimes got tongue-tied around men he was attracted to.

JJ looked at his phone and then at Brandon. "In the spirit of influencing each other, you want to go get a drink or something? Grab dinner at America House before we head back to the dorm?"

Brandon was about to say no, because mostly he just wanted to sleep, but then his phone chirped. He looked at the screen. Jamal's name popped up above a text telling him not to come back to the room for the next hour. He wanted to get his swerve on.

And so it began.

"Yeah, all right," Brandon said. Because, well, he liked JJ. He pushed his nerves aside. It wasn't like anything would really happen here. JJ was way out of his league. A guy who seemed as casual and comfortable in his own body as JJ would never be interested in a guy as gawky and awkward as Brandon. But a guy had to eat, didn't he?

Brandon followed JJ out of the stadium. As they waited for the shuttle bus, JJ said, "So, if you train with Grady, you must live in California."

"I live in University Park."

"So right near USC, then?"

Brandon tilted his head. "Yeah, I'm a student there. I'm in my last year of a five-year engineering program."

"Wow, engineering." JJ slid a pair of sunglasses on his face. "I live in West Hollywood. The drive to USC for training is a nightmare, but I do it."

"I ride my bike to school most days."

JJ turned toward Brandon with a grin on his face, and Brandon regretted saying it immediately. Was he the biggest dweeb or what? There was no way a guy as hot—and cool—as JJ would ever even speak to Brandon if not for this proximity.

"So, what's your deal?" JJ asked. "Tamika said you're some kind of genius. Why the hurdles?"

Brandon shrugged, unsure how to answer. "I like running. My high school coach had me try a lot of things, and hurdles was my best event. Then I won a bunch of junior championships and got a track scholarship to USC."

"You didn't deny being a genius."

Brandon shrugged again. He didn't like talking about it… or drawing attention to himself in this way. "I don't know about that. I do well in school, but I've never had my IQ tested or anything. What does *genius* even mean?"

Brandon couldn't read JJ's face behind the sunglasses, but he felt the scrutiny anyway. Luckily, the bus pulled up then. The day's events were still going on as planned in the stadium, so the crowd waiting for the bus wasn't too bad. Everyone filed on, and Brandon followed JJ to a seat toward the back.

"So, Mr. Engineering, do you have a job, or do you just go to school and jump hurdles?"

"I work in the dean's office at the School of Engineering. It mostly involves answering the phone, but it pays the bills."

JJ nodded. "I'm not in school. I basically just run and tend bar."

"You must keep strange hours."

JJ laughed. "I do. I usually close. Last call is at two. So I get home around three, sleep until noon, then curse whoever designed the roads in LA on my drive to USC, train with Tamika until I gotta be at work at eight, and then the cycle repeats."

Brandon leaned back in his seat as the bus pulled out of the parking lot. He had a hundred questions, and they all felt rude. Had JJ gone to college? If so, why was he working in a bar? Did he want to be a professional runner? Was that a thing?

"Do you plan to keep running after you graduate?" JJ asked.

"Probably, but I don't see myself continuing to compete at this level."

"No?"

"I intend to get a job that doesn't leave me enough free time to train."

JJ slid his sunglasses off and nodded, as if that were the answer he expected. "If I could make a career of running, I would."

"Yeah?"

"Yeah. Only thing I was ever good at."

There was more there than Brandon could unpack, so he just nodded.

"So…," JJ said.

Brandon had JJ pegged as one of those people who found silence unnerving and needed to fill time with useless chitchat. Brandon could have sat in contented silence for the rest of the bus trip, but apparently they were doing some get-to-know-you thing. He turned toward JJ and tried to look interested.

JJ laughed softly. "You find me annoying."

"I don't." And in truth, he didn't. But he struggled to keep up conversation and felt awkward about it. "I'm sorry if I come across as rude. Small talk is not my forte."

"All right. Well, if I ask you a question you don't want to answer, feel free to tell me to shut up."

"I can do that." Brandon liked having permission to shut this down if JJ started pushing, and Brandon suspected that JJ *would* push him. He reasoned that if they were following their coaches' advice, they should get to know each other. So he would put up with JJ asking him things, but he had limits. There were some places he didn't want to let JJ near, especially anything related to sex.

Particularly not when JJ was sitting this close.

JJ had a lot of smooth unblemished skin that had a bit of a sheen to it, thanks to the humid day. One little drop of sweat had made its way from his hairline, down the side of his face, to the dark shadow of beard on his chin. Brandon wanted to know what it would be like to touch that beard, if it would be soft.

Being attracted to JJ was bound to make this whole thing even more awkward. Awesome.

"School and a job and jumping hurdles must not leave a lot of time for dating," JJ said as he glanced out the window, sounding casual.

And there it was. Brandon sighed. "Not really, no. But not because I have any principles about it or anything. I'm just…."

After a moment JJ said, "Just what?"

"We've met. You must have noticed. I'm nerdy and awkward. In order to get a date, you have to talk to strangers. I'm not very good at that."

JJ smiled, which surprised Brandon. "You're doing fine."

"I don't go out of my way to meet people, which limits my dating opportunities. And I'm even worse online, so the apps and stuff don't really work for me. Plus, I dunno…." Brandon let out a breath. He couldn't believe he was talking this much.

"What else is there, Brandon?"

Something about the way JJ said his name was oddly soothing. So Brandon said, "This is going to sound silly, but I tried that whole swipe left thing, and it gave me a lot of anxiety. I kept worrying that I'd meet someone at a bar and they'd take one look at me and be like, 'Oh, that dork? No.'"

JJ balked, a little line of confusion forming between his brows. "Really?"

"Maybe it's irrational." It didn't change his thought pattern, though. He'd put some good-faith efforts into being on dating apps, but always panicked when the guy on the other end said, "Hey, let's meet." He felt more comfortable meeting people face-to-face rather than online, which was probably uncommon for people as chronically awkward as Brandon. But he reasoned that at least if he met someone in person first, they could see the real package. Because Brandon knew his way around Photoshop and could augment a photo of himself to look reasonably attractive, and he couldn't deny that he was in excellent physical condition given that he was here at the Olympics. But once he got past the superficial with someone, what would they even talk about? Running and circuits were about all Brandon knew. The few guys he'd dated hadn't cared much about either of those things.

Brandon sighed audibly.

JJ gawked at him. "Girl. It's completely irrational. Have you looked in a mirror?"

"Even if someone found me attractive, we'd talk for five minutes before my awkwardness took over and I'd scare them off."

"You're not that awkward. You're talking to me fine, aren't you?"

"I guess."

And Brandon felt mostly okay talking to JJ, but in truth, he was still struggling and wanted to hide his face in the back of the seat in front of him to escape the fact that he'd been very careful with pronouns. Brandon was starting to trust JJ, who seemed friendly and genuine, but he didn't know JJ, and he was terrible at reading people.

JJ squinted at Brandon for a moment, but just as Brandon started to pray he'd spontaneously combust so all this would end, the bus pulled up to the stop at the Olympic Village.

"If I bought you a beer, would it loosen you up?"

Brandon stood and took a deep breath. "Only one way to find out."

JJ THOUGHT he had Brandon's number now. He was a hard-core introvert, the sort of guy who was more comfortable with books and math problems than other people. That was fine; JJ could work with that. And, well, he wanted to work with… or on… or just work it with Brandon. The fact that Brandon had no clue he was sexy and adorable was kind of a turn-on, in fact. Brandon thought others would think him an incurable dork not worth dating? JJ would show him otherwise.

But he needed to clarify a few things before he really went for it.

They walked toward the America House, the main gathering spot for athletes and their coaches, friends, and families. Except for the athletes, everyone was banned from the athlete dorms, so this was a popular postevent celebration spot. From the outside, it looked pretty crowded.

JJ glanced at Brandon, still trying to get a read on him, and asked, "But you're not, like, a virgin, are you?" He immediately regretted the question because it felt too personal and invasive.

Brandon tilted his head in confusion. "No. I've met a few people who don't seem to mind my dorkiness."

Brandon's frankness surprised JJ, but at least he wasn't offended. JJ smiled. "I don't mind your dorkiness."

"Oh."

The bar was packed. JJ looked around. He'd walked by the building that morning, but this was his first time inside. It wasn't vastly different from the America House at the previous Olympics; one of these existed in every Olympic Village, and many other countries had their own gathering spots. The interior here looked just like every sports bar he'd been to in the States, with lots of brass and wood paneling and big televisions everywhere showing various events. Random Olympics-related memorabilia was tacked up on the walls. JJ had done this rodeo four years before, so he knew a crowd like this probably meant an American athlete or team had won a final or something that day. The tables were mostly occupied, but there were two empty stools at the bar. JJ motioned for Brandon to follow him and then snagged those stools.

The bartender walked over. "What happened?" JJ asked.

"Women's gymnastics. Chelsea Mirakovitch, the tiny brunette over there? She won a medal in all four event finals. Best gymnast in the world."

JJ followed the bartender's gesture and took in a gaggle of petite women fussing over a brunette in a blue tracksuit with glittery trim. Her gold medals hung around her neck.

"American?" Brandon asked.

"From Texas."

JJ didn't care that much about gymnastics. He'd met a few gymnasts in his time running at the elite level, and he was in awe of their strength and conditioning, but he knew also that it took a certain type of athlete to be a gymnast, and JJ was not it. What JJ had always liked about track—or *athletics* as the international organizations all referred to it—was the low barrier to entry. Gymnasts needed access to equipment, and the elite ones began training at a very young age. JJ bet he could count the number of elite gyms—or pools, or places to train for any of the winter sports on skates or skis—on one hand, but all he needed access to for running was a hard surface and a decent pair of sneakers. He'd started sprinting on the blacktop behind his elementary school when he'd been a kid, and his shoes had been whatever had been on sale at the local department store.

Of course, things were different now. JJ had his own shoe line with a major sneaker company, not to put too fine a point on it, and they supplied all of his running shoes now. He had special lightweight shoes made specifically to fit his feet, and they had spikes on the soles meant to grip the track so he didn't slip as he ran. He ran on the state-of-the-art track at USC most days. So it wasn't like running when he'd been a kid, but he'd managed to get to this level without any special equipment. Running was pure that way. Just the human body powering itself.

He turned his attention back to the bartender and ordered a vodka soda. "What are you drinking?" he asked Brandon.

"I'll have a beer, I guess."

JJ had a hundred questions he wanted to ask Brandon, and for some reason Brandon's reluctance was more intriguing than a deterrence. Maybe the beer would loosen Brandon up. Or maybe it would give Brandon the courage to tell JJ to fuck off. As Brandon had said, there was only one way to find out.

JJ watched Brandon, who gazed at the TV over the bar. Maybe dating wasn't the best topic, but any athlete worth his salt could talk about his sport all day. "So, what's your secret? Tamika told me you have some kind of strategy for running the hurdles that gives you a competitive edge."

Brandon shrugged. "It's not really a secret. It's just math. I try to only take a certain number of steps between hurdles, which makes me a more efficient runner. Too many steps or too few will cause you to miss the hurdle. And obviously, the more steps you take, the longer it will take you to run the race. There's kind of an ideal ratio that I strive for."

JJ nodded. "Could you apply math to the one-hundred-meter sprint?"

Brandon took a sip of his beer and tilted his head as if he was considering the question. Yes, this was safe ground. Brandon understood this. "How many steps?" he asked.

"I don't know. I never counted."

Brandon pulled a phone from his pocket and swiped at the screen a few times. "Okay, it says here that when Usain Bolt ran the one-hundred in 9.63 seconds, he made forty-one steps, for a stride rate of 255 strides per minute, or…." He closed his eyes for a moment. "Four-ish… uh, four and a quarter strides per second. So your goal should be less than five steps per second."

JJ was particularly impressed that Brandon had done all that math in his head. "Wait, that's it? Five or fewer steps per second?"

Brandon shrugged. "I mean… yeah. That's how you run faster. It's a concrete goal that isn't just 'get from point A to point B as fast as possible.'"

JJ was skeptical, but he nodded. If he counted steps as he ran, it would slow him down. Brandon's approach was interesting, but it was the sort of thing he should have implemented at the start of the season, not right before the Olympics races.

He glanced at Brandon's glass. The beer was half gone. JJ opted for warm-up questions. "So engineering. What kind?"

Brandon gave JJ a shy smile. "Electrical."

"Sounds challenging."

"It is. That's why I basically only have time for school, work, and hurdles."

JJ leaned forward a little, determined to push through the door that had been opened for him. "But no dating."

For the briefest of moments, Brandon met JJ's gaze full-on, and that sent a sizzle up JJ's spine. Oh, yeah. He understood what was going on here. Probably better than Brandon did.

"No… dating," Brandon murmured.

"I don't date much either. When your dating pool is limited to whichever guys are left at the bar when you're closing up, it's slim pickings most nights."

That seemed to snag Brandon's interest. "Is it… do you work at a gay bar?"

JJ smiled. "I do." His sexuality was hardly a secret. He got press all the time for being a little too flashy when he ran a race. But he liked some bling, and he figured he was just one in a long line of American sprinters who had style on the track, like his hero Flo-Jo.

"Oh," said Brandon.

JJ read that as mild surprise, but not any disdain, so he asked, "These people who have overlooked your dorkiness in the past… they were men, yeah?"

"Yeah." Brandon's voice was low, practically a whisper.

"There's no shame in that, honey."

"I don't feel shame. I'm just used to… not talking about it, I guess."

JJ leaned back because he didn't want to make Brandon uncomfortable, although he noticed now that the beer glass was almost empty. "You and I are teammates. We could be friends. We could help each other out." At the startled look in Brandon's eyes, JJ hastily added, "That came out sounding more suggestive than I meant it. But… it's good to have an ally at an event like this. Someone to talk to about whatever. The anxiety before the race, the soreness in your body, the dread you feel when someone in a white doctor's coat approaches you holding a cup and a clipboard."

Brandon grimaced. "They tested me the first day I showed up at the track. I had to pee in front of someone, which was almost impossible because he stared at me the whole time. I've never felt so mortified."

"You kind of get used to it after a while, but I have a positive test on my record, so they come at me with needles and test my blood now."

Brandon balked. "Really?"

"I didn't dope. I would never do that. It was a bullshit charge and I was exonerated. But this is my life now. It's not the best."

"I'm not sure which is worse—peeing in front of a stranger or dealing with needles. I don't like needles."

JJ couldn't help but smile at that. He wasn't a fan of needles either. He was squeamish about blood, even, and just the sight of a few drops would make him nauseous. So the blood testing was a particular trial. But if that was what it took to prove he played fair, then that was what he'd do.

Brandon drained the rest of his glass. JJ was done with his drink too. Cautiously, he touched Brandon's arm. When Brandon didn't pull away, JJ wrapped his hand around Brandon's forearm and squeezed it gently. Brandon blushed in the sweetest way.

"Refills?" asked the bartender.

Brandon looked at the bartender in surprise, as if he'd forgotten anyone else was around. He glanced at JJ, then said, "Okay. Also a hamburger?"

"Same," said JJ.

"Coming right up."

CHAPTER FIVE

IT WASN'T that Brandon was drunk. Tipsy, sure. Impaired enough that he shouldn't operate a motor vehicle, yes. But he understood a few important things.

First, he was at the Olympics and had to compete in a matter of days, and even if he hadn't finished that third beer, ordering it had been a tremendous mistake. Practice tomorrow was going to *suck*.

Second, sometimes he needed a social lubricant, and those beers had loosened his tongue in a way that he didn't regret exactly, but he still felt weird about it. Because he'd told JJ some things he didn't normally talk about. The second beer had somehow unlocked the story about how his best friend Zach had dragged him to a gay bar one night sophomore year, and Brandon had felt so uncomfortable there he hadn't known how to act. But then this god of a man had sat next to him at the bar and they'd talked about circuits and things for an hour and Brandon had dated that guy for three months, so gay bars weren't *all* bad. And that yeah, he'd had a little bit of a crush on Zach for a hot minute, but Zach had just graduated and moved up to Oakland, so clearly nothing would ever happen there, and Brandon was okay with that because it wasn't even like Brandon thought Zach was the love of his life so much as that he was close by and easy to talk to.

Phew.

And third, Brandon had noticed that JJ was basically sex on legs.

Then, somewhere between the second and third beer, Brandon realized JJ was flirting with him, and there'd been some kind of short circuit in his brain.

And now they were walking across the Athlete Village together and Brandon was definitely tipsy.

"You okay, babe?" JJ asked.

"Yeah. I think that last beer was a mistake, though."

JJ grinned. "Ooh, girl. You will only be twenty-two at the Olympics this one time. Experience it to the fullest."

"Well, there's experiencing things to the fullest and then being hungover at practice and getting murdered by your coach."

JJ laughed, and Brandon wondered if anything ever bothered him. He wondered what it would be like to feel so at ease all the time. On the other hand, he felt pretty mellow now, but… the world was spinning a bit.

He also couldn't help wondering, what would it be like to be *with* someone so calm and cool and sexy? If he couldn't understand the intricacies of social things like small talk and first dates, what would it be like to be with someone who did?

What would it be like to be with JJ?

But no, that was preposterous. JJ… well, JJ seemed interested, but how real was that? Was JJ *actually* interested in Brandon, or was he just being nice because their coaches wanted them to hang out? Brandon wished he could tell. And he really wished he could make his brain focus, but the alcohol was making everything a little fuzzy, and—

"Woah, hey. Be careful."

Brandon must have stumbled, because suddenly he found that JJ's hands were wrapped around his upper arm, holding him up. Brandon paused to get his bearings, then stood a little taller when he felt steady on his feet. He looked around to see what he'd stumbled over, but there was nothing. It had probably been his own big feet.

"That last beer was *definitely* a mistake."

JJ let go of Brandon's arm but didn't step away very far. "You okay?"

"Yeah. The dorm is right there. Twenty more feet. I can make it."

Brandon was a hurdles jumper; his whole goal as an athlete was to stay on his feet and leap cleanly over obstacles. He should be able to walk on flat ground.

JJ's presence beside him was a little distracting, though.

"I like you," Brandon said.

JJ shot him that wide grin again. That grin was going to kill Brandon. "I like you too. Keep walking."

It took some effort to focus on his steps enough for Brandon to make it through the door, to show his ID to the security guards, and to follow JJ to the elevator.

"Which floor?"

"Eight."

JJ nodded and pressed the elevator button. “I’m on seven.”

Before Brandon’s brain caught up, he stood inside an elevator car, the doors slid closed, and he and JJ were alone.

For a shiny new building, the elevators were surprisingly clunky, and every time Brandon got in this one, he thought about what he could change to make it go faster. He knew the athlete dorms had been built quickly on the cheap and would likely be either torn down or converted to apartments after the athletes were gone, but still…. He pushed that thought aside when he noticed JJ staring at him.

Brandon stared back as the elevator stalled for a moment. JJ’s beautiful eyes seemed to see right through Brandon. Brandon’s heart pounded as he took it all in: JJ’s striking face, the fierce quality of his gaze, the unquestionable strength and physique beneath his loose clothing. Brandon wanted to touch him, to kiss him, to throw his whole body over JJ until they were both writhing against each other….

So Brandon went for it.

One second he was looking at JJ’s plump lips pulled wide into a grin, and then he was kissing that grin off JJ’s face. JJ’s hands were instantly on Brandon, sliding up his arms and down his back, and JJ was groaning or Brandon was groaning or they were groaning together. JJ pressed Brandon’s back into the cheap faux wood paneling of the elevator and ground his hips against Brandon’s, and Brandon thought they might just catch fire right there.

Then the elevator dinged.

“This elevator is too fast,” JJ said breathlessly as he pulled away.

Brandon laughed, despite being turned-on and embarrassed and drunk.

JJ stepped out of the elevator but held his hand over the doorway to keep the door from closing. "You've, ah, given me some things to think about. I'll see you tomorrow, okay?"

Then he was gone and the doors slid closed before Brandon could respond.

It was only after Brandon stepped onto his own floor and took a moment to stand in the hallway and get his breathing back under control that he remembered that Jamal had sexiled him. Annoyed, he marched down the hall and opted to knock on the door instead of barging in on something he didn't want to see.

Jamal opened the door, wearing only black sweatpants, and the girlish giggle in the room indicated Shara was still there.

"Is it safe to come in?" Brandon asked.

"Yeah, it's fine. Shara's on her way back to her room."

Shara sauntered to the door, fully dressed at least, and kissed Jamal on the way out.

"Sorry," Brandon said as he walked into the room. "Didn't mean to interrupt anything, but I gotta get some sleep."

"Me too. It's fine." Jamal moved out of the way but then said, "Were you… drinking? You smell like beer."

"I had a drink with my training mate at the America House." Jamal did not need to know that it had been two and a half beers and that Brandon definitely had a crush on said training mate and they had just made out in the elevator.

Holy shit, he'd just made out with JJ in the elevator.

"I have to pee," Brandon said, then ran for the bathroom. And, well, he did, but more than that, he needed a moment to think about the fact that he'd kissed a man and hadn't been super weird and awkward about it. And he'd have to see JJ tomorrow. What the hell had he gotten himself into?

JJ SMILED to himself as he walked down the hall to his room. Before he got there, Clark, JJ's Olympics roommate and a pole vaulter who also trained at USC, left the room, holding a huge hiking backpack.

"Oh, hey," Clark said. "I was going to text you. Marla's roommate got eliminated this morning and decided to fly home today, so I'm going to move into her room." Marla was Clark's girlfriend and also the American high jump champion.

"Oh. Cool." And it was cool to have a room all to himself. JJ hadn't anticipated such a thing. He kind of wanted to run back to the elevator and grab Brandon so that they could finish what they'd started.

Clark looked at his backpack, then glanced back at the door to their room. "Are there, like, rules about this kind of thing? Do I have to stay in the room I was assigned?"

JJ shrugged. "I don't think anyone cares. We're adults."

"Well, most of us. Those rhythmic gymnasts next door are sixteen." Clark grimaced.

That had been the one drawback to this particular room. JJ could hear the giggles of young women as he fell asleep each night. Team USA took up an entire high rise in the Athlete Village and, as such, had some control over the rules for the housing. It was a lot like a co-ed college dorm, every floor an identical square made of long corridors full of doors, each leading to identical small rooms furnished with two twin beds. At least the rooms had their own bathrooms. JJ hoped to never have to deal with communal showers the way he had in college ever again. But unlike college, in these dorms, there were kids as young as sixteen and adults as old as the archer in his fifties, the oldest athlete on the American team.

JJ watched Clark walk toward the elevator before going into his room. Sure enough, Clark's half had been completely cleared out. JJ liked Clark but was thrilled to have a room to himself. No struggling to sleep through someone else's snoring, no one banging around the room in the morning before JJ was ready to get up. No competing for the bathroom when they both had to get to the track in the morning.

He flopped down on his bed and wished Brandon was with him. But it was probably a smarter move to send Brandon away. He had been drunk, and JJ didn't want to take advantage. Besides, now he really did have some things to think about.

Because, okay, Brandon was a little awkward, but he was also really cute and smart, and he kissed like a dream. JJ would have liked to explore that more. To get Brandon out of his baggy tracksuit. To touch all that smooth skin, get a closer look at what JJ could only imagine were phenomenal abs—jumping over hurdles required a lot of core strength—run his fingers through Brandon's dark hair. Maybe slide those old track pants down to look at Brandon's—

JJ's phone chimed. He looked at the screen. The text from Tamika read, *Anti-doping wants you to report for a blood test at 7am.*

Well, fuck. The blood test itself wasn't an issue; JJ hadn't taken anything, and the alcohol would work its way out of his system by morning—and luckily, vodka sodas were not on the current banned substance list. But JJ resented that he had to take the test at all. And he really hated needles.

He texted back: *Fine*. Then he set an alarm so he'd get up and make it to the stadium in time for that bullshit.

And he knew it was because once there was a doping charge on an athlete's record—even if he'd been exonerated of all wrongdoing—it hung over the athlete forever. He'd tested positive once, so he was assumed to be doping until proven otherwise. JJ knew how it went. He followed sports news well enough to know that any athlete with a positive test essentially had an asterisk after his or her name no matter the circumstances. There would always be doubts about him.

He spared a thought for Brandon, whose only performance enhancement seemed to be math. There was something charming about that. And a little naive.

With a sigh, JJ hauled himself off the bed so he could change. No sense in daydreaming about cute boys when there were bigger things to deal with.

CHAPTER SIX

Day 10

JJ STOPPED at a food kiosk in the Athlete Village to get a cup of coffee and an egg sandwich on the way to the stadium, and then his attention got snagged by a newspaper headline. He didn't speak or understand Spanish well, but he knew enough to work out that the headline said something about the Russian track team being in trouble with the World Anti-Doping Agency.

On the shuttle bus to the stadium, JJ ate his sandwich and looked at the news app on his phone. The story was that Russian athletes in a number of sports had tested positive for anabolic steroids and a number of banned substances—including a few that were very new to the market—and that the International Olympic Committee was considering banning the entire Russian team from the rest of the Games and rescinding the medals that had already been awarded. It seemed that the Russian team had not taken previous bans seriously but had instead been developing new drugs to get ahead of the official list of banned substances. The article further stated that there was some evidence that a Russian agency had attempted to hack WADA's computers.

When JJ arrived at the stadium, it looked like it was on lockdown. The security checkpoint all athletes, coaches, and staff had to go through was flanked on both sides by lines of Madrid police as well as a handful of men in military uniforms.

It reminded JJ of an article he'd read about "security theater." How often security checkpoints weren't much more than a demonstration to make people think they were walking into a secure area. That the security screenings at airports were not effective at doing much of anything except making passengers feel at ease. The show of force at the athlete entrance to the stadium looked like peak security theater.

The big guns in the arms of the soldiers and policemen made JJ really nervous, however. He never trusted anyone openly carrying a gun. Even understanding that he was in Madrid and not an American city, he held his hands up as he walked toward the metal detector, as if to say, *See? I don't have a gun. Please don't shoot me.*

He got through the detector with no issues and then showed his badge to a security guard, who pointed him toward a corridor on the right. JJ wasn't entirely sure what was happening until he saw the table set up with stacks of drug testing kits. He noticed belatedly that the tablecloth draped over the top of it displayed the WADA logo.

He sucked in a breath. He'd expected this and still felt surprised by it. He felt a long way from home, miles outside of his comfort zone, and wondered how it was that he'd stumbled into such a situation.

He had grown up a middle-class kid from the Vermont Square neighborhood in LA, right on the border of South Central. His parents were wonderful, warm, supportive people who were flying out later today to watch him run. He'd grown up in a black neighborhood, was often surrounded by his big black family, and had gone to neighborhood schools that were mostly black and Latinx. He'd left home for college, and being outside of the neighborhood bubble made him realize what the world was really like, made him wonder if the color of his skin had something to do with the increased scrutiny on him. JJ was black *and* gay, which made him feel disconnected from the rest of the world sometimes, and he wondered what these women at the desk thought of him. Thank God for his parents. He wouldn't have survived if he didn't have their love and support to fall back on.

Although he did wonder now what Jason Jones Senior would think of JJ bringing home a white kid in glasses who understood math better than human emotion.

He was probably being paranoid. WADA had its eye on JJ because of a positive test in his past, and he wasn't the only one. He shook off his thoughts and focused on the two women sitting at the table. One was Asian, the other was white, and the white woman had a French accent as she asked JJ a series of questions. After finding his name on her clipboard, she handed JJ a plastic pouch about the size of a one-subject notebook and told him to go down to Room 6.

Room 6 turned out to be a very tiny room with a hospital bed and a bunch of medical equipment. There was no doctor in sight, so JJ sat on the side of the bed and texted Tamika to let her know he'd made it to the stadium on time and was about to get a needle shoved into his arm. A poster that displayed the current list of banned substances hung on the wall, and the text was tiny in order to fit them all. There looked to be a couple hundred substances on the list.

Good gravy.

A woman in a lab coat walked in. "Jones?"

"Yes, ma'am."

"Hold out your arm."

"What, no sweet talk? A little flirtation? You want to just get down to business."

The woman raised an eyebrow. Her name tag said *Dr. Patricia O'Neill*. JJ thought he'd detected a British accent. Either way, she didn't look amused. She grabbed the test kit from where JJ had left it on the counter. Then she tied off his arm, poured some iodine on a cotton ball and swiped it over the inside of JJ's elbow, and assembled the syringe and collection tube.

"Uh, blood makes me dizzy," JJ said. "I'm gonna…." He turned toward the banned substance poster.

"That's all right."

"I also really don't like needles and I'm…." JJ started to feel woozy. "Uh…."

The doctor stopped what she was doing. "All right. Take a deep breath. Would you like a glass of water?"

JJ took a few slow breaths. "Sorry. This whole thing is…."

The doctor pulled over a stool and sat on it. "I suppose if you're this phobic of needles, it's unlikely you're injecting anything into your thigh regularly."

JJ understood that she was not letting him off the hook. If WADA, World Athletics, or the IOC had decided he should get a blood test, he was getting a blood test or he wasn't competing. "I can do this. I do this at least once a month. Just give me a moment."

Dr. O'Neill waited. JJ took a few more deep breaths and felt his heart rate fall back to close to its normal rate. Dr. O'Neill handed him a ball that JJ realized was a squishy stress ball. He squeezed it with his free hand a couple of times, then focused his attention on the poster. "I'm good. Go ahead."

He read the names of all the banned substances, which was difficult because a lot of them had long, unpronounceable names. Still, he focused on each syllable and tried to work out how to pronounce it.

Androstenediol.... Bolasterone.... Calusterone.... Fluoxymesterone....

He felt the sharp pinch of the needle going into his arm and had to close his eyes for a moment and concentrate on breathing. No matter how often he got tested, this never got easier. When he opened his eyes again, he could see the tube filling with his blood in his peripheral vision. The room started to spin, so he focused again on the poster.

Prostanozol.... Quinbolone.... Stanozolol.... Stenbolone.... Tetrahydrogestrinone....

The pressure on his arm changed, and Dr. O'Neill said, "That's it." He stared stubbornly at the poster while he waited for her to put a Band-Aid over the puncture wound. He listened for the sounds of her cleaning up, and once the top of the trash can fell, he turned his head.

"Sorry," he mumbled.

"It's fine. I don't see a lot of patients as phobic of blood as you are, but it happens."

"There's a reason I didn't go to medical school," he tried to joke, his voice still shaky.

"Unfortunately, this is the most accurate way to test. And you don't need needles to dope these days. Did you know there are some banned substances that can be inhaled now? And that's just the anabolic stuff. Most athletes are smart enough not to ingest steroids in competition these days, but we still test for stimulants, narcotics, and those kinds of things. Don't need syringes for most of that either."

JJ knew all about testing for stimulants, of course. After his positive test, WADA had changed the guidelines for pseudoephedrine to be over a certain amount in urine, an amount four times as much as JJ had taken in the decongestant Franco had given him. So he wouldn't even have tested positive if he tested now. It made that invisible asterisk after his name feel like even more bullshit.

But he understood that "I didn't know" seemed like a flimsy excuse to basically everyone, and that wanting to run without that cold slowing him down had doomed him to periodic blood tests for the rest of his career. And if the Russian delegation had been suspended again, they were really going to crack down here.

Of course, JJ also understood a lot of this testing was for show. It was more security theater so that the television networks would do splashy stories about how WADA and the IOC were cracking down on doping, to make it clear that the sports being aired on television were pure, untainted by doping or cheating or anything scandalous.

JJ knew better than that.

"When is your first race?" the doctor asked.

"Wednesday."

"We'll have test results done before then, and they'll probably want to test you again before or after your races. You have a flag on your file."

"I took some cold pills."

Dr. O'Neill nodded. "I've run into that a few times. Thank God they raised the limit for pseudoephedrine. It was nonsense to have it that low. We kept snagging runners in the UK who didn't know they'd taken a banned substance. A couple of cold pills shouldn't make a difference, and anyway, you have to take a lot of pseudoephedrine before it has enough of a stimulant effect to enhance performance." She sighed. "I've been trying to argue that sure, fentanyl and oxycodone should be banned, but there are some things that need a more nuanced approach. A kid tested positive at the European Championships because he was taking antidepressants and the tester thought it was a stimulant."

JJ appreciated the sympathy, but he glanced at his phone, and this talk was eating into his practice time. "I gotta meet my coach. Thanks for not thinking I'm ridiculous for being weird about blood and needles."

Dr. O'Neill nodded. "Good luck out there, Mr. Jones."

BY SOME miracle, Brandon was not hungover, and Jamal was even pleasant company on the shuttle bus ride to the stadium.

When the bus pulled up to the athlete entrance, Brandon was shocked by the sheer volume of people at the security checkpoint. There were far more police officers and security personnel than there had been the day before. "What is all this?"

"Russians got caught doping again." Jamal held up his phone, which displayed a news story. "My coach texted me to expect extra drug testing."

"Oh, great." Brandon appreciated that some of these athletes who had been competing longer didn't seem to think peeing in a cup in front of a stranger was that big a deal, but Brandon's stomach flopped as he thought about having to do it again.

Brandon had read a lot about doping in the lead-up to the Olympics, not because he had an interest in doing it, but because the science of it fascinated him. The science of athleticism fascinated him generally. Certain muscle groups could be developed with specific exercises, and strength in certain parts of the body allowed an athlete to excel at certain tasks. Now sports scientists thought some athletes had certain genes that made them stronger or faster or able to move in certain ways. Technology affected performance as well. The reason that Usain Bolt or Jason Jones Jr. could run one hundred meters faster than Jesse Owens had a lot to do with shoes and the material the track was made out of. The general public sometimes assumed everyone was doping because how else could they destroy all those old records so easily? And probably some doping did account for it, but better training and technology had a lot to do with it too.

Still, the idea that an athlete could take something that would make him even better at something he was already very good at must have been tempting for a lot of athletes. Brandon had no interest in the side effects, everything from acne to sexual performance issues—Brandon hardly ever got to, er, perform sexually, so he would like to be able to do it well when the occasions arose, thank you—but that didn't mean he didn't want to know how each drug affected the body. The black market for these drugs kept making new ones faster than WADA and its list of banned substances could keep up with. The FDA didn't regulate or test any of it. How could the athletes who took these drugs know what they were doing was even safe?

"How many athletes from one country have to test positive for the whole country to be banned from competition?" Brandon asked Jamal.

"Dunno, but a lot, I'm guessing. It says here that fifty-four of the eighty track athletes Russia sent to the Games tested positive. Swimmers, gymnasts, most of the water polo team, and also a few archers also tested positive. Like, it's all over their whole athletic program." Jamal squinted at his phone. "Archery? How could PEDs help someone with archery?"

"Not sure, but… wow." Oddly, it made Brandon feel a little better. He'd be shocked if the American track team was completely free of performance-enhancing drugs and expected a few athletes to test positive, but he didn't want that to hurt his own medal chances.

Because Brandon might have viewed the four-hundred hurdles as a math problem, but he wanted his method to yield results. Well, he wanted to win—that was really the thing. He was here, wasn't he? His mother kept telling him that it didn't matter if he won or lost because he had made the Olympic team, and that was something so few athletes got to do, but he'd blown the rest of the competition out of the water at the Trials, so he knew he could win the race. The US team was so dominant in a lot of the short distances—except the one-hundred, which no American had won at the Olympics in a couple of decades—that Brandon had to assume that if he could beat a bunch of American runners, he could beat anybody.

When they got through security, Jamal and Brandon were both informed that they didn't need to test today, but they should be ready to test at any time for the rest of the week.

Brandon thought of JJ and his fear of blood and needles. He was surprised to find he felt concerned for JJ, a man he'd known less than twenty-four hours. Granted, they had made out in the elevator last night, which did up the stakes some. Brandon wondered if they'd make out in the elevator—or anywhere—again soon. He wanted to. He had no idea how to ask JJ about it, though. They hadn't even exchanged phone numbers, after all. Brandon could only hope JJ showed up at practice today.

"My coach is waiting at the practice track," said Jamal. "I'll see ya, Brandon."

"Sure," Brandon said with a little wave.

After a stop in the locker room, he found Grady with one of his other runners, running drills on the main track. Grady had his ubiquitous stopwatch in his hand and was yelling at the runner, so Brandon held back until the guy finished his drills. Grady told the runner to take five, then turned to Brandon.

"Surprised you got here so early. I saw they were randomly drug testing. It's holding up athletes and messing with the practice schedule."

"I was randomly not chosen."

"All right. Well, you ready? I'd like to have you warm up and do some speed drills. We can only do hurdles practice on the lower track after eleven."

"Yeah, that's fine. Whatever you think."

Grady operated on the theory that more practice was always better. The more Brandon got acclimated to this track, the more familiar he was with how his shoes gripped it and how much bounce he got off the surface, the better prepared he'd be on race day. Brandon could see the wisdom of that, and luckily he'd slept well the night before—the alcohol had put him out almost as soon as his head hit the pillow—but he worried he'd be tired if he trained this hard before his race. On the other hand, he'd learned the day before that "training" at the Olympics often meant sitting around and waiting one's turn a lot, since several hundred athletes wanted to use the same practice spaces.

Grady dictated a series of warm-up exercises, and Brandon stretched and jumped and jogged in place to get his heart rate up. Then Grady held up the stopwatch. "Lane 5, buddy. I want to see you run four hundred meters in less than fifty seconds."

Brandon jogged over to the blocks Grady had already set up. As he checked them, he saw JJ walk out onto the track. Brandon took a deep breath but then focused on the block—he couldn't let JJ distract him from what he was here to do. Satisfied that his blocks were set up correctly, he put his feet in them and signaled to Grady that he was ready. When Grady said, "Go!" Brandon took off.

Chapter Seven

JJ sometimes thought his trip to the Olympics was preordained. He'd always excelled at running—he'd gained a reputation for being one of the fastest kids in his class by the time he was seven or eight, and had easily made the high school track team. He'd grown up close to what had been the very first Olympic Village ever built, for the 1932 Olympics, and he could walk to LA Memorial Stadium from his parents' house. He'd stared up at the Olympic rings over the entrance to the stadium plenty of times. He'd close his eyes and fantasize about walking into some Olympic stadium one day, about being a part of this huge global movement in which the very best athletes in the world competed. He'd dreamed of being the fastest man on earth, of taking home that one-hundred-meter gold medal, and he'd dreamed of standing atop a podium as the national anthem played.

Most days he trained at the Cromwell track at USC, but Memorial Stadium was in Exposition Park, adjacent to the USC campus, and every now and then, JJ got to run there. He'd picture the stadium full of people cheering for him to win. He imagined crossing the finish line first and running a victory lap while waving an American flag in the wind. He thought about standing atop the medal podium. He'd lived his big Olympic moment over and over and over again.

That moment had never involved syringes and people in white lab coats.

He was still a little woozy as he walked onto the track to train with Tamika that day.

"You okay?" she asked.

"I *really* don't like needles."

She patted his shoulder. "I know, honey. Grady's got a cooler full of water and Gatorade if you need some before we get started."

"Cold water would be good."

Grady stood beside the track, holding up his stopwatch. Brandon came around the turn with a look of determination on his face, and he plowed right past the start line. Grady hit the button on his stopwatch. "Forty-seven seconds. Very good!"

Brandon jogged off the track, dodging another runner passing in Lane 2, and then stood beside Grady and panted for a moment. He looked up and saw JJ, and their eyes met for the briefest of glorious seconds.

"Uh, Tamika said you had water?" JJ said to Grady.

"I do, yeah. Follow me."

JJ followed Grady over to a cooler, and Brandon trailed behind. JJ grabbed a bottle of water from the cooler and took a few gulps, trying to let the cool water soothe his rattled insides. Then, because it was already a hot day, he dumped the last bit of water on his head.

When he looked again, Brandon was staring at him. And not in a "you're crazy" way, but definitely in an "I want to do you against a locker right now" way. JJ smiled at him.

Brandon's face flushed.

JJ grabbed another water for the road. "Thanks, Grady. I'll see you later, Brandon, yeah?"

"Um, yeah."

And JJ did indeed see him four hours later, when his legs felt like spaghetti and all he wanted to do was lie flat in bed for a while. He was, in fact, lying perfectly horizontal on a bench in the locker room, his running shoes already stuffed in his duffel bag. It had been a challenging practice, and he'd blown up at Tamika at one point because he was frustrated by his slow time and "you have to run faster" was not useful advice. But he'd pushed and finally run a hundred meters in a time fast enough to be competitive. He could run no more today. His last task was to summon the energy to get up so he could catch the bus back to the Athlete Village.

"You okay?" Brandon asked.

"Yeah. Just tired. Trying day."

"Um. Yeah."

Brandon was cute when he was nervous. From this angle, JJ could only really see his fingers, which tangled together, and the bottom of his chin. It didn't look like Brandon had shaved today. JJ was deciding whether he thought that was hot when he realized he probably looked like a weirdo. He took a deep breath and slowly pulled himself into a sitting position.

"Are you going back to the Athlete Village now?" Brandon asked.

"That was the plan, yeah. I'm wiped."

Brandon looked around. JJ followed his gaze and realized Brandon was probably trying to see if there were many other athletes around. There were three or four events happening on the main track right then, and athletes not competing that day had been asked to leave the practice track a half hour ago, so the locker room was pretty empty. Still, Brandon spoke under his breath.

"Can we talk about last night?"

"Yeah." JJ tried to read Brandon's facial expression but couldn't; this kid was impenetrable.

JJ hauled himself off the bench. Brandon continued to wring his hands, so maybe that was the tell. But did he regret making out with JJ in the elevator? Because JJ regretted nothing.

"Let's go," said JJ, grabbing his bag.

Brandon nodded and walked beside him out of the stadium.

"When is your race?" JJ asked.

"Heats Thursday, final Friday."

"So you still have some time."

Brandon got twitchier the closer they got to the bus stop.

There weren't a lot of other people around when the shuttle bus pulled up. JJ led Brandon to the back of the bus, where they could speak with relative privacy. Once the bus got rolling and the roar of it would drown out their voices to the people sitting in the front, JJ said, "Let me ask. Are you upset about what happened?"

Brandon looked startled. "Upset? No. I just… I don't really know how to do this."

Brandon was wildly twitchy. JJ had an idea of what Brandon wanted to say. He was charmed by how nervous Brandon seemed.

"Deep breath. It'll be okay. You wanted to talk about last night. So, tell me what's on your mind."

Brandon looked up and met JJ's gaze. His fingers were basically knots in his lap now, and he seemed to be shaking a little, but he said in a low voice, "I really like you and want to kiss you again."

JJ grinned. "I really like you too."

Brandon let out a breath. "I was worried I acted too fast and you'd think I was pushy and Lord knows why you're even attracted to me, but I want to do it again."

"Fun story. My roommate moved out last night. I have a room all to myself if you want some privacy."

Brandon swallowed so hard, JJ was worried he'd choke. "I don't know if I'm ready for all that."

"All right. Just saying."

"Not that I don't want to, because I totally do, but I… I'm trying to wrap my head around all this. Like, one of the sexiest guys I've ever met invited me to his room, and what even is that?"

JJ laughed. That Brandon found him sexy was a good sign. "Hey, no pressure."

"Okay."

Brandon's nerves were endearing, and JJ didn't want to push against that too much because he wanted Brandon to feel safe with him. They'd talked enough the night before that JJ knew, at least, that Brandon was a little awkward and didn't have a wealth of experience, but he wasn't a blushing virgin either. They'd get where they both wanted to go eventually. Because JJ definitely wanted to go there. Brandon had beautiful eyes magnified by his thick glasses and unblemished skin and the kind of slamming body only runners who worked out a lot could develop, strong but not over-the-top. And JJ really wanted to get a look at that body-ody-ody when Brandon wasn't wearing any clothes.

So JJ decided the best approach would be not to push it. Instead, he changed the subject. "I don't know about you, but I'm starving. When we get back, let's go check out that cafeteria. See if they have anything good. One of my training mates said they make decent sandwiches."

Brandon let out a breath. "Yeah, okay. I can do that."

BRANDON HADN'T felt this nervous the day before, but maybe the difference was that he'd tasted what could be, and he wanted more of it.

JJ was laid-back through their early dinner, making quick work of a turkey sandwich and some house-made potato chips. Brandon ate a piece of chicken slowly, knowing he needed to replace the protein in his body, even though what he'd really wanted was pasta. The cafeteria food included a strange mélange of ethnic cuisines, probably trying to appeal to as many athletes as possible, so there were actually a lot of options, but Brandon had been so shaky, he'd just chosen the first thing he saw that seemed appetizing.

"There were no homosexuals involved in the design of this cafeteria," JJ said at one point, looking around.

"No?"

"No. Yellow walls and blue tables?" JJ shook his head.

Brandon didn't know how to respond. He had no eye for design.

"It's not hideous," JJ said, popping a chip into his mouth. "There's just no life to it." He glanced at

Brandon. "Sorry, I kind of mentally make everything over. I do it with men on the street too. Straight dudes have no idea how to make themselves look attractive. Not to generalize."

Brandon couldn't help but laugh at that. He suspected he had a similar issue—his wardrobe was fairly bland—but that wouldn't be obvious this week since he was mostly wearing clothes provided to him by the USATF or the same kind of athletic wear everyone here wore between events.

Brandon bet JJ dressed well when he wasn't competing. He glanced at JJ's sparkly nails. Yeah, he could see JJ in a lot of bright colors, well-tailored shirts, pants that showed off his….

"Did you say your roommate moved out?" Brandon asked.

"He did, yeah. It's nice, I have the whole room to myself."

"My roommate wishes he was in your shoes. He's hooking up with another athlete and seems more interested in having sex with her than training."

JJ didn't say anything, so Brandon looked up from his meal. JJ squinted at Brandon as if he was trying to see something.

"What?" Brandon asked, wondering if he had food on his face.

"Just when I think I've got you figured out, you surprise me again."

"How so?"

JJ pressed his lips together. "Usually when you meet Olympic athletes, they all have kind of the same attitude. They've trained for this opportunity most of their lives. They want to win a medal more than anything else in the world. I've met runners who think sex is bad luck or throws them off their game. I know guys on strict diets who will not deviate until after all their races are run. Some of us sprinters, we train for years to spend mere seconds proving ourselves. I want to win the one-hundred meter more than I want to take my next breath. But you? I don't know what moves you. Sometimes I think you're here on a lark."

"I want to win. Of course I want to win."

"Not solve a math problem?"

Brandon was a little offended. He recognized that JJ was teasing him, but it felt a little like being in high school again, of being acutely aware that he was a Smart Kid and thus would never be a Cool Kid. JJ was definitely a Cool Kid. Brandon also understood that he was a grown man now and that these distinctions were meaningless, but it was hard for him to adjust to social situations, and he was intimidated by the ease JJ had in them.

He took a deep breath. JJ had said he liked Brandon. He wasn't really making fun.

"The math problems are in the service of winning. The number of steps between hurdles, the number of steps per second—calculating all that helps me run my race faster. The goal of doing all the math is to run the best race."

JJ nodded slowly. "Math was never my best subject in school."

"But you understand the basic mechanics of a race. If you have a long stride length, you can finish the race in fewer steps. If you take more steps each second than your opponent, you will get to the finish line sooner. And so on. It's all a math problem. I do all this math because it makes me a better runner. I'm not saying it's the best method, but it helps me." Brandon paused to drink some water. When he looked up again, JJ smiled. "What?"

"I like how passionate you are about math."

"Oh." Heat rose to Brandon's face.

JJ pulled out his phone. "Give me your phone number so I can text you. I want to be able to see you because I want to, not because I randomly run into you at the track."

"Doesn't it cost extra to send texts in Spain?"

"Nah, I have an app for it. As long as there's Wi-Fi, I can get in touch. Since there's Wi-Fi at the stadium and in the Athlete Village—the only places I go—I figure I'm good."

They exchanged phone numbers, and JJ added, "You can text me anytime too."

"Thanks." Brandon felt giddy at getting a hot guy's number, and it was all he could do not to hug his phone. Which was dumb because he was twenty-two, not fifteen, but he didn't feel very rational where JJ was concerned.

After they ate, they walked back to the American dorm building together again, and once they were in the elevator, Brandon let out a little giggle.

"You have all the maturity of an eight-year-old," said JJ, though he was smiling.

Brandon felt giddy. It wasn't a sensation he was familiar with, but this bubbly feeling in his chest was thrilling in a way. Oh, he'd had crushes on boys and had sex with men and had what he'd thought was a wide array of human experiences, but this silly relationship with a very sexy man was different from anything he'd experienced before.

"All I can think about is kissing you," he blurted.

JJ smirked. "No one's stopping you, babe."

So Brandon kissed JJ, and it was just as thrilling as it had been in this same spot the night before. But then the elevator doors opened. And Brandon did not want JJ to get off. JJ must have felt the same, because he stepped toward the elevator door, then held his hand over the opening to keep it from closing.

"No pressure, I promise," JJ said, nodding toward his room. He stepped off the elevator onto his floor. And Brandon followed him.

Brandon didn't have any superstitions about sex and athletics; such things weren't logical. Flukes happened in sports sometimes, especially in track and field, because athletes had bad days and good days, and sometimes an underdog did everything right but the veteran made mistakes. And sometimes an athlete you expected to come in last won gold and the athlete you expected to win gold finished off the podium. Things happened; sports were unpredictable. But at the same time, there were logical explanations for every outcome. So Brandon didn't think more time spent with JJ would affect his performance.

He followed JJ down the hall to his room and inside. The left side of the room was basically empty aside from a twin bed with a bare mattress.

Brandon stood in the middle of the room, unsure of what to do.

JJ approached him. "I can see the gears turning in your head."

Brandon bit his lip but then admitted, "Mostly in the past, I've let the guy I'm with take the lead and tell me what to do because I never really know what I'm *supposed* to do. Like, do I say something? Do I make a move? Do we make small talk for a few minutes? Do I wait for him to do something? And then I get so far in my thoughts that it's awkward and not sexy. By then I've ruined everything."

JJ leaned close. "You've ruined nothing. Push all that aside. I don't care what you think you're supposed to do. What do you *want* to do?"

"I want to kiss you," Brandon admitted.

JJ smiled. He had the most compelling smile, plump lips, wide grin, white teeth, and some kind of hidden knowledge, as if he knew a secret Brandon would never be privy to.

"Here's how we're gonna do this," JJ said. "When you're with me, when it's just the two of us? Never worry about what you're supposed to do. Do what you want to do, because you want it, and I probably want it too. If you ever do something that crosses a line for me, I'll tell you, and you should do the same. Deal?"

That seemed reasonable. "Deal."

JJ stepped forward, closing most of the space between them. He put his hands on Brandon's shoulders. "So, what was it that you wanted to do?"

Brandon recognized the invitation, so he kissed JJ. It was just as electric as it had been before, which was wild because Brandon thought the first time was a lightning-in-a-bottle situation. How could kissing one man feel this amazing? And yet, the way their lips slid together was basically perfect, and JJ tasted kind of sweet and metallic, and he was so responsive that Brandon didn't feel awkward and stupid for once. It felt right.

JJ tugged Brandon toward the bed, and Brandon went willingly, excited now to see where this might go. It took the rest of his body a moment to catch on that this was about to get exciting, but suddenly he was hard and tingly and happily fell onto JJ's bed and tangled his limbs with JJ's. JJ had on a T-shirt and a pair of shiny basketball shorts that went to his knees, and Brandon wore a T-shirt and old, worn sweatpants, and neither of them had enough fabric on their body to leave much of anything to the imagination. As they rolled as much as they could on a narrow twin mattress, Brandon felt JJ's hot, hard cock against his thigh. He groaned in response.

Brandon tried to shut off his brain and focus only on the sensation of JJ's big hands roaming his body, of JJ's hot skin under his own hands, of the insistent press of JJ's cock against Brandon's thigh, his hip, his own hard cock. He arched his back, pressing forward into JJ, under him now, and he spread his legs to make room for JJ to settle between them. JJ grunted and groaned as they writhed together, as JJ's hands snuck under Brandon's shirt and he nibbled at Brandon's chin, his neck, his collarbone. Brandon wrapped a hand around the back of JJ's head and discovered that JJ's barely-there hair was surprisingly soft, as was the beard on his face.

What did Brandon want? He wanted JJ inside him, definitely, wanted to feel JJ moving in him. He reached into JJ's shorts and wrapped his hand around that cock, and it was substantial. Brandon probably could have calculated its exact length based on the width of his own hand, but now was not the time.

"What do you want, Brandon?" JJ asked, breathless and shaky.

"I want you inside me, but…."

"Mmm, I want that too."

"Not actually, though. I mean, I do, but I'm trying to be smart about this…."

JJ pulled away slightly. "What do you mean?"

Brandon struggled with how to say what he meant. He wasn't shy about sex, but sometimes being explicit made him self-conscious. But JJ had said to do what he wanted, and Brandon took that to mean he should say things the way he wanted too. "I just thought we'd kiss now. I mean, I *want* to have sex with you, but also, I haven't bottomed in quite a long time, and you're quite large, and I have to run in a few days."

JJ's expression smoothed over, perhaps because he understood. "Gotcha. You don't want to be sore tomorrow, in other words."

"Yeah. It's not like getting drunk and sleeping it off, you know?"

JJ rolled away slightly and propped himself up on his elbow. "You've already broken rules you've set with yourself while with me, I take it."

"Yeah. I mean, they aren't really rules. You didn't make me do anything I didn't want to do, just… I don't know. You asked me before if I wanted to win and I *do*, and I don't want to do anything that might put that in jeopardy."

"So what do you want to do now?"

"What I want and what I should do are different things in this case. I'm glad decision-making happens easily for you, but it doesn't for me. I think what I *should* do is go back to my room and get a good night's sleep so that I can get up tomorrow and do drills with Grady until it feels like my feet will fall off in the interest of sailing through the qualifying heats to make the final. Even though I *want* to have sex with you."

The moment felt anticlimactic, and Brandon felt the disappointment on JJ's face in his gut, but he knew the right thing to do here would be to go back to his room so that he wouldn't spend all night making out with JJ, no matter how much his body screamed for release. He hated putting the brakes on this. Still, he knew he had to. He wasn't here to have sex with hot men; he was here to win a race. All summer, this one race had been his singular focus. The plan had been to run this race, win his gold medal, then go home and finish his degree and walk into the future he wanted.

Did that future include a man like JJ? It seemed so unlikely. They had so little in common. And yet….

"You think a lot," JJ said.

"More than I should."

"I didn't say that. Maybe I should think more. Maybe I'm too impulsive."

"I'm sorry. This is killing me. I don't want to leave, but I know I should."

"No, you're right. I agree, the best thing is a good night's sleep, and I won't sleep if you're here with me. I've been wanting to win this race since I ran my first sprint when I was, like, seven years old. I had to have a blood test today, which is basically my least favorite thing in the world. And if I could get past watching a tube fill with my own blood, I can peel myself away from you now."

Brandon rolled out of bed and stood up. He was still half-hard, and looking at JJ lounging on the bed wasn't helping with that much. He grabbed his bag where he'd left it on the floor when he'd come in and said, "I'm sorry."

"No need to apologize. It's probably the right thing to do. But know that if you change your mind, you've got my phone number now."

"Right. Um. Good night."

Brandon didn't wait for a response. He slipped out of the room.

Chapter Eight

Day 11

Brandon's practice times were solid. The current world record time was just under forty-seven seconds. Brandon's hero Edwin Moses's best time had been 47.02. Brandon had finished his race in forty-seven flat twice that day. Who knew if he'd be able to do it during the competition? But still, he felt good about it.

He'd only seen JJ in passing that day and felt weird about it. He didn't know what to say or what to do where JJ was concerned. His desire to be sweaty and naked with JJ somewhere had not faded at all, and he was starting to think it might be better to get that out of his system rather than try to postpone the inevitable.

But JJ was off somewhere, probably doing drills with Tamika, and Grady said, "Jamal is competing in the long jump right now. Do you want to go watch with me?"

"Sure," Brandon said.

He and Jamal weren't really friends, but they'd known each other since Jamal had joined the USC track team, and Brandon wanted him to do well. By the time he and Grady sat in the stands, a good number of Jamal's opponents had already been eliminated.

The individual events that comprised track and field were odd, Brandon reflected as he watched the officials record the distance one of the other competitors had jumped. Most of the athletes who competed in track and field, or athletics, trained and competed and got injured and struggled and triumphed for only a few seconds of competition. It wasn't like a team sport, in which there was round-robin play and many opportunities to win. It wasn't like gymnastics, in which there were several days of competition. He supposed a lot of Olympic sports lasted a few seconds—swim races, archery, rowing, shooting, and weight lifting could all be over quite quickly—but it felt strange that he'd logged hours and hours of practice and drills and training to run for forty-seven seconds.

And Jamal had even less time than that to prove himself, since he literally just ran toward the jumping area, jumped on a line, and tried to get his body to travel through the air as far as it would go. Jamal had won the competition at the Olympic Trials but didn't have a lot of world experience. Brandon and Jamal had talked about that briefly in their time sharing a room for the past week, and Jamal seemed confident, so it was anyone's guess how the international competition was affecting him—if it even was, because he was jumping very well.

Brandon sat forward in his seat as they waited to see if any of the remaining jumpers could top Jamal's 8.74 meter jump. Long jump was a sport that couldn't be improved upon much, since the equipment was still largely the same as it had always been. According to the scoreboard, the Olympic record hadn't budged since 1968. And yet Brandon was already trying to calculate how to do it better. Would running faster or slower in the approach make a difference? How fast should the athlete accelerate? What kind of force needed to be applied to the takeoff board? Was the athlete's weight thrown forward at takeoff?

Maybe nobody could do it better than Jamal, who took another turn but only inched forward 0.02 meters. Two measly centimeters.

"His technique is not as good as it could be," Grady said.

"No?"

"No, he usually accelerates better before hitting the takeoff board." Grady was not Jamal's coach and didn't specialize in the jumping sports, but he'd spent enough time at the USC facilities that he had likely seen Jamal jump plenty of times. "Not that it even matters, because none of these guys are getting close. And they're all about a foot off the world record, give or take." He glanced at Brandon. "My math skills are not as good as yours."

"Less than a foot. Nineteen centimeters. That's about like this." Brandon placed his hands about twenty centimeters apart to show Grady.

Grady chuckled. "You're too smart for your own good, kid."

A runner from Canada approached the jump. His approach looked perfect; he accelerated gracefully, hit the takeoff board right in the middle, and launched himself in the air. When his score flashed up a moment later, he'd jumped 8.80 meters.

Grady clapped. “That was very good. If Jamal had technique like that, he’d jump nine meters, easy.”

Jamal would have a chance to see if he could top that distance. His jump looked decent, but when his score came up, it showed he’d come up short, unable to top his top jump. That meant Jamal had earned himself a silver medal.

“Can’t be mad at that,” Grady said as he stood to clap for the winners.

Brandon scanned the stadium to see what other events were happening. Nothing excited him much. The first day of the decathlon was wrapping up. Over to the right, they were setting up for the hammer throw. One of the long-distance races was about to start. Brandon liked watching sprints—he was prepared to do anything to be in the stadium during JJ’s one-hundred-meter race—but the long distances and the throwing events didn’t interest him much. He wondered what JJ was up to and considered texting him, but his most immediate need was to take care of his growling stomach, so he decided to go back to the Village to find something to eat.

He walked with Grady back to the practice track, and on the way, Grady said, “Have you talked with JJ at all?”

Brandon almost laughed, but instead he said, “Yeah, the last two nights, actually.”

Grady nodded. “Tamika thought you two would get along.”

“Really? I mean, I like him and all, but I can’t imagine anyone on this planet is more different from me.”

“I think that’s the point. Tamika thinks you might… balance each other, is how I think she put it.”

Brandon could see that, although he wasn't altogether convinced that JJ wouldn't grow bored with him. But the way Grady phrased it, it almost sounded like…. "Wait, is Tamika trying to set us up? Like, romantically?"

Grady waved his hand. "Don't sound so scandalized. And no, I don't think so. But maybe? My woman has strange ideas sometimes." He laughed. "Don't worry about it. At this point, anything that helps you prepare for and stay calm before the race is good. Did talking to JJ help?"

"Ah, in some ways." But he felt worse in others. Brandon felt wound up even thinking about JJ. Not in a bad way, though; an excited tension rolled through his belly.

They paused near the practice track. It was an oval directly under the main track upstairs, intended to be a spot athletes could train and warm up while the official races took place above. Since this area was not intended for public viewing, it wasn't as nice as the main track. It was made of a similar synthetic material, and it had a similar stick and bounce, but otherwise it looked like someone had plunked a track in the middle of a parking garage. Huge metal pillars surrounded the track, and the floor was unfinished cement. Someone had rolled out some blue carpeting to lead the way toward the locker rooms, but it was otherwise quite plain down here. Brandon thought about what JJ had said about no homosexuals being involved in the design of the cafeteria and guessed that was the case here as well. It was functional, but there was no color, no life. Brandon put a hand over his face to hide the fact that he was smiling to himself.

"Do you feel ready for Thursday?" Grady asked.

"As I can be. The worst part is waiting for the competition to begin."

"I know. Hang in there. Soak it all in. It will be over before you know it."

Two hours later, after dinner at the cafeteria with a random assortment of track athletes and a side trip to the Athlete Village gift shop, Brandon rode the elevator up to his room. When he arrived, Jamal was there, already looking a little drunk.

"Congratulations," Brandon said, gesturing toward the silver medal that hung from Jamal's neck. "I watched from the stands." He thought he should throw in some platitude about how it was a great jump, but then he overthought it and too much time went by, so he just stood impotently by his bed, waiting for Jamal to respond.

"Thanks, man! I plan to celebrate tonight. My parents bought me dinner, but they've gone back to the hotel. Now Shara is headed over. We're going to do some celebrating of our own." Jamal thrust his hips a couple of times. "That is, if you have somewhere you can go."

Brandon's gut reaction was to panic, because he didn't want to deprive Jamal of his celebration, but he didn't really want to wander aimlessly around the Athlete Village either. Then he remembered he had JJ's phone number. "I might, actually. Let me see if my friend is back from training yet."

Brandon sent a text to JJ. *My roommate is about to sexile me. You back yet?*

Within thirty seconds, JJ responded. *In my room. Ur welcome anytime.*

There was nothing explicitly sexual in any of those words, but Brandon shivered anyway. Thinking fast, he went to the closet and pulled out a clean change of clothes and shoved them in his bag. It was probably presumptuous to assume JJ would let him stay the night, but somehow he didn't think JJ would object much.

Then he turned to Jamal. "I can get lost for the night, but I'll need to come back tomorrow."

"Shara is competing in the morning, so we'll clear out of here early to go to the stadium."

That was good knowledge to have. Brandon nodded. "Uh, have fun tonight."

He left the room and stood in the hall, and it hit him suddenly that he'd just decided to spend the night with JJ. This ran completely contrary to everything he'd said the night before. And yet he couldn't say he regretted anything or thought he was making a mistake.

JJ WAS exhausted. He'd been tapped for a random urine test and had peed in a cup while a guy in a lab coat watched. Thanks, Russians, for devising a system in which urine could be covertly swapped out so that now all urine had to be collected with people watching. Then Tamika yelled at him about pacing for what felt like hours because he was still trying to run the two-hundred the way he ran the one-hundred, which meant his starts were fast but his finishes were slow as he petered out and ran out of steam. And this was an issue because he was supposed to run qualifiers for the two-hundred *tomorrow*. He'd finally started getting good times by the end of the day, but those last two practice runs had taken the last of his strength.

A few hours later and he was back in his room, basically immobile. He lay on his bed contemplating sleep, a protein-heavy burrito from the cafeteria sitting on the side table waiting for him to eat as soon as he could summon the strength to lift it. Then Brandon texted.

JJ hadn't given much thought to his response. He wanted to see Brandon, full stop. But after he hit Send, he started to wonder if this was a mistake. Was Brandon a distraction? Did JJ have any business doing anything in Madrid besides sleeping, eating, and running? He was so tired now, he could feel the weariness in his bones, in his teeth, in his toenails. What he needed was to eat dinner and sleep so he'd be refreshed to run prelims tomorrow.

Too late now, though. And if Brandon was getting kicked out of his room, JJ didn't want to leave him in the lurch. JJ also regretted not getting the extra key from Clark when he moved out so that he could give that key to Brandon. That way he wouldn't have had to get up when Brandon knocked on the door.

And there was the knock.

With a groan, JJ hauled himself up.

He opened the door and saw Brandon had a bag.

"Oh," JJ said, pointing to the bag. "You're… oh."

"My roommate won a silver medal today and plans to celebrate all night long with his girlfriend. But if this is too much, I can just sleep on the other bed there. If that's okay. I didn't mean to impose on you."

JJ realized quite suddenly that he was hungry enough to feel a little light-headed. He should really eat that burrito. "It's totally fine. I mean, I think there's an extra set of sheets in the closet if you want to… but I mean…." JJ sighed and sat back down on his bed. "Sorry, I'm wiped. I still haven't eaten. I can barely put two thoughts together. Do you mind if I…?" He gestured toward the side table.

"Oh, no, not at all."

JJ peeled the foil wrapper from his burrito and took a huge bite as Brandon put his bag on the other bed and sat on the bare mattress.

"How was your day?" JJ asked after he'd chewed.

"Oh. It was okay. I did the race in forty-seven flat twice."

Brandon's affect was sometimes so stoic, JJ couldn't tell if he was happy or not. "Is that good?" JJ asked.

"I'm running about four-tenths of a second off world record pace. So, yes, it's good. If I can run the race in under forty-seven, I'm basically assured a medal."

"But of course, you're running against other people, so if it's a slow race, you won't need to run it that fast."

"Correct."

JJ took another bite of the burrito. It was bland as hell, but he was starving, so he took a few more bites hoping a jalapeño had slipped in there, maybe; then he said, "Hurdles was never my event. I tried a couple of times in high school. I tripped over a hurdle and skinned the hell out of my knee during a meet once, and that was enough of that. I just want to run fast. I don't need to jump too."

Brandon shrugged. "I like the challenge."

JJ found a miraculous piece of chorizo in the burrito. Spanish chorizo was garlicky rather than spicy, but it was seasoned, which was the key. Would it kill the chef at the cafeteria to use some pepper? "You have any time to walk around at all? Soak up your Olympic experience?" JJ asked, trying to make conversation.

"Actually, I went to the gift shop tonight because Grady said I should soak it all in, and I was looking around at all the Olympic-branded merchandise and it really hit me that I'm *here*. I started running because I needed a physical outlet. I used to watch the Olympics with my mom when I was a kid. I never imagined I'd be good enough to actually *be at the Olympics*. It's so strange."

JJ knew the feeling. He'd hit the ground running when he'd arrived in Madrid, so he hadn't had much time to even acknowledge where he was or the weight of everything. It hadn't really hit him yet.

But he was at the Olympics. That gold medal he'd won at Worlds, the one that had been taken away? He'd earned that, but it had been on a much smaller stage. This was the *Olympics*. Millions of people from around the world would be watching his races. And given how often he was getting tested, no one could argue that he was running clean. On *this* stage, he could prove to the whole world that he really was the fastest man alive and he didn't need drugs to win the title.

He polished off the rest of the burrito while Brandon described what he'd bought at the gift shop: a T-shirt, a gift for his mother, and a paperback novel. JJ's dinner had been unsatisfying, but he had some hope that the rest of the night would be different.

He popped into the bathroom to wash his hands, and when he returned, Brandon was still sitting on the bed.

JJ felt strange simply propositioning Brandon, because his suspicion was that Brandon was extremely cautious. So maybe talking it out or presenting an argument would be the right tack. On the other hand, maybe they should just retire to separate beds and get the sleep they both needed. "You said a bunch of things last night about sleeping and getting ready for competition, and Lord knows I could use a solid night's sleep tonight. But at the same time, I was sad you left last night and I'm pretty happy to see you now."

"Everything I said last night was stupid."

JJ laughed. "Girl, sometimes you say exactly the right thing."

Brandon stood up finally and stepped into JJ's personal space. Then he put his hands on JJ's face, rubbed JJ's beard with his thumbs, and lowered his face to press their lips together in a fierce kiss. JJ sank into it, putting his hands on Brandon's waist and leaning close.

Then Brandon pulled away slightly. "You said I could do what I wanted with you. Is this okay?"

"Yeah, baby. This is perfect."

Brandon laughed under his breath and leaned his head against JJ's shoulder. "I didn't come here meaning for anything to happen. I just needed to not be in my room. Still, all I thought about all day today was you and hurdles."

"So if I said, 'I'm gonna hop in the shower, and I want you to come with me so I can see you naked and we can make out,' would you be down?"

Brandon lifted his head and met JJ's gaze. "I mean… obviously."

"Come on, then. Although fair warning, I'm totally going to crash after this shower. So if you want some action, now is your only chance."

JJ grabbed Brandon's hand and led him to the bathroom. Brandon didn't understand subtlety well, and JJ was too tired to fuck around, so once he was in eyeshot of the shower, he dropped Brandon's hand and started peeling off his clothes. Brandon followed his lead and pulled his shirt off over his head.

And whoa. Brandon's chest was a wide expanse of peachy pink skin covering tight muscles. Brandon apparently had that core strength good hurdlers needed in abundance, because he was *cut*. Which of course made sense—any world-class track athlete probably was, and JJ had figured Brandon had a good body—but somehow JJ hadn't expected *this* body. It was as if the body didn't match Brandon's math nerd personality. Lord Almighty.

JJ stopped disrobing when he got to his briefs and walked over to Brandon, who stood there in only his sweatpants, giving JJ a curious look. JJ trailed his thumbs down Brandon's abs.

"Hey, sexy," JJ said.

Brandon blushed, his face and chest going crimson. The sexy plus the adorable was an interesting combination, but JJ liked it. He kissed Brandon and ground his hips against Brandon's, deriving deep satisfaction from the moan that escaped Brandon's lips.

"Hey," Brandon whispered.

JJ put his hands on Brandon's waist and pulled him close. "You know what I think? I think you've got this nerdy exterior, but inside you're just as horny as the rest of us. You're in this place with all these people in peak physical condition, and you're dying to touch them, to be with them."

"No…," Brandon whispered.

"There's something animal in you that I need to unleash. I can get you grunting and moaning and falling to pieces under my hands."

"Maybe… but it's not just any athlete I want."

"No?"

"No, I only want you."

Brandon crushed his lips against JJ's. They kissed hard, and JJ grabbed the waist of Brandon's sweatpants. "Get naked," he said against Brandon's lips. "Let's get in the shower."

Brandon eyed JJ as he peeled off his sweatpants and underwear. So much pink skin. Brandon was hard, his cock jutting away from his body.

This was one sexy math nerd. He had defined pecs, tight abs, rounded muscles on his arms, developed calves. Men like Brandon had long been models for marble statues, because everything was in perfect proportion. He had long legs to help him leap over hurdles, long arms to balance out his legs, long fingers, a long cock.

And two could play at that, because JJ was no slouch. He pulled off his briefs and let Brandon get a look at everything.

Brandon flushed, the pink starting near his collarbone and spreading down his chest. He murmured something JJ couldn't quite hear but thought might have been "Jesus."

"I love that I can see your arousal on your skin," JJ said.

Brandon ducked his head, then rotated to turn on the water.

Brandon had a great backside too. The long line of his spine led to a tight, round butt and powerful thighs. JJ decided to press against that long back as Brandon fiddled with the knobs in the shower. Brandon groaned.

"I can feel your cock," Brandon said softly.

"Is that okay?"

"Yeah. You're just…." Brandon sighed and pressed his ass back against JJ's cock. "I like it."

"Yeah?"

"Yes."

"Do you want me to fuck you?"

Brandon let out a shaky sigh. He lifted his arm and cupped his hand around the back of JJ's head. "So much," he said. "Not tonight, but I want it."

JJ put his arms around Brandon and let his cock settle between the cheeks of Brandon's ass. He thrust a few times and Brandon moaned, so responsive, so ready for JJ.

"Shower," Brandon said with a shudder.

Brandon pulled out of JJ's embrace and stepped into the shower. He adjusted the temperature as the water started to stream down his body, making him look slick and inviting, and then he turned around as JJ stepped in behind him, so that they faced each other.

JJ had left a bottle of bodywash on the corner of the tub, so he grabbed that. He poured some on his hands, then decided to soap up Brandon. He took the opportunity to touch Brandon everywhere, to get soap all over his skin, in every crevice, over his pecs, his abs, his arms, his ass, his cock, his legs. Brandon's knees seemed a little shaky, and he pressed one hand against the wall and grabbed the curtain rod with his other, bracing himself.

JJ kissed him. He wrapped one hand around Brandon's cock and stroked it. He reached the other behind and ran his hand around Brandon's ass. He pressed one soapy finger against the entrance of Brandon's body, and Brandon sighed and pushed down on it.

"All in good time," JJ said.

"Let me touch you."

Brandon grabbed the bodywash, poured some all over his hands, then soaped up JJ. And holy Jesus. Everywhere Brandon touched, JJ's skin tingled. Brandon's touch was assertive. He took what he wanted, and JJ was only too happy to give. But Brandon, of course, was an athlete and had a sense for the pain limits of the human body. He'd probably gotten enough sports massages to know what amount of pressure felt the best on tired muscles.

Things got a little messy after that. They explored each other with soapy hands. JJ got soap in his hair, on his beard, a little in his eyes, but he didn't care because he loved feeling Brandon's hands on him, seeing Brandon's intense gaze on his body. And he loved touching Brandon, finding the places on his body that JJ could dig his nails into or nibble on that would get the best reactions from Brandon.

When JJ was painfully hard and couldn't stand it anymore, he leaned back against the wall across from the cheap showerhead and pulled Brandon with him. He grabbed Brandon's ass and pressed their hips together. Then he grabbed both of their cocks in one hand and stroked them together. Brandon groaned and braced himself against the wall, a hand on either side of JJ's head.

The expression on Brandon's face told JJ he was nearly gone. JJ wanted to join him. His hand was slippery with water and soap, and it glided over both cocks easily. He looked down. Brandon thrust his hips, fucking against JJ's cock, fucking into his hand. Their cocks looked hot and perfect at the same time.

"I'm gonna come," Brandon said on a shuddery breath.

And JJ wanted to be right there with him, so he tightened his grip around them and thrust against Brandon. Brandon came first, his whole body shaking with it, spilling onto JJ's hand, making the grip even slicker. That was too much for JJ, whose orgasm started somewhere inside his body and seemed to radiate out. He let his release come but rode it out, thrusting against

Brandon while he grabbed on to Brandon's shoulders and pressed them together.

When they were both spent and panting, JJ found he was reluctant to let go. He hugged Brandon instead and felt gratified when Brandon's arms came around him. They held each other as Brandon was pelted with the spray from the shower.

"That was so fucking hot," JJ said.

"I know," said Brandon.

JJ laughed at that. Brandon had a gift for saying kind of the wrong thing, but also, something perfect.

"I'm a little sticky," Brandon said.

"Good thing we're already in the shower. Shall I assist in helping you clean off?"

"Please do."

CHAPTER NINE

THE TWIN bed wasn't really wide enough to hold them both. Brandon made a halfhearted suggestion that they push the two beds together, but that seemed like too much work, so they pressed together in one bed instead. Brandon hooked his legs around JJ's, mostly so he wouldn't fall out.

He supposed people found this tangle of limbs romantic. And, well, Brandon was quite comfortable tucked against JJ. His feet were dangling off the end of the bed, but that would have happened anyway. Brandon had never met a twin bed that was long enough for his frame. He was just sleepy enough from the long day of training and the hot shower and the good orgasm that it wouldn't take much effort to fall asleep.

And yet now, JJ was awake. The lights were off, although there was a dim glow from streetlights through the cheap translucent curtains. Brandon could see that light reflecting off JJ's open eyes.

JJ trailed his fingers along the edge of Brandon's hair, and Brandon closed his eyes and leaned into the touch. Maybe he didn't understand much about intimacy or how to express emotion, but he understood what felt good, and this was like a balm. Just that light trail of fingers could soothe anxiety, or at least make Brandon forget he was ever anxious about anything.

"So when did you know?"

Brandon yawned. "Know what?"

"When did you *know*. Like, when did you realize you weren't like other boys?"

"Is this small talk?"

JJ chuckled. "I'm curious. I like this question more than asking when you lost your virginity. The first time you have sex, that's a choice most of the time. The moment you realize you're gay? That's a revelation."

Brandon had never given this much thought before. He settled against JJ and tried to remember.

"I'll tell you mine," JJ said. "When I was, I dunno, thirteen? My mom was really into this show about people who wanted to be models. Boys and girls, not just girls. The host was a former model himself, and he was *foine*, but there was this one guy on the show who just… made me feel things. There was one episode in which all the models had to do an underwear shoot, and here was this perfect specimen of a man with his brown skin and his waxed chest wearing only these tiny briefs, and something happened to me."

Brandon smiled to himself. He could imagine. He had to think about his own revelation. Had there been a precise moment or just a general feeling? "I had a crush on a guy in my biology class my freshman year in high school. That was my first real crush, I guess."

"Uh-huh. What did he look like?"

Brandon closed his eyes and tried to remember. "A little taller than me. Curly brown hair. Blue eyes. He was a junior when I was a freshman. Not the brightest bulb in the box, but gosh, he was pretty. I used to spend half the class wishing he would turn around and smile at me. In retrospect, I don't think he even knew my name. Also, he was dating the head cheerleader."

The whole situation had puzzled him at the time, because why should he have cared so much about what this kid, who wasn't even very smart, thought of him? But whenever he'd been nearby, Brandon had been unable to look away. It had been a confusing time.

"You're out to your family?"

"I am. My parents got divorced when I was eight. I came out to my mom when I was fifteen and to my dad about a year later. He got married again when I was in middle school, so he was preoccupied with his new family when I was first coming out. Honestly, I think my parents cared more about the fact that I struggled so much socially in high school than anything else."

"I'm sorry. High school kids are the worst."

Brandon sighed. "I suppose you didn't have any problem."

"Oh, I had my share of issues. I stayed in the closet until college, but I'm sure people knew. My parents were not at all surprised. Mom was like, 'And?'" JJ grunted and shifted on the bed a little. "They flew in today. I couldn't make time to see them before practice, and then I was too tired to deal with them, but my mother has called me twice."

"But I mean, you probably got along with everyone in high school."

"I did all right."

Brandon recognized that he was being a little pushy. "I'm sorry. The therapist I saw a few years ago would probably say that I'm projecting all my issues on you. I don't mean to. You just seem so cool and easygoing to me, and I'm a little jealous of that."

JJ settled back against Brandon's side, and Brandon held him, because if he put any distance between them, he'd fall out of the bed. But he wanted to hold JJ too. Making out in the shower had been hot and overwhelming, and Brandon still couldn't believe he'd let go like that. And even after that wallop of an orgasm, he still wanted JJ to fuck him. But not tonight. Not when Brandon had to run the next day, especially when the stakes were this high. Hopefully there'd be an opportunity for that before they tired of each other.

"It's not always easy," JJ said.

"Hmm?"

"I have to work to seem relaxed sometimes. I don't want to be… angry. I am, a lot of the time. Angry, I mean. I have to work to let that anger go."

"What are you angry about?"

JJ laughed. "Oooh, girl. What am I *not* angry about? But that's a talk for another time. We should probably try to sleep."

The warmth of the recent orgasm and shower and the press of JJ's body were making Brandon sleepy anyway, so he decided not to push JJ, even though Brandon suddenly burned with the desire to know everything there was to know about him. But apparently the day was catching up with JJ too, because he closed his eyes and his breathing evened out. So Brandon closed his eyes and sank into oblivion.

JJ WAS nearly finished painting his nails when Brandon finally stirred. JJ had brought his whole nail polish kit with him, but there was only one color appropriate for what he planned to do in Madrid: gold. He'd have custom gold running shoes on his feet, sparkly gold polish on his nails, and some bling around his neck. Some of his teammates wore gold crosses, but JJ wasn't religious. Instead, he rotated between a pendant his mother had given him, a small gold medal on a gold chain he'd won at one of his first track meets, and a medallion depicting St. Sebastian, the patron saint of athletes, that had been a gift from Tamika.

Brandon sat up and looked confused for a moment; then he murmured, "Oh, nail polish."

"Is that a problem?"

"No. I smelled something weird and couldn't figure out what it was."

JJ focused on finishing the second coat on his right hand. When he looked up, Brandon was staring at him. And that look got JJ's hackles up.

"You think it's silly, don't you?"

Brandon shook his head. "No. It's… weirdly sexy, actually."

JJ finished what he was doing and dropped the brush back in the bottle. He glanced at Brandon, who was looking intently at JJ's hands.

"Sexy, huh?"

JJ had pulled on shorts and a tank top when he'd gotten out of bed, but Brandon was still naked, the sheet draped over his lap now. His dark hair was disheveled and his pale skin was a bit flushed. His glasses were on the side table, and his eyes looked bigger without them, somehow. Brandon did not seem particularly invested in his appearance. He'd admitted during one of their late-night talks that he had his chest waxed before meets that he knew would be televised because he didn't like how his body hair looked with the Team USA uniforms they issued these days, but that seemed to be extent of his vanity.

"Is this part of your premeet ritual?" Brandon asked, running a hand through his hair.

"I would have done this last night, but, well…." JJ gestured toward Brandon.

"Sorry."

"Don't apologize. I have no regrets about last night. Do you?"

Brandon shook his head.

"Good." JJ blew on his nails. He'd learned over the years that the good polish that stayed on without chipping or peeling took a minute to dry.

Brandon tilted his head. "Can you paint my nails?"

"Really?"

"Forget it."

"No, I totally will if you want to."

Brandon took a deep breath. "It could be fun. I like how it looks on your hands."

On JJ's brown hands, the gold popped, but it would blend in a little on Brandon's lighter skin. "Do you want gold or another color?"

"You have other colors?"

"Girl, please." JJ pointed to the cosmetics bag full of nail polish on the little desk near him.

Brandon got out of bed and walked, stark naked, over to the table. He picked up the bag and started rif-fling through it. JJ didn't want to chip his new mani-cure, but he couldn't resist running a hand down Bran-don's bare ass, since it was right there. He loved that

Brandon wasn't self-conscious. He had a lovely body, and his half-hard cock plumped up in interest at the proceedings, and JJ kind of wanted to put his mouth around it, and—

"What about a red, white, and blue thing? Like, on alternating fingers. Or is that too complicated?"

"Nope, I can do that. Welcome to JJ's Nail Salon. Although you might want to put some pants on so you don't distract the manicurist."

Brandon looked down. "Oh!" he said with a giggle.

He went into the bathroom, where he'd left his overnight bag the night before, and came back a few minutes later wearing a clean T-shirt and warm-up pants. He grabbed the other chair in the room and sat next to JJ. Then he placed his hands on the table.

"I've never gotten a manicure," Brandon said.

"You don't know what you're missing. I will not do the experience justice. The place I go in LA is fantastic. When you leave, your hands and feet are soft, your nails all look the same, and they give you a shoulder and scalp massage as part of the deal. I don't have time for all that right now, but I can make your nails look neat."

"I washed my hands."

JJ chuckled. "Good start." He glanced at his own nails and decided they were dry enough. With great care, he picked up a bottle of lotion, put a generous amount on his palm, and smeared it all over Brandon's hand. He got in there and really massaged Brandon's large fingers. Fingers that had been wrapped around JJ's cock a few hours ago, hands that had….

No, not the time. Sex would *definitely* chip JJ's nails. He focused instead on making sure the tips of Brandon's fingers were well moisturized.

"This is some routine you have," said Brandon.

"Do you like it?"

"Yeah. The hand massage is nice."

Brandon did have lovely hands. Wide palms, long fingers. Strong hands, callused hands—perhaps not the hands of an academic but rather someone who tinkered with things. JJ got a mental image of Brandon hovering over some circuit board, fiddling with parts of it to see what would happen. JJ liked the image. He liked these hands. He really liked Brandon.

JJ glanced up and saw Brandon staring back at him. Unable to resist, he leaned over and kissed Brandon slowly. Then he pulled back slightly and smiled.

Brandon smiled back. "Why did you kiss me?"

"I wanted to."

"Okay."

JJ cleared his throat and got back to the task at hand. He carefully reached into his nail polish bag and extracted a bottle of red polish, a bottle of white, and an electric blue. "Hold very still."

"Okay."

JJ gave each of Brandon's nails a quick swipe with polish remover. Then he started with red. Left thumb, left ring finger. Right pointer, right pinkie. Then he painted white. Then blue. Red, white, blue, red, white, blue, red, white, blue, red. Before he did the second coat, JJ leaned back to admire his handiwork. "I like it. Very patriotic."

Brandon gazed at his nails. "It looks really cool."

"Is this really okay? Because I can guarantee that some asshole at the stadium will call you a fag when they see your nails."

"I am a fag." Brandon's tone was matter-of-fact.

JJ laughed. "All right, then. I wasn't sure if you wanted all that out there."

"You don't care, do you?"

"Not at all. If someone called me a fag, it wouldn't be the first time. I say embrace it. I'm a runner, I'm black, and I'm queer, and I'm never going to stop being any of those things, especially not on the track. Might as well show it all off."

"I like that. I don't think I really read as gay. I'm not in the closet or anything. It's not like I try to hide it or act any specific way on purpose—it's just something people have told me. How did you know?"

JJ grinned. "You made eyes at me."

"I did not."

"Girl. Were you not attracted to me when we met at practice the other day?"

Brandon ducked his head and blushed. "Okay. I was."

"There were hearts in your eyes."

Brandon giggled nervously. "There were not."

JJ leaned over and gave Brandon a quick peck. "You were vibing on me. I could feel it."

"All right."

JJ laughed. Brandon was too much sometimes. JJ knew that life wasn't this simple, but he liked living in Brandon's bubble, where it was.

Chapter Ten

ONE INESCAPABLE fact was that JJ's mother would not stop calling until he agreed to meet up with his parents, and he'd better do it before that day's race or else risk her wrath. Hence the early-morning nail polishing and having to let Brandon go with some very sweet kisses. Then he jogged over to the America House for coffee and pub breakfast before he had to be at the stadium.

He'd had dinner at his parents' house three days before he'd flown to Madrid, so it wasn't like it had been so long since he'd seen them, and still Mildred Jones's eyes filled with moisture when JJ slid into the booth across from his parents.

"I'm not… dying, Mom."

"We're just so proud of you, sweetie," she said.

JJ was sad sometimes that he'd been an only child, with the full focus of Mildred's motherly attentions on him his whole life. On the one hand, it was great;

she'd been unfailingly supportive of him. On the other hand, it was a lot. Like right now, when she was smiling through her tears, gazing at him as she lifted a glass of orange juice to her lips.

JJ glanced at his father, who shrugged but grinned.

A waiter came by, so JJ ordered eggs and bacon, because he wanted protein. Someone else came by and slid a mug of hot coffee in front of him. He certainly couldn't complain about the service.

Even if he did want to be back in his dorm room, in bed with Brandon.

He sighed and sipped his coffee.

"How are you liking Madrid?" Mildred asked.

"It's fine. I haven't really seen anything that isn't part of the Olympic complex here."

"They play a lot of sports here," Jason Jones Senior said. "I read on the plane that most of the Olympic venues were already here. Only the Olympic Stadium is new. Your mother and I haven't been there yet. Is it nice?"

"The stadium is very nice, yes. I mean, I can't speak to what the stands are like, but the track is state-of-the-art. It reminds me a lot of that track in Dubai where they had the World Championship a few years ago. Only it's a smidge less hot here."

"It has been quite muggy," said Mildred.

"How has practice been going?" asked Jason Senior.

"Well, Tamika has been making me work pretty hard, but I've been putting in good times. I feel ready."

Conversation continued in this vein for a while. JJ felt a little awkward, not for any particular reason except that he kept thinking of Brandon. Even now, JJ was picturing Brandon splayed on his bed, Brandon standing over JJ naked, Brandon's face as he came in the shower. Warmth spread through JJ. He sipped his coffee to hide how he felt.

"You meet anyone new here?" Mildred asked.

JJ choked and almost spit out his coffee. He took a slow sip and then put the mug down. "Sorry, went down the wrong pipe." He cleared his throat. "Uh, well, Tamika's husband, Grady, you remember him? He has a hurdler he's coaching, and Tamika suggested we train together. So we've done some speed drills, that kind of thing. Other than that, I haven't really talked to many strangers."

"I always thought the Olympics were kind of romantic. Like, you might look across the way and see a handsome swimmer or gymnast or something and have an unlikely love affair."

Jason Senior rolled his eyes.

"Gross, Mom."

"I'm just saying. But finding a new training partner isn't so bad either. I only want…."

When she trailed off, JJ glanced at his father, who shrugged like he had no idea where she was going.

"Look, you can't run forever. I only want you to be happy. And I want grandchildren, but I'd settle for you finding a nice young man to settle down with."

JJ sighed. He had no particular desire for children, but he and his mother had spoken on this many times in the past. She knew his feelings on the matter. He also didn't see himself settling down anytime soon. His body still had a lot of races in it, he still had more people to meet, places to see, life to live.

He also knew that his parents had dated for only a hot minute before deciding to get married, that they'd literally spotted each other across a crowded bar when they'd both been in college, and that had been it. They'd hardly ever been apart since. Part of JJ kind of thought that when he found the right guy, he'd know, just like his parents had known they were meant to be together from the beginning.

Brandon popped into his head again. Was Brandon the man for him? JJ didn't know, so probably not, but he sure was a fun diversion during these Olympics.

A waiter showed up with his eggs, so JJ dove in.

"Anyway," said Jason Senior, "we have tickets to the stadium for the next four days, so we'll be at all your races. Our seats seem to be in the south side of the stadium about halfway up. I guess the section was reserved for parents of American athletes."

"Yeah, that's so they can get your reactions on camera when I run," JJ said between bites. The eggs were a little runny for his taste, but suddenly he was ravenous, shoving food in his face.

"Oh." Mildred touched her hair. She kept it cut fairly short these days, but it looked like it had been relaxed and flat-ironed recently, into kind of a spiky pixie cut. Jason Senior had recently given up on not being bald and just shaved his whole head, which JJ feared was in his future, although not for a few more years. Jason Senior had never been too concerned with appearances, but Mildred was the sort of woman who never left the house without full hair and her makeup done to perfection. Even now, she had on a floral dress that was only one step below what she would have worn to church. Jason Senior looked more appropriate in a navy T-shirt with *USA* in big white letters across his chest.

"You look great, Mom."

"Thank you, dear. I forgot that we might be on camera."

"Well, that assumes I make it out of prelims, of course."

"You will, son," said Jason Senior. "You looked amazing at the US Trials. You've been running great all year. I'll be shocked if you don't make the final. Plus I heard half your competition got DQ'd for doping."

"Well, just the Russians. And there weren't any in the field for my races anyway." JJ then related what he'd experienced with the drug testing so far.

"It'll all be worth it when you win gold," Jason Senior said.

"And no matter what, we love you and support you," said Mildred.

"Thanks."

"Aunt Ruthie and her family are watching from home too, and Gladys, of course," said Mildred. She had two sisters, Ruth and Gladys, and JJ had always kind of liked that they had names that sounded old-fashioned. Ruth and her kids lived a few blocks from JJ's parents, and Gladys and her husband had recently moved to the Bay Area to be closer to their daughter, who worked for a huge tech company in Silicon Valley. "Your whole family is behind you."

Jason Senior chuckled. "Uncle Joe says hi, by the way." Joe was JJ's uncle on his father's side. Joe had five kids, spanning in age from fourteen through twenty-seven. JJ's maternal grandparents were also still alive and lived in Vermont Square, as did many of his parents' close friends. Gatherings at the Jones house were often big, raucous affairs with lots of people and food and laughter, and JJ loved them, though he also loved being able to go back to his own apartment on the other side of the city afterward.

This was apparently on his mother's mind too. "You should think about moving back to the neighborhood," Mildred said.

"We've discussed this already."

"I know, but it doesn't make sense for you to live in West Hollywood. We live closer to USC than you do. There are hundreds of bars in the area where you could work."

"I'm still in LA. It's not like I live in New York. Also, if you want me to meet a nice young man, there sure are a lot of them in West Hollywood."

Mildred sighed. "We don't see you enough, JJ."

"The season's almost over. I'll come by more often when I'm not training as much."

"You'd better. We miss you."

JJ sighed and finished off his eggs.

BRANDON HAD two older brothers who had been hard on him for most of his childhood. He'd been an awkward, skinny kid who studied a lot and had few friends, something his more popular brothers had often brought up as a way to paint him as a loser. Their mother had always just said that boys would be boys, but as a kid, Brandon had hated that. After a long day of being picked on in school, he came home to more of the same, and nobody said a word about it. The only thing that had made life bearable for him was the fact that Danny and Mike had moved out of the house when Brandon was still in middle school—he knew he'd been a later-in-life, last-ditch-attempt-to-save-the-marriage baby—meaning they were mostly away during his most awkward years.

And yet Danny and Mike were here, in Madrid, with their wives, Danny's five-year-old son, and

Brandon's mother, Janine, all staring at him expectantly as he sat with them in a little food court area within the stadium. The only thing that could have made this worse would have been if Brandon's father—who was distant and sometimes acted like he was embarrassed to have a gay son—had flown out here too.

"I can't get over how you look these days," said Danny.

"I need to train," Brandon said, hooking his thumb back toward the athlete area.

"You can sit and talk to your family for five minutes," said Janine.

Brandon knew they meant well. He also knew that no one in his family really understood him. They didn't understand the work he did or the subject he studied. They often had very little to talk about. Even Janine, who had become his main ally in recent years, didn't fully understand the way his head worked. Brandon had spent a lot of his childhood feeling like an alien in his own home. His brothers had both made efforts in recent years to maintain a relationship with him, which Brandon appreciated, though he was still wary, wondering if the fact that he was outwardly a jock now somehow made him seem cool to them even though nothing had really changed. Brandon could run fast and jump over things. But he still loved math and putting things together and taking things apart, and he still liked to read long books and watch documentaries. He and his brothers still had nothing in common.

He hoped JJ was faring better with his family.

JJ got him, didn't he? Maybe JJ didn't understand all the math stuff, but he understood something crucial about the way Brandon saw the world, and he knew how to let Brandon be in his world.

Well, and he was really sexy. Brandon couldn't deny that.

He rubbed his forehead and looked at his gathered family.

"I'm just saying, you have muscles and things," Danny, who had a bit of a potbelly, said, gesturing at Brandon. "How do you keep in shape like that?"

"Training and diet."

Danny laughed. "Sure."

"We wanted to tell you," said Mike's wife, Amy, "that we're really proud of you and we're happy to be here to cheer for you."

Brandon smiled. Amy really was very sweet. Brandon liked her a lot. "Thank you. I appreciate it."

"What are your plans for after the Olympics?" asked Lucy, Danny's wife.

"Luce, give him a chance to compete first," said Janine.

"No, it's fine. I mean, I still have one more year of school." Brandon shrugged.

What Brandon really wanted to do was be involved in designing the electronic devices of the future. He wanted to build better tablets or play a role in figuring out whatever the next big thing would be. He liked the puzzle of figuring out how things worked, and once he understood how something functioned, he could figure out how to improve it. It was like the hurdles. Once he'd figured out the mechanics of it, the steps between hurdles and the force he had to jump, his race had improved significantly.

"What about running?" asked Amy.

"I'll stay on the track team until I graduate. I don't want it to be my full-time job, though."

"It's a shame, since you're so good," said Lucy.

Mike hadn't spoken at all, something Brandon found a little disconcerting. He wondered if Mike didn't want to be here.

They didn't even look alike. Danny and Mike were closer in age, of course, both of them in their thirties now, but they'd inherited their mother's sunnier coloring, lighter hair and tanner skin, whereas Brandon looked a lot like their father, with dark hair and pale skin. And maybe that didn't matter at all, but it didn't help Brandon not feel like an outsider. He was taller than his brothers, more awkward socially, and gay. Now that he'd made the Olympic team, he felt like a bit of a spectacle, and the center of attention was not his favorite place to be.

He'd taken up running because being around these people stressed him out, if he was honest. And he definitely wanted to run away now. He could have dealt with his mother one-on-one, but his brothers and their families too? It was too much.

His phone vibrated on the table. It was a text from Grady asking where he was. Thank goodness. He pointed at his phone. "That's my coach. I should go."

"You're not racing until tomorrow," said Danny. "Do you really need to train?"

"Yes, actually. Do you know how I got here? By training a lot. I need to continue to practice so that I get used to this track and give my best performance when I run." Brandon stood.

"Don't stalk off, Brandon," said his mother. "We just got here."

"I'll see you later, okay? I'm glad you're coming to see me run tomorrow. Jason Jones Jr. is running the two-hundred-meter sprint shortly, and he's wonderful. You should watch that race."

"He's the flamboyant one, right?" Mike asked.

"I… guess," Brandon said. Brandon hadn't given that much thought—he'd noticed that JJ painted his nails and wore brightly colored sneakers, and he'd heard other people describe him as flamboyant—but to Brandon he was just… JJ. The way he decorated himself was part of the package. Brandon put his hands behind his back, hoping no one had noticed his nails.

"We'll watch," said Mike.

"I'm sorry," Brandon said. "I love you all. We can do something later. Okay?"

"Be safe," said his mother.

"I will, of course. Um. I've got to get going." Brandon walked away.

CHAPTER ELEVEN

Day 12
Transcript from the TBC Broadcast of the two-hundred-meter sprint, qualifying heats

CASSELLO: NEXT we'll be seeing the qualifying heats for the men's two-hundred-meter sprint. There are four Americans in this field.

GRAYSON: That's right, Jim. In the first heat is Franco Greer. He's a veteran athlete out of the program at USC. He came in second at Trials. He's got a good shot at making the final.

CASSELLO: Just so the audience knows what we'll be seeing today, there are six qualifying heats for the two-hundred-meter sprint. The top sixteen times from those heats will advance to a semifinal, which they will run this evening, and the top eight from that race will run in the final tomorrow.

GRAYSON: Correct. So, the rest of the Americans who qualified include Rafael Martinez, who is stronger in the one-hundred-meter run, DeShawn Latrell, who has a good shot to make the final, and the runner who I think has the best hope—Jason Jones Jr. He goes by JJ. He's a… character.

CASSELLO: And you think he has a shot to win the gold medal?

GRAYSON: I mean, it's the Olympics. Anything is possible. But this year's Jamaican team is young and inexperienced, and their reign as the sprint champions may be coming to an end. This is JJ's second Olympics, he has a couple of World Championship medals under his belt, and he won this race at the Olympic Trials by a wide margin. But you may recall that he also tested positive for a banned substance a few years ago. He was cleared of those charges, but it makes you wonder, doesn't it?

CASSELLO: Track and field fans want to see the pure sport. No doping, no cheating.

GRAYSON: The World Anti-Doping Agency is here doing random testing. So far the entire Russian delegation and a handful of other athletes have been disqualified. And any athlete with a whiff of impropriety in their background is being subjected to extra testing, and that includes athletes like JJ. So we can assume he's being tested while he's here.

CASSELLO: We haven't talked much about doping in the past.

GRAYSON: No, but we should. It's a major issue in a number of sports now. The IOC is trying to make it clear it will not tolerate cheaters. I wouldn't be surprised if more athletes get DQ'd before this week is over.

CASSELLO: Let's hope it's none of these American athletes. I'd love to see Team USA bring home gold medals in the sprints once again.

GRAYSON: JJ could do it. He won this race at the Trials by almost half a second. He's… flashy.

CASSELLO: I've heard he models himself after Florence Griffith Joyner.

GRAYSON: Odd choice. But he's also openly gay. And anyone who has followed him for a while knows he's definitely not shy. JJ has a big personality. He paints his nails, he likes to wear a lot of bling during his races, and he designs his own running shoes. I heard a rumor he has custom gold shoes for his races this week because that's the color medal he intends to win.

CASSELLO: He stands out in a crowd, that's for sure….

RACE DAY started with a massage. When JJ arrived at the stadium after breakfast, Tamika directed him to a little area set up in the locker room for the American athletes. USATF had a physical therapist on staff who spent a half hour massaging JJ's feet and legs and then stretching him out. Once JJ got all soft and loose, he got off the table and hopped up and down a few times, ran a few slow laps on the practice track, and was ready to run a few sprints when Tamika pulled him into a team meeting.

He resented this meeting. JJ just wanted to get to the practice track so he could run two hundred meters a few times before he had to race officially.

JJ was less proven at the two-hundred than the one-hundred. He won it almost as much as he didn't in competition. It didn't have the same glory as the one-hundred, but JJ still liked the challenge of it. The one-hundred was an all-out sprint, less than ten seconds to prove a runner was the Fastest Man Alive. The two-hundred required a little more strategy. He wanted to practice his own strategy a few times more before he had to do it for real, but Tamika wanted the American relay team to meet.

"Ten minutes, JJ," she said. "You can give me ten measly minutes."

The four-by-one-hundred-meter relay team was composed of the four fastest American one-hundred-meter sprinters, with a couple of alternates in case someone got injured or otherwise bombed in competition. JJ had actually run his first relay at the previous Olympics when a teammate had lost most of his races by wide margins and the coach had pulled him from the relay team at the last minute. The team had come in second after the Jamaicans. Now that most of that Jamaican team had retired, everyone was putting pressure on the American relay team to win.

JJ looked at those assembled. There was Rafael Martinez, a dark-skinned Dominican guy from New York City whose father had played first base for the Mets, and probably JJ's main American competition in his other races; DeShawn Latrell, a sprinter from Detroit who had come in second to JJ in the one-hundred at the Trials; and Darrell Oakley, a career runner who had once beat Usain Bolt in a small meet no one watched but who was now a little past his prime. The alternates were a USC sophomore named Pete and a white guy named George, who hung back as if they didn't think they belonged in this scrum.

The American coaching staff had full reign of the practice track for a half hour, and someone decided it was a good opportunity to do a relay practice run.

When JJ started to protest, Tamika held up one finger and said, "The actual run-through will take less than a minute. I know you're worried about your race today, but we have plenty of time. Indulge me."

"Fine. Am I anchor?"

"No, third. I want DeShawn first, then Darrell, then you, then Rafa finishing it up."

JJ nodded. He could see the wisdom of that. The Jamaicans often put their fastest guy third so that he could build on the lead enough for the last runner to basically coast the last one hundred meters.

"I want DeShawn to practice the exchange." Tamika reached into her bag and pulled out a baton.

So JJ went through the motions of doing practice for the relay when he had to run the two-hundred in a couple of hours. He got into his position and watched DeShawn get a great start but then fumble the pass and drop the baton. Darrell grabbed it and ran toward JJ, so JJ jogged ahead a little and reached his hand back. Darrell slapped it into his hand rather hard, but he caught it and took off around the turn. He got the baton to Rafa, who grabbed it and sprinted toward the finish.

"Forty seconds," Tamika said with a grimace.

"Can we practice again tomorrow?" Rafa asked. "I gotta get ready for my race."

"Me too," JJ said.

Tamika looked around. "Fine. But we need to practice this more. The baton pass needs to be a lot smoother."

JJ wanted to tell her to run drills with DeShawn and Darrell so they could pass the baton better. JJ had run in dozens of relays and knew how this went. But he kept his mouth shut. He understood Tamika was taking advantage of the American team having a reservation on the practice track, but he didn't need this aggravation on race day. And truth be told, he was freaking out but trying not to show it. He felt nervous but couldn't put a finger on why. He should have been able to make the final easily, but sometimes just a few tenths of a second kept an athlete from advancing, and if he was slow because he was tired….

"You're really going with the nails thing, huh?" Darrell asked.

"It's my thing." But JJ already knew where this was going. He didn't know Darrell well, but he did know that the guy considered himself an elder statesman and didn't have time for any kind of ornamentation on the track. He wore simple black sneakers, no jewelry, and he kept his hair in a high fade, short on top, nothing interesting or controversial.

"Your thing is being a fruitcake?" said Darrell.

JJ rolled his eyes. He didn't have the bandwidth to engage with this. He wanted to get a few practice runs of the two-hundred in before their half hour on the track ran out.

"You don't have anything to say to me, faggot?" said Darrell.

"Come on," said Rafa. "We're teammates. Don't do this."

JJ decided to turn on the swish. "Girl, I like to paint my nails. I like to bring a little flash onto the track. And yes, I am a gay man. Nothing I do affects how fast or slow you run on the track. Unless you're afraid I'll come up behind you and stick my dick in your ass. Good thing I'm running after you, huh?"

"JJ, come on," said Rafa, a warning in his voice.

"You asshole," said Darrell, advancing on JJ.

"Who's the asshole? You're standing here calling me a faggot. How do you expect me to react?"

"Boys!" said Tamika. "Knock it off. JJ, that was too far. Darrell, if I hear you talk like that to JJ again, you're DQ'd. Off the relay team, and I'll talk to your coach about scratching you from your races. We don't tolerate talk like that here."

Darrell said, "Fine," and stormed off.

JJ finally lost all patience. He didn't have time to stand around yapping. "Tam, I gotta get some practice runs in before time runs out."

Tamika looked over JJ. "Fine. Go."

He set up his blocks and got Grady to time him. His start wasn't very strong, so he tried to channel all of his anger into the run. But he was distracted, thinking about Darrell his whole trip around the track. He was normally better about letting this kind of thing roll off his back, but Darrell ragging on him had made him feel shitty. He ran past the finish but didn't want to know his time.

"You're over twenty seconds," Grady said, showing his time on the timer.

"Fuck."

"You're too worked up."

JJ took a deep breath. He was mad at Tamika for making him do relay practice, and he was furious with Darrell. "What gives that dickhead the right to—?"

"I know," said Grady. "Deep breath."

JJ took a series of deep breaths and counted to ten. One of JJ's cousins was a kindergarten teacher, and she'd mentioned this was something she made her students do when they threw a tantrum. Worked like a charm every time. JJ had tried it a short while later, after he'd gotten into a fight with another athlete at the track. He'd stopped what he was doing, taken a deep breath, and counted to ten. At the time he'd thought it was stupid, but it helped him cool off. He had to remember to try it more often when he got worked up sometimes.

Grady got behind JJ and dug his thumbs into JJ's shoulders. "Run a few laps, go see the physical therapist or go do whatever you need to do to cool down, because you're tensing up."

JJ took another deep breath and let it go with a sigh. "Yeah."

He opted to run a few slow laps. Every hundred meters, he felt more tension drain from his body. He knew he shouldn't let assholes like Darrell get to him. If he wanted to run his race in full Flo-Jo drag, he should be able to.

He was on his third lap when a few other American athletes arrived to warm up.

Franco was running in the two-hundred, which JJ knew, but seeing him here felt jarring. They'd been good friends once and still talked frequently when they were training at USC at the same time and occasionally grabbed meals together. But ever since JJ had left Marcus and he and Franco had stopped training together, they'd drifted apart. They'd hardly interacted at all since arriving in Madrid aside from quick nods at each other as they passed.

JJ watched him do his warm-up. Franco ran a lap and looked to be in good condition, but JJ couldn't help but wonder…. Was Franco clean? Had Marcus devised a drug regimen for him? Had any of the random drug testing caught him yet? JJ also still wondered sometimes if Franco had sabotaged him on purpose. It had seemed unlikely. He and Franco had been training partners for years. At the time, JJ had tried convincing himself it was an honest mistake, and the fact that the guidelines for the acceptable amount of pseudoephedrine an athlete could take before a meet had changed proved the rules had been wrong at the time anyway.

But what lengths would Franco go to in order to win?

Thinking about that make JJ tense up again.

He'd never confronted Franco about it. He'd been afraid to ask. After JJ's acquittal, he and Franco had run into each other at the track and had a conversation in which Franco seemed genuinely sorry that JJ had been forced to defend himself and glad that JJ had been forgiven. JJ had taken his word for it, because they'd been friends and JJ had trusted him. But as they'd grown apart, JJ had started to wonder more. And the fact that he knew Marcus had a line on some dealers who could get an athlete on a regimen….

But no, that was ridiculous. Well, JJ couldn't speak for what Franco was doing to his body now, but Franco would never have deliberately sabotaged another athlete. He'd always been the sort to cheer on his training mates. His sabotaging JJ didn't make any sense. Franco had finished out of the medals in that race, more to the point, so it wasn't like JJ losing the medal had bestowed any awards on Franco.

JJ gave up on running laps and jogged over to the locker room, hoping the physical therapist could recommend something, but instead he ran into Brandon, who looked a little confused.

"You okay?" JJ asked.

"Yeah. Sorry." Brandon blinked a few times. "Grady told me to go to the gym, but I want to watch you race first, and I forgot how to get to the stands from here. The last time I went, I followed Grady and wasn't paying attention to how we got there."

"You want to watch me?"

"Yeah. We're friends now."

The "duh" in Brandon's tone made JJ smile. "Yes, we're friends. Thank you. To get to the stands, you have to walk to the other side of the practice track and then take the B staircase."

"Thank you."

Brandon started to walk out of the room, so JJ snagged his arm. "Before you go, can you help me with something?"

"Of course."

JJ led Brandon toward the American corner of the locker room. The physical therapist was working Rafa's legs, but there were little cubicles made of curtains set up, and JJ pulled Brandon into one of those.

"Just…," JJ said. And then he hugged Brandon.

Brandon made a little sound of surprise but put his arms around JJ. "Are *you* okay?" Brandon asked.

"Rough morning. I'm happy to see you."

"What happened?"

"Nothing." JJ grabbed on to Brandon and let the soft stroke of Brandon's hand down his back soothe him. Softly, he said, "Remember how I told you someone would call you a fag if you painted your nails? Well, someone called *me* a fag. And I got really angry and worked up about it. And then I got to thinking about some old garbage that I shouldn't care about anymore. I kind of spiraled. But I need to calm down before my race, so I'm glad I ran into you, because this is helping."

"Okay." Brandon sounded like he didn't totally understand that.

JJ breathed in and out slowly as Brandon held him, and he tried to remember what was really important here. Not assholes like Darrell, not Franco, not even the relay. All JJ could control was his own races, and he had to either calm down or find a constructive way to channel his frustration into his race.

Maybe he should talk to Franco and try to put this nonsense to rest, even if just for his own edification. Or JJ should push it aside because it was old news and he'd been acquitted and he was at the Olympics.

He took a few more deep breaths and then eased away from Brandon. "Thank you."

"I didn't really do anything," said Brandon.

JJ smiled and patted his shoulder. Brandon was really something. Nothing seemed to bother him much. More importantly, he was completely guileless. It was refreshing. "You're going to watch me run?"

"Yes, I want to. Grady said I could sit in the Team USA section in the stands. I think Tamika will be there."

"Yeah, she likes to film my races so we can discuss how to improve later. Assuming I make it out of the first round of heats, she'll have notes for the semifinal."

"Smart." Brandon took a deep breath and looked around. "I'll admit, I'm also kind of avoiding my family."

"Oh?"

Brandon sighed. "It's nothing. My brothers both flew out to Madrid with their families. It's nice to see them, but my family stresses me out."

"Families are like that." JJ sensed there was a larger story here, but he didn't have time to ask about it now. Instead he said, "Are you okay?"

"Better now." Brandon smiled.

JJ smiled back. Brandon was too cute for words sometimes. "Glad we could help each other."

"Me too."

"We could help each other more," said JJ.

"How?"

JJ paused to listen for a moment. He heard Rafa and the masseuse speaking softly to each other but didn't think many other people were around. JJ and Brandon had the relative privacy of four curtains shielding them from prying eyes. So JJ leaned over and pressed a kiss against Brandon's lips.

Brandon sighed into his mouth and put his arms more forcefully around JJ, pulling him close. He opened his mouth and let JJ in. They kissed for what might have been thirty seconds or a lifetime, and JJ felt himself getting worked up in an entirely different but far more pleasant way.

Brandon pulled away gently. "I mean… that helped me."

JJ laughed and felt some of the tension drain from his body.

Brandon made a shooing motion with his hands. "Okay, you should go."

"Yeah. And you do a lot, Brandon. I like that you'll be in the stands. It feels like you're supporting me."

"I am supporting you."

"I know." JJ leaned over and gave Brandon another peck on the lips. "You probably don't believe in this sort of thing, but the Olympics have a kind of magic to them. It's like living in a bubble while they're on. You meet new people and make new friends and maybe have a little romance and it's this strange, otherworldly experience, until you crash back to earth and have to fly home and go back to your job. I'm starting to think you're part of my Olympics magic."

"We both live in LA."

JJ searched Brandon's face. "Are you saying you'd like to keep seeing me after we get home?"

"I don't see why not."

JJ grinned. Maybe things were really that easy. "I'll keep that in mind. Cheer for me."

"I will."

BRANDON WAS still feeling a little rattled from visiting with his family—and a little charged up from kissing JJ—as he settled into his seat in the stands. Fortunately his family was no longer in the stadium; apparently some of their party had gotten bored watching preliminary heats and they'd gone off to do some touristy things in Madrid. It was just as well—Brandon didn't want to have to explain sitting with the coaches and not with his family in the stands. He just… couldn't, not right now. He appreciated that they were trying, but sometimes the effort it took to play nice with his family was more exhausting than a long, grueling track practice.

He glanced at Tamika, who sat beside him. Based on information from Grady and Google, Brandon knew she was a retired runner herself, with a handful of titles and an Olympic silver medal in the two-hundred earned several Games ago. Brandon had always thought she was pretty, with smooth brown skin, long eyelashes, and a great smile. She changed her hair a lot; currently it was in braids that went about halfway down her back and were pulled into a loose ponytail. Grady was… somewhere, with one of his other athletes. Grady had been a coach at USC for decades, it seemed like. He was pushing fifty now, and what hair he possessed had gone gray, but he and Tamika made a handsome couple, and it was clear Grady doted on his wife. Brandon supposed they must really be in love to spend their days at work together and their evenings afterward. And yet for being together all that time, they still appeared to get along very well.

But that wasn't Brandon's business, so he turned toward the track.

"I heard that you and JJ have been spending some time together," said Tamika.

"Yeah," Brandon said, scanning the track. No Americans in this heat, so he could take a break from waiting for JJ to talk to Tamika. "My roommate won a silver medal in the long jump yesterday and wanted to, uh, celebrate last night, so JJ let me sleep in his room. His roommate moved out, so there was an extra bed."

"Uh-huh," said Tamika.

Something in her tone didn't sit well with Brandon. "What?"

"Grady has said you remind him of our friend Keisha, who is kind of a classic introvert. She's fine in social situations and can talk to people easily enough, but she'd rather be home reading than at a party and she doesn't always understand the finer points of human interactions. I see some of that in you, which means you probably don't always understand social cues. So I'll just tell you, without beating around the bush, that part of the reason I wanted you and JJ to meet is that I think you complement each other. He can be a hothead at times, and he's very emotional. You seem kind of cool and calm all the time. I thought that would be a good balance."

"Maybe," said Brandon, not willing to admit how much he liked JJ yet, or what had happened between them so far.

"I see you painted your nails."

Brandon looked at his red, white, and blue fingernails. The blue had a little bit of sparkle in it, which Brandon really liked. It was weird and silly, but looking at his nails made him happy. "Yeah, JJ did them this morning. What do you think?"

"They look good. Very patriotic. Maybe JJ will bring you out of your shell a little." She raised an eyebrow.

"I'm not, like, in the closet or anything."

"Okay."

"JJ said some people might see my nails and call me gay. Well, he used a different word."

"Right." Tamika nodded. "He's a little too liberal with that word, if you ask me."

"Well, I told him it didn't matter because I *am* gay. I just don't talk about it a lot."

Tamika grinned. "It doesn't affect your running."

"Of course it doesn't. It's not relevant to how I run."

Tamika patted his knee. "I am very proud of my thinking on this matter. You and JJ should get along very well."

"I think we're friends now," said Brandon.

"Good." Tamika glanced at the scoreboard. "He's up in the next heat. Let's watch him win, shall we?"

Down on the track, the next group of runners milled around behind the blocks. JJ was the only American in this heat. This year the American track uniforms were navy blue tank tops with a big red *USA* across the chest and navy running shorts. Brandon had been happy for the choice of navy, because the red shorts from the last World Championship had been tight and created shadows, which put everything on display, leaving no question as to who dressed to the right or left. The blue looked more modest. Brandon glanced up at the Jumbotron and watched as a camera panned across the gathered athletes. At some point JJ had put gold hoops in his earlobes, and he tucked a gold pendant into his shirt as the camera panned back to reveal the gold nails and the gold shoes. JJ wasn't subtle, that was for sure.

"On your marks," said the announcer.

All eight runners got into their blocks. For the two-hundred, they were scattered to account for the curve of the track. Two hundred meters was half a lap. It would be over in twenty seconds. According to the scoreboard, the world record was just over nineteen seconds. Brandon had seen JJ run it pretty consistently around 19.5.

Tamika got her phone out and zoomed in on JJ. Brandon wasn't sure where to look, but he decided to focus on the track. JJ was in Lane 4, right in the middle.

"Get set."

The runners pushed up into position. Up on the Jumbotron, the camera zoomed in on JJ as he placed his fingers right behind the starting line. There were those gold nails.

Pop! went the starting gun.

JJ got a great start out of the blocks. He was off cleanly and smoothly transitioned into standing at his full height. With the staggered starting blocks, Brandon couldn't tell who was ahead until the runners got to the turn, but JJ ran well. He led most of the field, in fact. His form looked good, his strides were long, and he was in the lead out of the turn. He seemed to find another gear during the straightaway and pulled even farther ahead.

He crossed the finish line a few strides before anyone else did. Brandon looked at the scoreboard. JJ had run two hundred meters in 19.4 seconds, about 0.4 seconds faster than the next runner.

"Yeah, boy! That's what I'm talking about!" shouted Tamika as she jumped out of her seat. "Woo!"

Brandon stood beside her. JJ squinted up at the scoreboard, nodded to himself, then walked off the track and back down toward the locker room.

"He looked good, right?" said Tamika. "I'll take another look at the video later, but his form looked great. What did you think?"

"I agree. That was better than he's been running in practice."

"JJ is something else sometimes. His warm-up was messy today. I don't know where he gets his resolve from."

Brandon wondered how much the moment he and JJ had shared had helped JJ. He hoped it had; the idea made warmth spread across his chest. He smiled to himself and pulled his phone from his pocket to look at the time. "Do you know what time the semifinal is? I'm supposed to meet Grady at the gym now."

Tamika pulled out her phone. "It's at five. You want to watch it with us?"

"Yeah. I'll be back then."

Chapter Twelve

Transcript from the TBC Broadcast of the two-hundred-meter sprint semifinal

CASSELLO: All four Americans have made the semifinal.

GRAYSON: That's right, Jim. This first heat will probably be the slower one. Franco Greer and DeShawn Latrell are in this heat. Then Jason Jones Jr. and Rafael Martinez are in the second heat, which also includes Ajani Blake from Jamaica and Ato Frederick from Namibia.

CASSELLO: All right, let's watch the first heat. You'll see the athletes all look pretty relaxed. That's Greer in Lane 2 and Latrell in Lane 6. And they're off!

GRAYSON: Great starts for both Greer and Latrell. Looks like Latrell is a little ahead at the turn. Greer is right on his heels, though!

CASSELLO: Pritchard from Great Britain is with them. If he can keep up this pace, he's got a shot at the final.

GRAYSON: Oh, here comes Latrell. I thought Latrell had a better shot at the one-hundred, but here he comes! And Greer's right behind him! And there it is, Team USA is one and two in this semifinal, with Pritchard in third.

CASSELLO: Will all four Americans make it to the final?

GRAYSON: It's definitely possible. Jones ran a fantastic qualifying heat, and Martinez is young but super fast. I would have told you they were the most likely to make this final before the semifinals started.

CASSELLO: Well, let's go back to the track and find out….

BEFORE FLYING to Madrid, JJ would have said that no athletes at an event at which WADA had such a strong presence would have dared to actually use any performance enhancing drugs at the Games.

And yet, when he went to change into his official uniform to run the two-hundred-meter semifinal, JJ spotted Franco popping a handful of pills in a corner of the locker room and downing them with a few swigs of red Gatorade.

Aside from the Russians, a few athletes had been snared by the WADA testers. JJ had been grabbed to do another blood test right after the qualifying heats and was glad the only thing in his system at the time had been a protein bar. He was dehydrated enough postrace, though, that getting stuck with a needle had been kind of a trial, with the doctor making lots of jokes about his veins hiding and JJ just praying for it to end soon.

Most athletes stopped using anabolic steroids with enough lead time before a meet for those drugs to completely leave their systems. But if Franco was popping pills, was anybody else? Were those pills vitamins or ibuprofen or something else? Should JJ report it, or would that make him a scab?

He didn't want to feel so suspicious. But he could have sworn that one of the British runners was also swallowing a pill.

JJ understood the temptation, or at least understood the drive to win, to a point but would never use PEDs himself. The probability of getting caught was too high, for one thing, especially now that he was under more scrutiny, and the side effects could be brutal. There'd been a guy on his college team who developed heart problems after doping, something that had terrified JJ at the time. JJ generally didn't like taking any kind of medication, not even painkillers and sleeping pills, if he didn't know how it would affect his body. And more than that, he didn't train his ass off to win by cheating. So he would not be doping, and he would submit to as much testing as WADA wanted to conduct, because he wanted to prove he was not a cheater.

But he wondered if these days, he wasn't so much competing with faster runners as he was with doping. If it wasn't better athletes or better training regimens or better strategy he was running against, but stimulants and steroids. There was enough talk around USC that JJ was aware that the drugs were often ahead of the tests, and by the time testing caught up, the athletes were on to new drugs. How many of the athletes competing were taking drugs WADA hadn't figured out how to test for yet? Was that what Franco was doing?

Franco was past his prime. Marcus was still his coach, and JJ knew now that he'd worked with Tamika for a year that some of Marcus's ideas about coaching were old-school and probably not as effective against the new crop of younger runners coming up now. The only race Franco had qualified for at Trials was the two-hundred. JJ was a better runner. He intended to beat Franco.

He watched the first semifinal on a monitor near the entrance to the track. Franco qualified for the final with a reasonably fast time, which would, at least, give JJ the opportunity to beat him one-on-one.

When it was time, he jogged out to the track. Tamika was in the stands somewhere, as were Brandon and JJ's parents. He didn't want to let any of them down, but this race was for him as much as anything. It wasn't the gold-medal final; he just had to run this race fast enough to be in the top eight, something he could probably do in his sleep. But he still wanted to win it.

Maybe he needed to prove that *he* could win, without any performance enhancements.

He went through his prerace dance. He checked his shoes. He kissed his Saint Sebastian medallion and dropped it under his shirt. He adjusted the blocks until they were the way he liked them; then he put his feet in them to make sure it felt right. He practiced his start and felt good off the blocks. Then he jogged back around to stand with the other runners who were getting ready for their races.

"On your marks."

There wasn't much time to dick around. A quick glance at the scoreboard showed that the time to beat was just under twenty seconds. Piece of cake. JJ's desire to get to that final and win was fueling him now.

He got his feet in the blocks and carefully placed his fingers behind the starting line.

"Ready."

JJ rose up, ready to sprint. He wanted this. He wanted to win. He wanted to be the fastest man in the world. He wanted gold. That rolled through his head like a mantra.

Pop! The push off the blocks was a Pavlovian response to the sound of a starting gun. JJ transitioned into his full height as soon as he could so he could lengthen his strides and pull into a full sprint.

If JJ was running against doping, he wanted to prove he could win without. His chest burned with his anger from a long day, from Darrell calling him a fag to Tamika holding relay practice today and delaying his own practice to spotting Franco and those pills. He wanted to win. He *needed* to win. And if he couldn't shake off this anger and tension, he needed to use it to propel himself forward.

So he ran as if he could escape all of it. He ran like the devil nipped at his tail. He ran for glory, for gold, for all the things he'd been told his whole life he couldn't have. His heart pounded, but with exertion or emotion, it was hard to tell.

Because JJ was the fastest man in the world, and he would damn well prove it here or die trying.

When he came around the turn and into the straightaway, there were no runners on either side of him. JJ knew there were some fast men in this heat, but he didn't care. He wasn't running against them, he was running against the system, against himself. He felt his feet pound into and then bounce against the surface of the track, felt fire in his chest, felt his muscles crying as he pushed himself to run faster.

And he ran right over the finish line, knowing he'd finished first. He ran another half lap, trying to slow down safely. As he turned to look at his time, his bones were suddenly made of Jell-O, and he dropped onto the track, landing on his ass. He'd finished in 19.2 seconds, just a hair off the world record. He'd qualified first for the final, the fastest time in both semifinal heats.

He would win the final.

Oh, sure, some runners decided strategically not to go into their top gear for the preliminary races. They were either conserving their energy or trying to fake out the field or both. The time only counted in the final, which meant Rafa or Blake or Frederick could turn it on and challenge JJ. But he had a whole day to recover from this and get ready for the final, so why not prove he could do amazing things now?

He'd put the field on notice. Bring your A game.

"You okay?" Rafa asked.

JJ held out his hand, and Rafa helped him up.

"Yeah," JJ panted. "Legs kind of gave out at the end there."

"You were so fast, man. No one could catch you."

JJ nodded, still trying to get his breath. He looked up at the scoreboard and saw that the top four in that heat had been JJ, Blake, Rafa, and Frederick, who would all be advancing to the final.

"Congrats on making the final," JJ said between sharp inhales.

"Thanks. I think I've got a shot at a medal."

"I think so too. And thanks for defending me against Darrell earlier. He's a dick."

"Not a problem. I like you. I want to beat you, but if I can't, it better be because you ran faster and harder than anyone. You gonna break the world record tomorrow?"

"I'm certainly gonna try."

JJ's heart still pounded as he walked into the locker room. Franco was sitting on the bench near JJ's locker.

JJ realized that a part of him had been waiting for this confrontation since he'd arrived in Madrid. He knew in the back of his mind that he'd have to talk to Franco, but he'd been kicking the can down the road so that this would not become a distraction during his races.

Only Franco had made the decision for him.

JJ walked to his locker and opened it. He pulled out a towel and wiped the sweat off his face. "Hello, Franco."

"Good race. I watched on the monitor."

JJ turned to face him. He debated strategy. He wanted to ask the question that had been on his mind since he got the call that he'd tested positive for a stimulant, but instead he decided to stall to see where Franco wanted to take this. "Your race was good too."

"You remember that meet in Doha, like, five years ago? When we came in second and third?"

"Yeah. Of course." The meet in Doha had been JJ's first international meet. He'd been twenty years old and ready to prove himself on the world stage, but he also hadn't yet understood a lot about race strategy. So he'd run his heart out every time he got on the track and got good results, although he didn't win any races, consistently coming in behind the more experienced runners or finishing just out of the medals. But in the two-hundred, he and Franco had finished second and third respectively, and they'd gotten a *Sports Illustrated* cover out of it, declaring them the future of U.S. track, even though Franco had been a few years older.

That night in Doha had cemented something in JJ's and Franco's friendship, particularly after Franco had procured a bottle of good whiskey from a British runner and they'd gotten sloppy drunk in their hotel room together. JJ remembered that night as being the greatest of celebrations—his first international medal!—and he'd been excited about what the future held. Franco had seemed to agree.

"Sometimes I think about the way I felt back then. What it was like to be twenty-two and winning my first medal in international competition. I had hope and idealism then. I don't feel that way anymore. I miss it." Franco let out a breath. "Do you?"

"I mean… it's different. Training is harder."

"Yeah. I gotta swallow a pile of ibuprofen every race day now. God, everything hurts."

JJ felt a little relieved that the pills he'd seen Franco take had probably been ibuprofen. He said, "We grow up and mature with the sport, I guess."

"Yeah. But for me, it's… well."

"Is something going on? We're friends, or we used to be. You can tell me."

Franco shook his head. "I have some regrets, I guess. Things I wish I'd done differently. I made some decisions in the heat of the moment that I regret."

"Such as?"

"It's not worth getting into now. I just… I saw you run, and I wanted to tell you that what you did on the track impressed me. I haven't run the two-hundred in faster than 19.5 in… God, in three years. If you run like that in the final, the gold medal is yours. And you'd deserve it."

"Wow. Thanks, Franco. But didn't you win your semi? That silver could still be yours."

"Maybe. But I'd still have to beat Rafa and Blake and Frederick and that British guy."

JJ peeled off his shirt. He could feel the fatigue starting to sink into his body, so he went about his business, peeling off his damp uniform shirt and toeing off his sneakers. He sensed that Franco had something to say but was still working out how to say it.

"I think you and I have not been friends for a while," said Franco.

"Maybe not."

"I think I know why."

"I do too." JJ took a deep breath. "Look, I'll be honest. Ever since I tested positive, I wondered if you giving me cold pills with pseudoephedrine was an accident or deliberate sabotage. You knew the rules about banned substances as well as I did because we were both getting regular briefings on what was allowed and what wasn't in those days. I always assumed that you didn't know, because we were friends and you wouldn't do me wrong like that. But in the back of my mind, through the hearing and having to give my medal back and all of it, a tiny little voice in the back of my mind always wondered."

Franco looked at the floor.

And there it was. JJ knew in an instant that he'd been betrayed.

"You *did* do it on purpose, didn't you?"

"JJ, I'm so sorry, I—"

White hot rage burned through JJ as it fully hit him that what he'd always kind of suspected but hadn't accepted was in fact true. And suddenly he could picture what had happened like a movie. JJ had called Marcus to say he'd had a cold, Marcus had probably mentioned it to Franco, and a half hour later, Franco had handed JJ two unmarked pills.

Fuck.

JJ was still only half dressed, but in a rage, he threw his locker door shut. "You gave me those pills on purpose."

"I did," Franco said quietly.

"You *motherfucker*. You were my friend. I *trusted* you. I *asked* if those pills would get me in trouble, and you said *no*. So when I tested positive, I assumed you hadn't known. But you *did* know. You cost me a medal that was *mine*, that I *earned*."

"It was a spur-of-the-moment decision."

"Was it? *Was it?*" God, now JJ was really angry. "The sort of spur-of-the-moment decision to go to a store on the way to the track? The sort of spur-of-the-moment decision that was premeditated by your decision to buy cold medicine with a stimulant in it? God, fuck you, Franco. I *trusted you* and you *betrayed me*."

JJ knew he was shouting now, but his rage was incandescent.

"I—"

"And for *what*?" JJ shouted. "You didn't even get a medal out of it. You finished in fucking fifth place. Maybe instead of trying to destroy other runners, you should have worried about your own fucking race."

"I'm trying to apologize, JJ. This has been eating me up since it happened."

"You think you deserve my *forgiveness*? I mean… have you met me? I can't forgive this. You destroyed something I'd worked my ass off for, and to what end? To get me in trouble? To make me quit running? To take out the competition because you're too much of a coward to compete fairly? No, I can't accept or forgive any of that, and if you think I would, you don't know me at all."

"I know. I made a bad choice, I—"

"Get the fuck out of my sight, Franco." Then JJ punched a locker, because he didn't know where else to put his rage.

As the sound echoed through the locker room, Franco stood up. He held up his hands.

"Don't ever fucking talk to me again," said JJ. "Don't approach me, don't try to apologize, don't ever share the same oxygen with me. You are dead to me. Now get out of here."

When Franco was gone, JJ sat on the bench and tried to get his breathing back under control. He didn't think he'd taken a breath the entire time he'd yelled at Franco. He wanted to push it all aside, but every time Franco's pathetic face floated back into his mind's eye, JJ just felt furious all over again. He couldn't believe he'd been right all along. He couldn't believe a fellow runner, let alone his training partner and friend, would do something like this to him.

He was more determined than ever to beat Franco in the final tomorrow.

But God. Now that Franco was gone and JJ's emotions were waning a little, he felt exhausted, like he needed to weep. He would not cry in the men's locker room at Olympic Stadium where his opponents were still changing into their street clothes, and he had to maintain some dignity here.

He sighed and reopened his locker so he could continue getting dressed.

THE CAMERA feeding the Jumbotron had zoomed in on JJ's face as he turned into the straightaway, and

Brandon could see more emotion than he expected there. Brandon wondered what JJ was feeling. Brandon often spent his races trying not to feel anything, to make his mind as blank as possible, to just do his job and make the right number of steps between hurdles and jump when he was supposed to.

Brandon had felt exhilarated watching JJ run. JJ had gotten a huge jump off the blocks and pulled into his correct form faster than any of the other runners. His long legs had eaten up the track as he'd gone into the turn. He was so far in the lead by the time he got to the last straightaway that it had seemed unlikely any runner could have caught him.

"What is he *doing*?" asked Tamika.

"Winning," said Brandon as JJ ran across the finish line.

"He's going to wear himself out."

"I don't think so."

Tamika glanced at Brandon. "Did you see him this afternoon? Was he upset?"

"I haven't seen him since right after the qualifier. He seemed all right when I left him, but I don't know if I'm the right person to ask."

Tamika gave Brandon a long look. "Come with me."

Brandon followed Tamika down to the locker room. He was about to tell her she couldn't go into the men's locker room—there were runners from cultures who did not share intimate spaces with the opposite sex competing here—but she shouted, "Female coach!" in three different languages and stomped over to the American physical therapy area.

"Go find JJ," she ordered Brandon.

Brandon wondered if she was always this way. It was pretty intense.

He found JJ on a bench near his locker, hunched over with his head in his hands. Brandon couldn't read him and wished now that he had more facility interpreting body language and facial expressions, because JJ seemed upset. But that didn't make sense because he'd just won a race.

"JJ? You okay?"

JJ jerked his head up at the sound of Brandon's voice. His eyes were red, but he nodded. "Showed them, didn't I?"

"That was a great race."

Brandon was searching for something else to say or ask when a guy wearing a lab coat and carrying a clipboard walked by the end of the aisle. "Jones?" he shouted.

"That's my date," JJ said.

"Date?"

"With a cup." JJ pulled himself up off the bench.

"Tamika sent me to fetch you. She's setting up something in the physical therapy area."

"All right. Tell her I'll be there after the pee test." With a sigh, JJ loped off after the guy in the lab coat.

Brandon watched him go. He wished he understood what was going on. Was JJ upset? Was he in pain? Was he angry? Was he happy?

Needing to know, Brandon jogged after him. "Wait. Are you okay? Did something happen after your race?"

JJ smiled slowly. "I'll be fine. But unless *you* want to watch me pee in a cup, you better go catch up with Tamika. I'll be over there in a few moments."

Brandon understood he was being dismissed, but he hoped he'd get the full story later. He turned and went to find Tamika.

CHAPTER THIRTEEN

JJ STARED down into the fresh hell of the ice bath.

"You have to cool down," said Tamika.

JJ stripped to his underwear but eyed the tub. He hated this part of the postrace treatment but knew it was for the best. His muscles still burned from the exertion of the run. Brandon held out an arm, because he probably knew exactly what this was, so JJ gripped it and stepped into the tub.

"Oh, holy Jesus."

"Don't blaspheme," said Tameka.

JJ let out a steady stream of curses as he lowered himself into the water. Brandon let go of his hand when JJ's ass hit the bottom of the tub, and JJ let out harsh gasp.

"You gotta stay in there at least five minutes," said Tamika.

JJ whimpered and looked up at Brandon, who gazed back with a furrowed brow.

"What does this do?" Brandon asked.

"It helps sore muscles and speeds up recovery time," said Tamika. "Brings down any inflammation. He does this now so he can run again for the next three days."

"Does it hurt?"

JJ shifted in the tub, the cold water sluicing over legs. His whole body was numb now. "No. It's a shock to the system, though."

"Does the cold, like, shrink blood vessels or—?"

JJ barked out a shaky laugh. "Listen to Science Boy trying to break this down. Yes, it shrinks blood vessels and inflammation, which is how I recover faster."

Brandon stared at him for a long moment, probably wondering what to say.

"This'll wake you up," said JJ. "Could even replace coffee in the morning."

"I bet," said Brandon.

"Good thing I'm gay, 'cuz I'm never having kids now."

"Oh, here we go," said Tamika.

"My balls are up in my throat."

"He always does this," Tamika said to Brandon. "Thinks he's a stand-up comedian when he gets in the ice bath."

"I have to make this bearable somehow." JJ huffed out a breath and looked at Brandon. "Good thing you saw my dick in all its glory last night. But I want to emphasize that the cold water causes shrinkage."

Brandon went scarlet, which JJ enjoyed. To Tamika, he said, "We didn't—"

"It's fine. I'm used to him," said Tamika, completely unfazed.

JJ shifted his weight, hoping he'd adjust to the cold water, but moving it around just shocked him again. He let out another gasp.

Tamika raised an eyebrow and looked at Brandon. "Want me to tell Grady to set one of those up for you tomorrow night?"

"It seems unpleasant," said Brandon.

"Girl." JJ laughed despite himself. Brandon was going to kill him.

"He keeps calling me *girl*," Brandon said to Tamika.

"Don't take it personally. He calls everyone *girl*."

JJ leaned back in the tub and tried to get comfortable, closing his eyes and blocking out the conversation Brandon and Tamika were having, until he only heard low murmured voices. His teeth started to chatter. Finally, blessedly, Tamika said, "All right, kid, you can get out of the tub now."

"The clouds have parted. I hear angels singing."

To Brandon, Tamika said, "Help me get him out."

They each took one of JJ's arms and helped him out of the tub. When JJ's feet hit the mat beside the tub, he lurched forward, and Brandon caught him. Tamika handed Brandon a towel, which Brandon wrapped around JJ, hugging him a little as he did so. Burrowing into Brandon's warmth was a significant temptation, but not now, not with Tamika looking on. So JJ stood there, dripping, his teeth chattering.

Of course, if Brandon was here, Tamika already knew. She was a sharp one. She'd probably orchestrated this whole friendship. To what end, JJ wasn't entirely sure, but he wasn't in a position to question anything right then.

JJ shivered. "Can I go to sleep now?"

"Yeah. Brandon, can you make sure he gets back to his dorm okay?"

"Of course."

"Good. I'm gonna go find Grady and head back to the hotel. But good job today, kid. Be back here at eight for physical therapy."

"I will."

Tamika patted his shoulder and headed off. JJ shivered again but followed Brandon back to his locker. Brandon sat on the bench as JJ stood and dripped for a moment, warmth starting to seep back into his body. Not many athletes were still around, since competition had wound down for the day. JJ thought about giving Brandon a bit of a show, but he opened his towel and looked down and realized his penis was still sad and shriveled. He grunted and peeled off his wet underwear and grabbed a clean pair from his locker. He glanced back at Brandon, who was looking at his phone.

No one was around, so JJ said, "I had it out with Franco."

Brandon looked up as JJ slid his dry briefs into place. "Who?"

JJ let out a breath and went about getting dressed. He briefly recapped the story of his bad cold and the cold pills and the medal and everything. He wrapped up by saying, "He was my friend, so I didn't believe that he could have sabotaged me like that, but part of me always wondered. He came to see me after the race today, I think to apologize for slipping me pseudoephedrine all those years ago, but he was wishy-washy about it. So I confronted him and he confessed and, well, long story short, he's dead to me."

Brandon nodded slowly, likely absorbing all that. "Is that why you were upset?"

"Yeah. But I don't want that asshole to bring me down today. Not when I ran a race like that. But I just… I wanted to let you know what happened."

"Thank you for telling me."

JJ pulled on a clean shirt and turned to look at Brandon, who was still watching him. Their eyes met. It wasn't like Brandon had a right to know what was going on with JJ, but JJ had wanted to tell him. What brought on this compulsion? He didn't know, but he knew Brandon would listen if JJ talked. And sometimes JJ didn't need advice, he didn't need someone to tell him he'd overreacted or he was too hotheaded. He just needed someone to listen.

The moment passed and Brandon glanced at his phone. "Jamal hasn't left yet."

"What?"

Brandon cleared his throat. "My roommate. Jamal. I thought he was supposed to fly home this afternoon, but he didn't. He texted me to say he wants the room for a few hours."

"If you want to stay in my room again, you can. Hell, you can move in if you want to. I bet I'm a better roommate."

Brandon made a noncommittal noise.

JJ turned around. "I'm a sexier roommate."

"Well, that's true." Brandon fiddled with his phone a bit more. "All right. Let me tell Jamal I'll come by to grab my stuff."

"You want to get some dinner?"

"Sure."

JJ pulled on a sweatshirt, because even though it was still hot in Madrid, he'd never be warm again. After his head popped through the head opening, he looked at Brandon, who was staring at him.

"What?" JJ asked.

"Are we, like, dating? I mean, I know dinner can be two friends sharing a meal, but after what happened last night…."

"We can be dating."

"Is that not what you want?"

JJ laughed. It was a little reassuring that Brandon was so… Brandon. Straightforward. No ulterior motive. Not the sort of man who would persuade him to take cold pills without telling him what was in them. "I'm happy to take you however I can get you for the rest of the week. We can just be two guys having fun together without putting any labels on it."

"Is that what you want?"

JJ narrowed his eyes at Brandon. Brandon's face was typically placid, not showing any particular emotion. JJ knew there was a passionate man in there somewhere, but right now Brandon mostly seemed confused. "What do you want? Just tell me without worrying if it will upset me."

Brandon shrugged. "I like the idea of us going on a date. But I know it's the Olympics and circumstances are weird and we both really need to eat after all the calories we burned today with practice and the gym and whatever, and you're probably tired, so if you don't want to… do anything, I understand."

JJ pulled on his sneakers and sat beside Brandon on the bench to tie them. "You know, as we've previously discussed, we do live in the same city. If you're in University Park, you probably live near my parents. I could walk to Memorial Stadium from my house when I was a kid."

"That's cool."

"What I'm saying is, after all this is over, we *should* keep seeing each other or go on dates or whatever. I think that would be fun, actually. There's an Italian restaurant near USC that is hella romantic."

Brandon shot him a sidelong glance. "Yeah?"

The coy note in Brandon's voice was so unexpected and delightful that JJ focused on tying his shoes so he wouldn't get distracted. He cleared his throat. "I had one of these event flings a few years ago. Banged a Canadian pole vaulter when we were both in Tokyo for the World Championship. It was fun while it lasted but didn't have much substance."

"Oh."

Ah, there was some real emotion. Brandon sounded disappointed. "No, you're misunderstanding me. My point is that I think you and I *do* have substance, so I'd love to take you out somewhere in LA when we get home. But in the meantime, I don't want to put any pressure on us because we both have enough other shit going on while we're here in Madrid. You want to call dinner tonight a date, that's cool with me, but it's also fine if we don't put any labels on anything. Just have fun."

Brandon nodded. "Okay. That makes sense to me."

JJ laughed. "Also, not everything is a logic puzzle. Listen to your gut. What does your gut say?"

"I don't know. I like you."

"Well, that's a good start. I like you too. And I'm starving. So let's get the shuttle and then stuff our faces full of food."

BRANDON SAT across from JJ in the cafeteria and ate a huge bowl of seafood paella, which was well-seasoned but overcooked. Maybe after his race, he could go into the city proper and eat some better-quality Spanish food in which the fish was not rubbery. But he was hungry, so this was getting the job done.

JJ had a feast spread out on his own tray: a piece of grilled chicken, a bowl full of mushy-looking steamed vegetables, a baked potato slathered in sour cream, a bowl of rice and beans, a little plate with a few slices of ham and some triangular slices of cheese, and finally a vanilla milkshake to wash it all down. It was a lot. JJ was halfway through eating it all.

"I'm almost warm again," said JJ, pulling his sweatshirt off over his head. The sleeves on JJ's shirt were ripped off, showing off the muscles on his arms. JJ really was incredibly strong, his body well-developed, his skin nearly flawless. Brandon enjoyed taking it all in as he ate.

Needing something to talk about, and since it was on his brain, Brandon asked, "I'm always surprised how strong sprinters are. How do you get all these muscles?"

"Training."

"Sure, but, like, you look like a guy whose genetics would have made you pretty lean. Maybe not super tall, but long arms, narrow torso."

"You calling me skinny?"

Brandon laughed. "No. Just describing what I see. You're really strong."

JJ crossed his arms. "I'll tell you a secret. I watched this documentary about Usain Bolt. And in it, there's all this footage of him running on a dirt field with a huge weight, like the size of a car tire, attached to his waist with a rope. And I went to my old coach and said, 'I want to try that and see what happens.'" JJ's eyes darted over Brandon's face. "You're trying to math that out, aren't you?"

He was. Brandon thought for a moment about how to explain. "The dirt is more slippery than a synthetic track. In that way, it offers more resistance and is harder to run on. It doesn't bounce the way a track does. So you have to work harder to get up to speed. And if you've got the weight pulling you back, that's more resistance, and you have to work even harder. So if you can get to a good speed and maybe you run the one-hundred in ten to twelve seconds, with all that pulling you back, then once you get to the track, in optimal conditions, it must be a breeze."

JJ smiled. "That's it exactly. It's Jesse Owens running the one-hundred in 10.3 seconds, because he had shoes that basically had nails sticking out of the bottom instead of proper spikes and was running on raw dirt. Now we have better engineered shoes, a track made of synthetic material, and all of it makes running easier. So that's why I didn't want to just train on the track. If I could run a hundred meters in ten seconds on a *dirt* track, I could do it for sure in less time on a synthetic one."

"Right."

"State-of-the-art is not always ideal. At least, not for training. I figure, if Usain Bolt can slay a bunch of world records by training on a good old dirt track, there must be something to it."

"Makes sense."

"It's all about what you want. Hurdles are tricky, and maybe you can math your way through them, but there are a few dozen sprinters in this world who want the World's Fastest Man title, and I am one of them. I train harder, I train more, I run faster than any other athlete I know, and I realize that so much of this is luck or God-given ability or genetics or the weather or whatever, but I get up every morning intending to train for this, and I'm going to win. If that means more training, if it means weird training, if it means I have to subject myself to shit talk from my teammates for more motivation, then that's how this is gonna go. Because running a hundred meters in less than ten seconds is really fucking hard, and you have to want it, to put your body through this nonsense every day. And I want it."

Brandon nodded but wasn't totally sure how to respond. JJ was right, but also, he was wrong. Brandon mostly kept his training to what he considered traditional methods—he ran long distances on the road sometimes, but he did pretty much all of his short-distance training on USC's synthetic track. He didn't generally do anything that was too weird or speculative. He liked the logic of applying math to the hurdles, and it had yielded results, so why not keep doing it?

"What?" JJ asked.

Brandon paused for a moment, not wanting to insult JJ. But he said, "It's still math. It's still strategy and physics. How hard do you push off the blocks? How long do you stay hunched before pulling yourself upright? How do you breathe? How often do you breathe? How many steps do you take? What is your stride length? That's how you win. You don't win races by accident."

JJ grunted, clearly disagreeing. "Easy for you to say, white boy. Sure, it's math. White men can walk out into the world and be mediocre and everyone falls at their feet in praise. Black men have to be spectacular. When a man like me shows up on the world stage, I have to be better than everyone. I have to be the best, I have to win the race, failure is not an option. If I lose, no one gives a shit, because I'm living up to expectation. I have to be *exceptional*. You can't… it's not possible for you to fathom that kind of pressure, is it? You're not even stressed about the Games. You just have to solve a math problem and you win a race."

Brandon hadn't really thought of it in that way. He wasn't blind to racism in sports, but he didn't think about it much, and maybe that was because of his own privilege. He thought JJ was an exceptional athlete. Was it possible people disagreed?

JJ grunted. "Don't you dare tell me you don't fucking see color, or I will punch you in the face."

"I wasn't going to say that."

"It's not just in here," JJ said, pointing to his temple. "It's in here." He tapped his chest with his palm. "You have to *love* it. Otherwise, why are you even here?"

"It's not correct to say I don't feel pressure. I do feel some. But you're right, I can't understand the pressure you're under. It is different."

"Do you love running?"

Did he? Brandon didn't know. He certainly enjoyed it. "I like it enough to compete and train. I enjoy pushing my body. I like racing. I want to win."

"But, see, it's different for me. I mean, yes, you can math some of this."

"Are you using math as a verb?"

JJ rolled his eyes. "Thing is, you can be a technically proficient athlete, but it takes heart to win races." He sighed. "And it takes perseverance, because everyone out here is trying to take you down. I mean, I took some cold pills at the World Championship two years ago, and now that's the only thing people know about me. *Of course* the 'poor' kid from South Central has a doping charge. *Of course* he was desperate enough to cheat."

"You didn't cheat."

"I know that. You know that. My coaches know that. Hell, WADA *knows* that. And yet every fucking article about me mentions that I was exonerated on doping charges. If I was exonerated, why not leave the whole incident out of the article?"

"It wasn't your fault. You just told me your teammate confessed to giving you the pills on purpose."

"He did, yeah. Good luck proving it, though. Besides, how could I have been dumb enough to just take them on faith?"

"He was your friend. You trusted him."

"I did. And I'll have an asterisk after my name forever now." JJ shook his head and shoveled some rice into his mouth, then took a sip of the milkshake. "You know, Tommie Smith actually used to increase his stride length later in the race when he ran the two-hundred. That's incredibly hard to do. He was the fastest sprinter of his time. Brilliant athlete. And we remember him because he raised his fist."

Brandon was having trouble following all this. He knew the name Tommie Smith; Smith had been one of the athletes who had raised his fist in protest of racism—specifically anti-black racism—at the 1968 Olympics in Mexico City. Brandon thought the raised fist might have been a black power thing, but he wasn't certain. He felt strange asking JJ about it, though, so he pressed his lips together. Of course, the fact that Brandon only knew who Tommie Smith was because of the black power salute thing proved JJ's point.

"Sorry, I didn't mean to get into a whole thing," JJ said.

"Please talk as much as you like. I want to understand you."

JJ smiled. "We all say the Olympics are the great equalizer, that the Games overcame Hitler and terrorists in Munich and the Moscow boycott and we're all wiser and more inclusive because of it, but you've been here long enough to know that the glossy finish the television broadcast puts on all this isn't reality. There's all kinds of bullshit happening behind the scenes." He put his fork down and rubbed his forehead. "Sorry, I'm in a mood."

Brandon nodded, still trying to put the pieces together. "It's all right. I completely understand why you're upset. It's terribly unfair, what happened to you."

JJ looked down at his food. "Some of the press about me coming into the Olympics was not the most flattering. I am a kid from South Central, and my parents are middle-class. I had a great childhood with a lot of extended family nearby. I started running because I liked it, not because I saw it as my ticket out of the 'hood or whatever bullshit thing an actual reporter put into an actual story about me that ran last month. But there's this assumption under everything that I'm black so I must have had a wretched life. *That's* racism, and it fuels all the other stories about me that aren't true. It's all part of a package of bullshit. And I let some of it get to me today. I don't want to let it. I want to be able to turn it into fuel with which to win races."

Brandon understood better now. "Did you see the story last week about the reporter who put a bunch of gay dating apps on his phone and outed some athletes?"

JJ howled with laughter. "Girl. You do know how to take a left turn."

"A lot of the press has been bad. The story didn't include anyone's name, but there were just enough clues that you could tell a few of the athletes it mentioned were from countries where being gay is not okay. Can you even imagine? Say you grew up in an oppressive society where you could be arrested or killed because of who you are, so you keep that a secret your whole life. But then you finally have an opportunity to be yourself because you're away from home and there are other LGBTQ people around, and some reporter ruins it all. I can't stop thinking about it. A friend sent me the story and it made me feel ill."

JJ sobered and frowned. He went back to eating his dinner. "Yeah, well. If anything, that says to me that I really need to make these people eat their words. I'm gonna win the gold medal, and you and I are going to have a lot of gay sex to celebrate it."

Brandon's face warmed. He tried to laugh, but he didn't think JJ was joking, and it came out as a strangled giggle. Some animalistic part of Brandon wanted JJ with a hunger he couldn't explain or account for, and he looked forward to all that sex.

This was not how he'd expected his Olympic experience to go. He'd anticipated tolerating Jamal in the dorm and then training his butt off on the track, and that was it, really. But JJ made him want more. JJ had uncorked something. Brandon generally kept his head down, stayed on top of his studies, and focused on what he needed to do to get the career he wanted. He'd been dreaming about building or inventing something that would help people live better lives since he'd been a little boy. He ran as a way to blow off steam, and he ran because he was good at it. He liked the thrill of competition and liked proving that his pragmatic view of the sport yielded results.

But something had changed in him since he'd arrived in Madrid. He didn't see the world so objectively, and he was frankly startled by how cold and analytical he'd been before. Now, not only did he want JJ, but something of JJ's determination was rubbing off on him, and he really wanted to win his race too. How wild would it be if he not only won but set a world record? The record time for the four-hundred-meter hurdles had stood since the early '90s, so that would be a real accomplishment. Could he do it?

He shook his head and looked at his nearly-empty bowl. He scooped up some rice with his fork. There was so much more to JJ than met the eye, that was for certain. So much of what he'd said made sense, even if it wasn't something Brandon had ever thought about. And JJ probably had dealt with a lot of adversity, but his attitude that he'd win just to prove all his haters wrong was admirable. Brandon blurted out, "You're amazing, you know that?"

"Why, thank you." JJ winked.

Brandon took a deep breath. "You want to know why I started running?"

"Tell me."

"I have two older brothers who are these huge guys. Danny used to lift weights and Mike was on the football team. I knew I'd never be strong enough to do things like that, but you know how we had to run a mile in gym class? Did you have to do that?"

"Yeah."

"So, I always ran pretty fast. I wasn't exactly cool, but the kids in my gym class used to fight over who got to have me on their team because I was fast and coordinated enough to catch dodgeballs pretty well. So I thought, fine, I'm reasonably athletic. Maybe I can play sports. And then one day, one of my brothers said something that upset me so much, I left the house and started running, and I just… kept going. I ran halfway across town before my mom found me and picked me up in her car."

"Your brothers, they bullied you?"

"I don't know if bully is the right word, and by the time I was old enough to realize I was gay, they'd moved out of the house. But they did pick on me a lot, and I always felt like I didn't belong, like I was too different to be their brother in the truest sense. It was a strange way to grow up. I didn't get bullied much in school either, but it was…." Brandon sighed. He hated talking about this, although he was glad JJ was here to listen. "I mean, I was a good student and a good athlete, the kind of thing that the USC admissions department ate for breakfast when I applied, but I didn't really have many friends."

And that was the heart of it. By the time Brandon had started high school, it was just him and his mom at home. He was friendly with some of the guys on the track team, but none of them were true friends. For a lot of his teenage years, he'd been incredibly lonely. Things had gotten better in college, and he liked being alone—Tamika was right that he would have preferred reading a book at home to attending a party. The track team gave him a group to belong to, even if there weren't many teammates he'd considered close friends. But it didn't mean that, late at night, he didn't often long for other companionship.

"Sorry," he said softly. "I didn't mean to burden you with this."

"You're not. You were a lonely kid."

"I was. I guess being athletic saved me from being a total nerd, but that's basically the story. I ran to get away from my problems and because running made me feel better."

"All those endorphins," JJ said.

"Maybe. How pathetic do you think I am?"

"Not at all. We each have our demons. Is this why seeing your family earlier upset you?"

"Yeah. My brothers and I barely talk to each other. I like their families, and they've tried for the sake of our mom, but we don't relate to each other well. We don't really have anything to talk about. I appreciate that they flew all the way out here, but I didn't know what to say when my mom made us all sit down together, and it just made me want them all to go home."

JJ reached over and took Brandon's hand. "I'm sorry you have to deal with all that."

Brandon tried to smile. "It's okay. But it's part of why I live alone, even though it would be cheaper to live at home. Although if you think the commute from West Hollywood is terrible, think about the drive all the way from Pasadena."

JJ chuckled. "Well, for what it's worth, all those people who couldn't see how great you are and decided not to be your friend are missing out. Because I'm really enjoying hanging out with you."

Brandon looked down at their joined hands. "You're holding my hand."

"Is that a problem?"

"No." Brandon took a deep breath and tried to shove all his family drama aside. "So, this *is* a date."

JJ smiled. "I think it might be. Although if we do this in LA, I'm taking you somewhere that has better food and some ambiance that reads a bit less hospital corridor."

Brandon laughed, despite still feeling a little out of sorts. "Deal."

Chapter Fourteen

Day 13

Transcript from the TBC Broadcast of the four-hundred-meter hurdles, qualifying heats

CASSELLO: Welcome back to the Olympic Stadium and the track and field events. First on the schedule for today is the four-hundred-meter hurdle qualifier. But before we get there, I understand we have some developing news from our correspondent, Leslie Boothe.

BOOTHE: Yes. Thanks, Jim. As you know, the World Anti-Doping Agency has had a strong presence at these Games. So far nearly a dozen athletes and nearly the entire Russian delegation have been disqualified after testing positive for banned substances. And now we're hearing that there is a fresh group of athletes who have been DQ'd for doping, and this group may include a few Americans. I don't have the names yet, but this is an evolving story.

CASSELLO: It would be terrible if American athletes have been caught doping.

BOOTHE: I have not been able to confirm which athletes have been disqualified, but we're following this story closely and hope to have an update for you soon.

CASSELLO: Thanks, Leslie. Any thoughts, Jimmy?

GRAYSON: What a heartbreak it would be if Americans were caught up in this scandal.

CASSELLO: Agreed. I hope that story turns out not to be true, although I am glad the WADA is trying so hard to shut down doping. But if you redirect your attention to the track, the hurdles qualifying heats are under way. There are four Americans in these initial heats. None of them were in the first heat, but here in the second, we have a young runner named Brandon Stanton out of USC.

GRAYSON: Stanton is a really interesting runner. He's only twenty-two. He's been something of a prodigy, coming out of practically nowhere to win the hurdles final at the US Trials. He has some international experience, mostly limited to a handful of World Cup races, but he's earned a few medals on the world stage. I've been watching him run in practice all week, and I have to say, his speed and his form are really fantastic. I think he has a solid chance at a medal.

CASSELLO: Those glasses are something else.

GRAYSON: Yes, I asked about that. He said he doesn't see depth well enough with contact lenses, so he has to wear his glasses to run. You'll see the little strap that keeps them on his head, though. Not the most glamorous look, but whatever works, right?

CASSELLO: Anyone else in this heat to look out for?

GRAYSON: A few standouts. Stefan Abramanian from Qatar in Lane 5 is in the mix. He came close to breaking the world record at last year's World Championship. I also expect José Sanchez from the Dominican Republic to run well in this race.

CASSELLO: Oh, will you look at that. Stanton has his nails painted, just like Jason Jones Jr.

GRAYSON: That's certainly some kind of statement. I never would have expected that from a runner like Stanton. He's so straitlaced. But, well, I guess it's the twenty-first century, eh?

CASSELLO: [laughs] All right. Let's watch the race.

GRAYSON: Wow, that's a great start from Stanton. He's such a platonic ideal for a hurdler, just perfect form. And here comes Sanchez, but oh, he misses a hurdle. That will slow him down. And Pierre in Lane 8 misses too. Oh, some of this is getting messy. But Stanton is running a clean race. And he's pulling ahead. If he keeps this up, he'll win the heat easily. He's on world record pace going into the turn. Wow, what a race from Stanton. He blew the rest of the field out of the water. And now Stanton is into the straightaway and… he wins the heat easily! Sanchez is second and Abramanian is third. But Stanton is the real story here. I thought he'd be in the mix, but that was amazing.

CASSELLO: 47.05 is the final time.

GRAYSON: That's a *great* time. A little more push and he could break the world record, which has been on the books since 1992, if you can believe it.

CASSELLO: So Brandon Stanton is one to watch, huh?

GRAYSON: Definitely. I'm excited to see him run again in the semifinal tonight.

BRANDON LOOKED up at the scoreboard. 47.05. That was a really solid time. He wanted to get his race under forty-seven seconds, and he thought he was close to doing so. Maybe in the semifinal, he could do it when he had more competition to spur him on.

He was completely covered in sweat. It was hot as blazes in Madrid, and the midday sun shone directly on the track. His glasses fogged because there was so much moisture in the air, so he carefully pulled them off and wiped the lenses with the edge of his jersey. He put the glasses back on his head but saw that he'd made the problem worse. With a sigh, he collected his things from the track and jogged to the lower level of the stadium to do a cool-down lap on the practice track.

Grady caught up with him as he got to the track. "That was really fantastic. Everything like we practiced."

"Thank you."

"How do you feel?"

Brandon hated this question because he was never sure if Grady was asking how he felt physically or emotionally. So he said, "I feel okay."

Grady rolled his eyes. "Just okay? You won that heat by a wide margin and you don't even seem to have tried very hard."

"I tried!"

"Yes, I know, but… I don't know. You make it look effortless. I've never met anyone this cool in competition. That's not a bad thing! I'm glad you're so chill."

"Can I cool off now?"

"Sure."

Brandon figured out which lane on the practice track was available and broke into a run, not pushing himself very hard, but not going at an easy pace either. Something was stirring in him. He felt… frustrated. A little angry, maybe. The win wasn't as satisfying as it should have been, but more than that, Grady seemed to have expectations that Brandon should feel a certain way. It was a preliminary heat, not a final. Brandon had done what he set out to do, and he'd do it again tonight, when he'd push himself to win his semifinal, and then he'd do it again tomorrow in the final.

Why did everyone have these sorts of expectations? Why should he be overtly emotional over a qualifying heat? Sure, it was the Olympics, but it was a meet like any other. A lot of the same runners he'd competed against in the past couple of years were here. The crowd sounds, the bounce of the track, the height of the hurdles, all of that was familiar.

JJ would probably say he was trying to math this again.

Brandon wasn't a robot. He had feelings. He felt fatigue in his muscles now that the adrenaline from the race was wearing off. He was happy he'd won and he was satisfied with his time, which was close to his personal best. But he'd have to run again tonight, so he couldn't take the time to really feel anything yet.

More than that, though, he *was* capable of getting excited about races. He had a hard time expressing his emotions, but he felt a lot of them. He was starting to feel a little homesick, wanting to be home in his apartment, sleeping in his own bed. He wanted to talk to his mother without his brothers around; she knew Brandon well enough that she didn't ask him these dumb questions about how he felt. And he felt giddy where JJ was concerned. JJ had been too tired the night before for them to get into much more trouble than mutual hand jobs, but Brandon enjoyed it immensely, and he liked sharing a bed with JJ, even while he'd wished it was bigger.

And the remarkable thing was that JJ seemed to understand him and didn't ask Brandon for anything more than he could give. It was strange, because most of Brandon's past romantic prospects had thought him too odd, too nerdy, too awkward. Too cold, too robotic. JJ didn't seem to think any of that. And JJ himself was his own kind of amazing: passionate, smart, confident, and incredibly sexy.

Brandon's feet pounded into the surface of the practice track as he realized he'd run three laps very quickly. He slowed down to a jog to give his legs a rest and tried to empty his mind. When he finished and jogged over to where Grady stood watching him, Grady said, "Did you work out whatever was happening there?"

Brandon sighed. "Yes. I think so."

"What do you want to do now?"

"Eat lunch." Which was true, although he'd committed to eating with his family, which he was not that excited about.

Grady smiled. "All right, kid. Take it easy for a while. The semifinal is at seventeen hundred, so try to be back here two hours before that so we can get in a few practice runs during your warm-up."

"No problem." Brandon wondered when Grady had picked up the habit of using military time. Probably here, since all the digital clocks showed the twenty-four-hour time; Brandon's own phone, which he took from Grady now, displayed the time as 13:24.

Grady patted Brandon's shoulder. "You did good today, kid. Keep it up, all right?"

THE RUMOR that one or more Americans had tested positive for a banned substance shouldn't have made JJ paranoid, and yet his heart pounded whenever he spotted anyone in a white lab coat.

JJ was slotted to run about an hour after the four-hundred-meter hurdle semifinal. He'd watched the qualifier from the stands and had been blown away by how good Brandon had looked on the track. But watching the semifinal from the stands was just not an option if he had to run so soon afterward. Still, there were monitors near the practice track that showed each event live, so JJ planned to pause his warm-up to watch the race.

But first he had to deal with the fact that several television crews were hanging around the practice track. Reporters from networks around the world were trying to get some kind of scoop related to the doping rumors.

"You want to do a few practice runs?" Tamika asked.

"With the whole world watching?" JJ hooked his thumb toward the TV crews standing behind him. "Not really."

A woman in a polo shirt with the logo from the American TV network on her breast pocket approached slowly. "JJ? I'm Leslie Boothe from TBC. Can I ask you a few questions?"

JJ glanced at Tamika. He didn't want to but recognized he'd probably have to. Tamika said, "A few questions, but then he has to warm up for the two-hundred final."

While Tamika made Leslie promise to talk to JJ for no more than five minutes, a camera guy got into place and shone a blindingly bright light into JJ's eyes.

He took a deep breath. He was frustrated but knew better than to be anything but unfailingly chipper and polite with the reporter. He knew one furrowed brow was enough to get him painted as the angry black man. He knew that well enough from experience; he'd blown up at a reporter at an World Athletics meet in Dubai the previous year and had been raked over the coals by the international sports press. He couldn't pull a John McEnroe without it following him the rest of the Games.

"Well, first, can we talk about your race bling?" Leslie asked, sounding like the whitest white lady the network had available. "I see you've got your nails done and ready."

"Yeah." JJ held up his hands for the camera and wiggled his fingers to show off the manicure. "And I worked with Nike to design custom gold shoes for this week's races, because that's the color medal I intend to win."

Leslie asked a few more questions about that, and JJ dropped the name of the shoe company about eight times because he was contractually obligated to, but then Leslie took a left turn and said, "You've got quite a story, right? Grew up in South Central, and now you're here. How amazing does that feel?"

JJ glanced at Tamika, whose eyes widened. "Ah, well," JJ said, trying to hold back. "I mean, my family is great, and I've trained really hard for this." There, that sounded pretty diplomatic.

"You must have had a difficult childhood."

What was wrong with this reporter? "Uh, no, not really. Like I said, my family is wonderful. They've always been very supportive."

"You're a gay athlete, though. That must be hard."

JJ tilted his head. He felt bile rising up in his throat, felt the anger spreading across his chest, but he saw the camera hovering in his peripheral vision, so he didn't give in to it. "I gotta be me," he said. "Where I grew up and who I love has zero bearing on how I run a race. I'm here to win a gold medal, and that's really all I have to say about that." There. That should shut her up.

"JJ," Tamika said under her breath.

JJ sighed. "Look, I'm proud of who I am. I have a great life and I want to celebrate it."

The reporter nodded and jotted something down on a pad in her hand. Then she looked up at JJ again. "There's a rumor one of your teammates has tested positive for a banned substance." Then she stared at JJ expectantly.

He resisted the urge to pointedly ask "Is that a question?" and settled on "I don't know anything about that."

"You have a doping charge in your history."

Something toxic and terrible bubbled up in JJ's chest. He swallowed and said, "I took some cold pills before they adjusted the allowed amount of pseudo-ephedrine. I was cleared of all charges. I've never deliberately taken any kind of performance enhancing substance and never will."

"What about your teammates?"

"I can't speak to what anyone else does." He glanced at the clock on the wall to his left. Ms. Boothe had gone far over her five minutes.

She seemed to understand that. "Okay, JJ. Thank you for your time."

She smiled, but the damage was done, and now everything in JJ swirled around as he considered the larger implications of what had just happened. He'd held it together, at least. That reporter had been goading him into saying his life had been a struggle, which struck him as the worst kind of bias. Just because he was gay and black, he must have endured woe and tragedy? Sure, he'd experienced homophobia and racism, mostly via subtle microaggressions—like Boothe's faux sympathy for an imagined terrible childhood—rather than blatant prejudice, but he loved his parents, and his childhood had been a happy one.

More than that, though, Boothe's questions implied he was under suspicion, at least from the network, despite all the vials of blood WADA technicians had drawn from his arm and tested. He was under suspicion, even after having to pee in front of a stranger three times already that week. He wouldn't be surprised if he was one of the most frequently tested athletes at the Games, all because Franco had lied about what was in those fucking cold pills.

And very likely Franco was the one who'd been caught doping. And if he had been caught, he would not be at the two-hundred final happening in less than an hour. JJ felt like redemption had been robbed from him.

"Practice run!" said Tamika.

JJ shook his head and tried to focus on the task at hand, hoping he could channel some of his anger at the reporter and this situation into a fast two-hundred. His blocks were already set up in Lane 4 of the practice track, so he got his feet in them and waited for Tamika to signal he should go. When she did, he took off, but his head was still somewhere else, angry at Franco, angry at the WADA, angry at Leslie goddamned Boothe. He couldn't quite switch gears, and when he crossed the finish line, Tamika said, "22.04," with a frown on her face.

"Shit." There was no way he'd win if he couldn't get his time under twenty seconds, and over twenty-two was the slowest he'd run all week.

"You're rattled. Do whatever you need to do in order to calm down."

"Okay. But I want to see Brandon run his semifinal. On the monitor over there." He pointed.

Tamika glanced back at it. "Sure. I'll let you know when he's about to be on."

The other two-hundred finalists had drifted out and were doing their warm-ups on the practice track. JJ stayed in his lane and ran a few laps, trying to forget whatever had been in his head. But then he noted that all of the two-hundred finalists were out here warming up—except Franco.

Which totally pissed JJ off.

The fucking gall of that guy. He'd taken a World Championship medal away from JJ for no real reason other than his own pettiness, and JJ wanted to beat him on his own terms, but he'd been robbed of that opportunity too.

Shit, shit, shit.

Tamika waved him over just before the four-hundred hurdles semifinal. Well, if JJ was about to flame out, at least he wanted to see Brandon win first.

"On your marks."

On screen, Brandon got in his blocks and placed his hands behind the line. The camera got a good shot of his painted nails, and JJ felt a little gratified by that. Brandon's big glasses were held on his head with a stretchy strap, and he looked like such a dork, but also a really hot dork. JJ guessed most engineering students did not have six-pack abs and corded muscles on their arms and legs the way Brandon did. They also didn't have Brandon's tousled hair or intense blue eyes or completely unassuming demeanor.

JJ liked him a whole lot. It was getting dangerous.

But none of that mattered now.

"Get set."

When the gun went off, Brandon got out of the blocks fast, breaking into a run and hitting his stride in time to leap over the first hurdle. And so it went around the track, Brandon clearing each hurdle like it was his job to demonstrate how to do it, while competitors around him had far messier races. One guy tripped over a hurdle and completely wiped out, but Brandon kept running, as if he wasn't aware of anything happening behind him. He probably wasn't.

Brandon cleared the last hurdle with only one runner anywhere near him, and broke into an all-out sprint toward the finish line. He finished the semifinal in first, of course, with a time just under forty-seven seconds. The camera zoomed in on his face as he walked out of the way of the finishing runners. He put his hands on his waist and looked up at the scoreboard. Satisfaction crossed his face. He nodded once, grabbed his things from the starting line, and headed back into the stadium as if it were nothing.

This kid. He was gifted and didn't even know it.

"He won his heat, didn't he?" Tamika asked.

"Without breaking a sweat."

She nodded. Quietly, she said, "This is not public yet, but Franco Greer was DQ'd, and your old coach is in a lot of trouble."

Hardly a surprise, but something about that made JJ furious. "That's why I changed coaches," he said with all the calm he could muster. Because fuck Marcus too. If he thought encouraging his athletes to cheat was the way to win, then he had no business being a coach.

Tamika smiled. "I know. I really appreciate that."

Watching Brandon run had been a good distraction, but now the anger was seeping in again. Franco had been DQ'd. "Fucking Franco," he muttered.

"Do you feel ready for your race?"

"No. I'm freaking out, honestly."

Tamika crossed her arms and gave JJ a long look from head to toe. "Why? What is making you freak out?"

"Have you seen the news reports? Everyone suspects I'm doping; everyone suspects half the sprinters are doping. I have to run clean against these guys who are using God only knows what to get ahead, and I can't even beat Franco on my terms because he's been DQ'd. And I really wanted to beat Franco." He thought he might vomit. He wanted to calm down, but he couldn't seem to get a handle on his anger at this situation. He pulled Tamika into a dark corner, and when he felt fairly confident no one was in earshot, he added, "Franco confessed that he gave me those cold pills on purpose."

Tamika gasped. "When?"

"Yesterday. So it wasn't enough for him to cheat. He had to sabotage someone else. I mean, what the fuck?"

She frowned and nodded. "I understand why you're upset. You have every right to be. But you also have races to run."

"I know." JJ sighed. His heart pounded. He pressed a hand to his chest in a futile attempt to get his breathing back to normal, although every time he thought about Franco, his pulse spiked again.

"Go see the physical therapist. Get a massage. Do what you can to calm down."

JJ took a deep breath and nodded.

He retreated to the locker room and lay on the table for ten minutes while a physical therapist named Travis tried to rub the anger out of his muscles. It helped some. JJ just hoped he could figure out how to channel this into a victory. It wouldn't be easy.

CHAPTER FIFTEEN

AFTER HIS cool-down, Brandon checked in with the team physical therapists, who suggested a massage to soothe Brandon's tired muscles. That seemed like a solid idea, so Brandon lay down on the table and let the therapist go to work. It felt so good and so relaxing that Brandon was pretty sure he fell asleep for part of it. So by the time he was back at his locker, he was feeling pretty mellow.

He'd had a moment where he'd contemplated following JJ's lead and dunking in an ice bath, but he didn't really want to shock his body that way, especially not now that he felt so warm and sleepy. He doubted the ice bath had much therapeutic value—the science of it didn't quite add up—but he also knew athletes were superstitious, so if JJ and Tamika thought it helped, he wasn't going to intervene.

Brandon thought he heard JJ's voice echoing through the room, but he ignored it, knowing JJ was probably preparing for his race. Brandon changed out of his uniform and figured he'd go watch the two-hundred final from the stands.

But then JJ appeared at the end of the aisle of lockers. "Good race."

Brandon pulled on a T-shirt. "Thank you."

"How do you feel?"

Brandon swallowed a sigh. "I'm all right. You?"

JJ looked off into the distance. He stepped closer to Brandon and lowered his voice. "One of the American sprinters was disqualified for doping. He was that former training partner of mine I told you about."

"Wow." Brandon had thought most of the athletes were too smart to dope with this many WADA technicians around, but apparently not. Brandon had not been particularly tempted by the stuff. He knew there were athletes who would do literally anything for a shot to compete at the Olympics—he'd recently read a book about the 1984 US cycling team, which had done blood doping to gain a competitive edge, despite the fact that the practice was incredibly risky—but he was not among them. The science seemed sketchy, since none of these things were tested or regulated. Did more red blood cells really boost performance? The cyclists thought so, but Brandon remained skeptical that some of these practices would have more than a placebo effect. Certainly anabolic steroids boosted muscle mass, but the extra testosterone did some other odd things to the body. Brandon wanted to win, but not badly enough to risk his health; if he didn't win, he'd still have a career ahead of him as an engineer.

JJ leaned against the locker. "Did you know Tamika's older brother is a runner? He made the Olympic team twice."

"No, I didn't know that."

"Tamika is very firmly antidoping. That's because her brother took some experimental drug before his last Olympics. He won a medal in one of the middle-distance races. And he thinks that medal is tainted. It's in a box in a closet somewhere. He won't even acknowledge it. See, there's shame in doping, and athletes know it's wrong, but they feel desperate. It's not as bad as it used to be, but you know it's still happening."

"Some coaches promote drug use, I've heard."

"Mine did. My old one, I mean, not Tamika. He offered to put me on a regimen. I said no. And I tested positive anyway. And even though I fucking hate needles and I hate blood, I have to get blood drawn at least once every other day the whole time I'm competing to make sure I'm not cheating. And it doesn't matter if I'm not. I'll do these tests because it will prove I'm not doping, but I still hate that I have to."

"I'm sorry." Brandon wasn't entirely sure what to say to JJ to help him calm down. A crease formed on JJ's forehead, foretelling his distress.

"I can beat the drugs. I can do it. Maybe this one guy is gone, but that doesn't mean that there aren't other athletes who are using something the tests can't find yet." JJ kicked a locker. "God, it pisses me off."

Brandon stared at JJ.

"There are cheaters in your races too. Maybe drugs can't teach you how to count steps or leap over hurdles or solve math problems, but they can improve your speed, strength, and dexterity, like experience points in a video game. And isn't that fucking rich."

"JJ."

"And no one will just fucking let me be. No one will trust me. I test positive once, and it turns out it's because someone I thought was my friend gave me cold pills with a stimulant *on purpose*, and it's like an albatross around my neck for the rest of my career. I lost a bunch of endorsement deals and it took me a year to win some of them back. Because you test positive only once and everyone still suspects you after that. The facts don't matter. *Perception* is what matters. And everyone will always wonder."

Brandon tried to process what JJ was saying, but couldn't help feeling that JJ was overreacting. "I think you might be overestimating people's memories."

JJ wheeled on Brandon. "How would you know? You don't even try. You look at some hurdles and turn around some numbers in your head and win races. And it's not even fucking fair because this isn't your career. You can lose and go home and get your engineering degree and be famous for something else. But this is everything I've worked for most of my life. This *is* my life. Running is my life. And losing is not an option for me."

"No one would judge you if you lost." Brandon wasn't sure why it suddenly felt like his job to talk JJ off the ledge, but he knew JJ was getting so worked up that it might affect his performance.

"*I* would judge me."

Brandon couldn't deny that anything JJ said was true, but he was also a little offended at JJ's accusations. "I know you think I don't feel any passion for this, but you're wrong. I do. I want to win, or I wouldn't try so hard. Just because I don't wear my heart on my sleeve like you do doesn't mean I don't want the medal."

"You could act like it sometimes."

"That's not really how I operate."

JJ kicked a locker again and let out a groan. "Right. Because I'm too much. I'm flashy and aggressive. I'm too *emotional*."

Okay, now Brandon was getting mad. He didn't deserve to take the brunt of this. "Did I say that?"

JJ just grunted. "It doesn't matter. I may lose today. And if I do, and if it's because runners cheated, then I don't even know what to think of that."

"You've been running so well all week."

JJ pointed at Brandon, his finger brushing over Brandon's chest. JJ was close enough to kiss, but his rage came off him in waves. Brandon thought JJ's anger justified—he was right, the system was unfair, and if these drugs really did enhance athletic ability, it was very possible that JJ could lose because someone cheated—but having this amount of anger leveled at him was making him uncomfortable. And now Brandon was pressed against the lockers, JJ barring his escape.

"You don't get it," JJ said, sounding furious and exasperated. "You *can't* get it. You are constitutionally incapable of understanding. This is all a game for you, but the stakes are so much higher for me, and I'm gonna need you to get it through your thick skull that that you don't know or understand everything, even if you are a genius."

"JJ, I—"

"Stand down, JJ," said Grady as he walked down the aisle.

JJ took a step away. "Fuck."

"You okay, Brandon?"

"I'm fine."

Grady looked at JJ. "Is yelling at people part of your prerace routine?"

JJ glanced at Brandon. "No."

"Tamika wants you on the practice track. Try not to bite anyone's head off."

JJ stormed off. When he was gone, Grady turned to Brandon. "You okay?"

"I'm fine. JJ was just… blowing off steam, I guess." But the more Brandon thought about it, the more he found the whole thing unfair. JJ had mentioned he had anger issues, but Brandon had never seen JJ blow up this way. It highlighted how little they knew each other. But more than that, Brandon hadn't deserved JJ's rage. Was this how things would go in a relationship? If JJ was mad about something, would he take it out on Brandon because he was there? And what if JJ was upset about something he wasn't saying? Maybe he was worried about his race. Maybe he was trying to tell Brandon something else, and Brandon was too dense to understand it.

Grady sighed. "You need anything else for cool-down? You good?"

"I ran a couple of laps and got a massage. I feel good now." Although he was also tense, after having endured JJ's shouting.

"Good. Come with me. I want to talk to the physical therapist about tomorrow; then you can go watch JJ run if you want."

"I do want to watch him."

Although JJ's words continued to bounce around Brandon's head. Brandon was irritated now that JJ didn't seem to take him very seriously. It was as if he thought Brandon didn't belong here because he wasn't a career runner. Had JJ really meant that, or had he just been shouting? Brandon couldn't quite sort it out.

"How well do you know JJ?" Brandon asked Grady.

"Not well. Tamika has told me a few things. He's great most of the time, but he's got a bit of a chip on his shoulder."

"I can't tell if he yelled at me because he wanted to yell at *me*, or because I was the first person he ran into that he knew and needed to unload."

"Probably the latter, but hard to say."

"Hmm."

Brandon decided to push it aside and focus on whatever postrace treatment Grady had in mind for him, but he was starting to rethink moving into JJ's room. Maybe he'd be better off staying in his own room tonight. Give JJ room to cool off.

JJ HAD gone to a summer camp in northern California when he'd been seven or eight. One of his counselors had liked to play a game she called Primal Scream. The gist was that all the kids stood in a row at one end of a field. When they were given the word, all of the kids would take a deep breath and scream as they ran across the field. When they took a breath, they had to stop running. JJ had won a lot, mostly because he ran faster than most of the other kids and could get a lot of mileage out of that scream.

He'd learned that a good scream could do a lot to defuse his anger, although it wasn't polite to scream like that in polite company.

And yet, as he crossed the finish line of the practice track and Tamika yelled out "20.01!" he let out the most primal of primal screams, a groan meant to let out all his anger and frustration.

Tamika jogged over. "Right before the final is a terrible time for a nervous breakdown," she said.

"Why can't I run this fucking race under twenty seconds?"

"I don't know, but you've only got about twenty minutes to figure it out. What is bothering you?"

JJ took a deep breath and tried to calm down. His muscles were tied in knots from tension, which was why he was running slowly. He couldn't get his body to cooperate. He wasn't as loose as he should have been. "Well, I'm mad about being suspecting of doping, I'm mad Franco was DQ'd, and I'm so worked up about everything that I just picked a fight with Brandon, so he probably won't be speaking to me again." JJ regretted yelling at Brandon, but staring at Brandon's placid face had rubbed JJ the wrong way. He hadn't felt like Brandon had understood the source of JJ's frustration. But JJ hadn't given him the chance to, had he?

Running was the only thing JJ had ever excelled at. Brandon needed to understand that so he could understand why this race unnerved JJ so much.

"I doubt that's true. Brandon clearly likes you. And not in a training partner kind of way."

"He's not good at sorting through emotions. He may think I hate him. He's probably confused about why." JJ let out a breath. If Brandon never spoke to JJ again, he'd be justified, because he hadn't deserved the full force of JJ's wrath. JJ knew that. He knew he'd crossed a line. He wished he could have found a more constructive way to convey what he meant. But instead he'd gone off half-cocked and screamed. He didn't know if any amount of groveling would win Brandon back, but he was genuinely sorry for the yelling. He sighed and kicked a stray bit of detritus on the track.

Tamika frowned at him, then glanced at her clipboard. "Well, you'll have to win a gold medal to impress him."

JJ laughed despite himself. "Come on, girl. That doesn't make any sense."

Tamika laughed too, and shrugged. "I tried. Look, let me tell you something, okay?"

"Is this going to be an inspirational speech?"

"Yes."

JJ groaned.

Tamika put a hand on his shoulder. "My grandpa was an Olympic champion long jumper. You know that?"

"No."

"He was on the San Jose State track team in the sixties. You may recall that the establishment, including the president of the IOC, didn't have much respect for black athletes. Generations of Olympic committees and the powers that be didn't have any respect for black athletes. We had to prove ourselves over and over and over again. Jesse Owens, Tommie Smith, Carl Lewis. All these men who came before you. And you, JJ, are living in a time in which you *are* taken seriously. Now, I know there's all this bullshit with WADA and the drug testing, but you know you're clean, I know you're clean, and as long as your tests keep coming back clean, no one can take what you've achieved away from you. No one expects you to fail. No one will be surprised if a black man wins this race. Hell, there's only one white guy in the final."

"Do you have a point?"

Tamika frowned. "You know, in 1968 when the white establishment thought the black athletes on Team USA were getting too uppity, they called in Jesse Owens to talk them off the ledge, and it only made things worse because the contemporary athletes resented him for trying to stop the protest. They called Jesse Owens an Uncle Tom. Can you believe that?"

JJ narrowed his eyes at Tamika. She did this sometimes, talked in circles, pulled in all of her knowledge of the history of track and field, which was extensive. JJ tried to wade through everything she'd just said. He couldn't figure out what she was trying to tell him or what this had to do with his present situation. "Are you telling me not to resent my predecessors?"

"Each generation has its own shit to deal with. Jesse Owens had to run in front of Hitler. Tommie Smith protested even when everyone told him not to, and he got told to leave Mexico City. Some of the most successful runners of the past few years overcame racism and poverty and training programs lacking in resources to get where they are. You have to deal with the fact everyone is so determined to show the world that our sports are clean that innocent people get caught in the net sometimes. I know this doping accusation is hanging over you. But it doesn't matter. Nothing matters. When you are on the track, the only thing that counts is what you do there. I know you can run two hundred meters in nineteen seconds because I've seen you do it. So do that. Forget about everything else."

JJ sighed. He supposed what Tamika was trying to tell him was that generations of runners that had come before him had managed to shake off whatever else was going on and run the races of their lives. JJ could do that, because he'd done it before.

He spared a thought for Jesse Owens having to run a race in front of Hitler. He was reminded of the internet truism that if one was involved in an argument, once Hitler was invoked, the argument was over. But in this case, JJ tried to imagine what it must have been like if he had to literally run in front of a man who thought men of his race should not exist. A doping scandal seemed like nothing in comparison.

He had to shake it off, in other words.

"These pep talks," JJ said, "they often ramble and take wrong turns, but I think I get what you're saying."

"Good." Tamika smiled. "Leave your shit here. Run a lap now, do whatever you have to do mentally so that when you hit the field, all you have to do is run two hundred meters."

"In less than twenty seconds. Sure. That's all."

Chapter Sixteen

Transcript from the TBC Broadcast of the two-hundred-meter sprint final

GRAYSON: BEFORE we get to the race, I hear we have an update about the doping disqualifications.

CASSELLO: What we know, as of a few minutes ago, is that American sprinter Franco Greer has been disqualified after testing positive for a banned substance. Unfortunately, we don't have any information about what drug he took or the circumstances around it. But it's good to know that WADA is maintaining the integrity of the games.

GRAYSON: That's right. Athletes I've talked to have said that the WADA officials have been quite aggressive about testing. Some of the athletes in this very final have been tested repeatedly all week. So I think we can feel good about who is left in this race.

CASSELLO: Let's run through who we have on the track.

GRAYSON: Of course. In Lane 1, we have one of the Americans, DeShawn Latrell. He's a sprinter originally from Detroit, trains at the University of Michigan. In Lane 2, we have Jeremy Partridge from Great Britain. He's the European champion in this event. They call him "White Lightning," if you can believe that. He actually trains at the University of Oregon but is here representing his home country.

CASSELLO: [*laughs*] That nickname is a little on the nose.

GRAYSON: True, true. In Lane 3, that's Lanny Eldridge from Jamaica. In Lane 4, we have Jason Jones Jr., who won both his prelim and his semifinal to get here, so I think he's likely our front-runner, although Leslie passed along the news that he struggled a bit in practice this afternoon, so he could be having an off day.

CASSELLO: Is that something that happens?

GRAYSON: Sure. The Olympics put so much pressure on these athletes that sometimes they get tense, or they come down with a virus or something and don't feel a hundred percent. It's hard to say what will cause an athlete to have a bad day; it could be any number of things.

CASSELLO: All right. Who else?

GRAYSON: In Lane 5, it's Ajani Blake from Jamaica. In Lane 6, we have Rafael Martinez from Team USA, another sprinter out of the USC program. And finally, in Lane 7, that is Ato Frederick from Namibia.

CASSELLO: Aside from Jones, who do you think has a shot at the gold?

GRAYSON: Based on how these runners looked in the earlier heats, I'd say Blake from Jamaica and probably Rafael Martinez have the best odds. Martinez looked very good in the earlier heats, and Blake is blazing fast. Blake has won this event at a number of World Cup events. So I guess we'll see. If JJ pulls it together and runs the way he did in the prelims, he'll win, no problem. If he doesn't, anyone in this field has a shot at a medal.

CASSELLO: JJ wants everyone to know he wants that gold medal.

GRAYSON: No denying the sneakers and the nail polish.

CASSELLO: I guess we'll know in twenty seconds….

JJ PUT his feet in the blocks. He wasn't religious, but he caught a few of the men in his peripheral vision gesturing toward heaven and wondered if he shouldn't send up a prayer, just in case. Instead, he touched the St. Sebastian medal on his chest and made sure it was tucked under his jersey.

The polish on his right forefinger had chipped at some point this afternoon, and JJ was only noticing it now. That was a shame, but there was nothing he could do about it. He placed his fingers in their proper position behind the line.

He tried to make his brain go blank. He'd heard of runners who could channel their emotions into a run, but he wasn't sure he could do that here. His last few practice runs had been too slow, and all he'd been able to think about was the crap that had been plaguing him all day. So he tried to empty his mind now.

He focused his attention on the mission: stay in his lane and get to the finish line on the other side of the track.

"Get set."

JJ pressed his feet into the blocks and raised his back. He focused on the track, on the long line ahead of him, the maroon color of the synthetic surface, the starkness of the white lines that demarcated the lanes.

The gun sounded, and JJ pushed off. It was a good start, a smooth pop off the blocks and into racing form. He saw in his peripheral vision that one of the runners to his right did not get off right and stumbled out of the start. Any mistake in a race like this would take a runner out, so JJ only had to beat six other runners now.

He chased the runners in the right lanes that were staggered ahead of him. He passed the white guy, the runner from Great Britain, who seemed to be struggling. He couldn't see the runners in the lanes to his left yet, but they were probably gaining on him as he went into the turn. The runners all seemed to be side-by-side for a brief moment as they entered the turn, but by the time JJ got to the straightaway, he, Rafa, and Blake from Jamaica were ahead, with Blake just slightly ahead of JJ.

JJ couldn't have that. He couldn't let another runner win, not after the week he'd had. He dug into himself, tried to find another gear, ran harder. He made a conscious effort to make longer strides, to breathe the way he was supposed to, to leap ahead if that was possible.

He and Blake were right beside each other down the straightaway, with Rafa falling farther behind as they ran down the track. JJ only had to beat Blake, and he wanted to beat Blake more than anything. He had to push himself beyond anything he'd ever done before. The crowd roared around him, the sound echoing through the stadium, more a loud hum in his ears than anything else, and that spurred him on too; if this crowd wanted a show, he'd give one to them.

He thought he might have pulled ahead of Blake a little, but as they crossed the finish line, he wasn't sure. He ducked his head when he got to the line, thinking that might give him the edge—if it was close, whoever got a body part ahead of the other runner would be ruled the winner.

Then he kept pounding his feet against the track but pulled on the brakes as he rounded the next curve, trying to slow down. Blake, Rafa, and Ato from Namibia were there with him.

But had he won decisively, or had it been a photo finish?

JJ stopped running, closed his eyes for a moment, took a deep breath, and looked up at the scoreboard.

JJ had finished first. 19.2 seconds. Gold medal.

Blake had won the silver. Rafa the bronze. Ato had finished 0.3 seconds out of the medals, and they had collectively smoked the rest of the field, who all finished over twenty seconds.

Dear God in heaven.

Tamika ran onto the track screaming, two American flags in her hand.

"You did it! You did it!" she screamed.

She was probably right to be surprised, given how poorly he'd run during the practice sprints. And now he was covered from head to toe in beads of sweat—it was a hot summer in Madrid—and he was panting so hard, he couldn't speak. But he took a flag from Tamika as she handed the other to Rafa. Before he could get his bearings, Rafa had thrown his arms around him and was panting and laughing. Rafa was screaming in his ear, and he looked down at the flag in his hands, which still had the crease marks from being folded inside a plastic bag until now. JJ shook it, tried to get some of the creases out. Then he wrapped it around himself for a moment and held it around his neck so it unfurled like a cape.

Tamika was still screaming, tugging on her braided hair, jumping up and down on the track as if she'd been the one who won. He was still having trouble wrapping his head around it.

Suddenly he was exhausted. His knees buckled and he sank onto the track, kneeling there for a moment. Tamika and Rafa helped him back up and draped the flag around his shoulders, like he was James Brown toward the end of his set. JJ took a moment to wave up at the stands at about the spot he thought most of the US delegation was sitting.

Had Brandon seen that? Had he been watching? Or had he given up on JJ and gone back to the Olympic Village?

God, Brandon. JJ had really given it to him earlier, and Brandon hadn't deserved that. So JJ would have to apologize.

But first he had to get his gold medal.

BRANDON SANG the national anthem with the rest of the USATF staff and athletes around him in the stands, and he watched JJ standing on top of that podium, staring at the flag with his hand over his heart and a little toy bull in his hand. The plastic toy represented the official Madrid Olympics mascot and was allegedly a greener alternative to a bouquet of flowers. And yes, on the surface, they weren't mowing down a field so the athletes could hold some flowers for a few days, but how green was the manufacturing process for those toy bulls?

Brandon shook his head. He was mortified by his own thought processes sometimes. Why was he thinking about toy manufacturing and not the fact that JJ just won a gold medal at the Olympics?

"JJ wants the one-hundred more," Grady said when the anthem ended and the athletes were escorted off the podium by the president of the IOC and a group of women in beige suits, some of the officials who helped give out the medals. "The two-hundred is the trial run, basically. Tamika told me JJ was worried that if he didn't win the two-hundred, he had no shot at all at the one-hundred, because the competition there will be more difficult."

"Prelims for that are tomorrow, right?"

"Yes. Do you plan to watch?"

"If I can before my final."

"So you still plan to hang around with JJ, even though he picked a fight with you?"

Brandon shrugged. "He can be intense sometimes."

Grady laughed. "That's an understatement."

Brandon wasn't ready to say this aloud, but he thought understood JJ a bit better now. JJ hadn't been mad at Brandon, although what he'd said had bothered Brandon. JJ had mostly been expressing frustration. JJ was mad about WADA and doping and some of the racist microaggressions he'd had to deal with since getting to Madrid; Brandon understood the world well enough to know that. And because Brandon was not good at expressing emotion, JJ had interpreted Brandon's outward ambivalence as indifference, when the reality was that Brandon felt anything but indifferent. He wanted to win, he wanted JJ to win, and he cared about JJ.

Was he wrong to still want to be with JJ after JJ had yelled at him? When they were alone together, JJ kept saying Brandon should express what he wanted, do what he wanted. Well, Brandon still wanted to be with JJ. So that's what he'd do.

He and Grady chatted as they walked back into the stadium. Brandon decided he'd wait for JJ in the locker room while JJ wrapped up with whatever he had to do on the track, likely interviews with the press. They ran into Tamika at the entrance to the men's locker room; she smiled broadly.

"Well, my love," said Grady, "you have officially coached a gold medal athlete."

Tamika threw her arms around him. "Can you believe it? I really didn't think he could win. He was so far in his head before the race started. I don't know where that last burst came from, but wherever he found the energy to finish ahead of Blake, I hope he can find it again in the one-hundred."

"He will. That kid wants this more than anything."

Tamika stepped away from her husband and patted him on the chest. "If I feel this good, I can only imagine how JJ feels."

"That was a great race," Brandon said.

Tamika grinned and hugged Brandon. "I'm so thrilled right now. I can't even."

Brandon stood there awkwardly for a moment. He wasn't sure if he should leave or if these two would include him in the conversation or what would happen. But Tamika said, "Hey, let's celebrate. We'll get JJ's parents in on it too. Drinks at the America House. Well, one drink. You boys have to run tomorrow. You want to come, Brandon?"

"Sure." Did this mean he'd meet JJ's parents? Did that mean anything? Would he have to pretend he and JJ weren't together?

Or were they?

Brandon didn't want to overthink this. JJ had made his feelings pretty clear, despite picking that fight. Brandon felt confident JJ liked him. He worried briefly that he was giving JJ too much slack, but they could talk about it later and Brandon would explain his feelings, and maybe it would all be okay.

Still, he asked, "You guys think JJ was just blowing off steam when he picked that fight with me earlier, right?"

Tamika nodded. "Yeah, that seems likely. He gets heated at practice sometimes too, and yells at me. I'm pretty used to it now. I haven't seen him worked up quite as much as he got this afternoon before, but I figure that's because it's the Olympics and he was anxious about the race. I wouldn't take anything he said personally. He'll probably show up to apologize in a few."

"Okay. I'll take your word for it."

JJ did show up a few minutes later, though his facial expression was unreadable. Was he happy? Angry? Confused?

"There's the man of the hour!" said Tamika.

JJ ducked his head but smiled. "It hasn't sunk in yet."

"How did you do it?"

JJ shrugged. "I really wanted to win. Blake was on me the whole race, so I pushed myself to go past him."

Grady chuckled. "Oh, is that all?"

"Go get changed, JJ," said Tamika. "I'll buy you a drink."

Chapter Seventeen

JJ's MOTHER gave him a big sloppy kiss as they stood in front of America House. Fatigue was sinking into JJ's bones now and he really just wanted to go back to his dorm and lie down, preferably with Brandon, to whom he still hadn't been able to apologize.

It had been a whirlwind from the moment JJ had crossed the finish line. There'd been the victory lap on the track, followed by a few frenzied moments when television crews shoved microphones in his face. Then there'd been the medal ceremony, and JJ had felt so overwhelmed, he'd forgotten the words to the national anthem and had hummed it instead.

On his way off the track, he'd been stopped by several other reporters, and before he had a good grip on what was going on, he was shoved in a cab with Grady, Tamika, and Brandon. Then he'd held court at a big table in America House with this gang, plus his parents. And Tamika hadn't even tried not to make it seem like

Brandon was JJ's boyfriend, which had made things a little awkward. JJ had said lamely, "Brandon and I are good friends," and let everyone draw their own conclusions. He could explain whatever was happening to his family when he got back home.

Mildred still had hearts in her eyes as Jason Senior gave him a hearty handshake. They congratulated JJ about seven hundred more times as they started their retreat toward the taxi stand. Then Grady and Tamika hugged him and shook his hand. Tamika did the weird thing all the athletes did when they won a medal and picked up the one hanging from JJ's neck and pretended to try to bite it.

"Is it real gold?" JJ asked.

"Sure is. I'm so proud of you, JJ."

"Well, I'm not done yet."

"No, but take tonight to celebrate. You've earned it."

Then Grady and Tamika left, leaving JJ and Brandon alone at last. The fact that Brandon was still there seemed like a good sign.

"Listen, about earlier...," JJ said.

"Do you really think I don't care?"

JJ supposed he deserved that. "No. I know you do. Can we talk?"

"Yeah. Let's walk back to the dorm."

When they fell into step beside each other, JJ said, "Franco getting disqualified threw me for a loop. He's the training partner I mentioned."

"Yeah, I saw he wasn't in the final."

"Look, I realize I'm probably being paranoid, but I feel like I'm being led into a trap. Anytime someone in a lab coat gets near me, I kind of freak out. I know I'm clean, but it sort of feels like they *want* to catch me, and after past experience, I have to wonder. Like, if I drink a Coke will they DQ me for taking a stimulant?" And if Franco had sold him out as easily as he had, after all those years of friendship and training together, who could JJ even trust?

"There isn't enough caffeine in Coke to meet the threshold for—"

"I know!" JJ groaned. "I'm sorry. I don't mean to take all this out on you, but here's where I am right now. But worse than that, I'm worried that even though I haven't had anything more potent than a cup of coffee all day, no one will believe me if I say I'm clean."

"I believe you."

Aw, poor, sweet Brandon. "Thanks, babe, but that's not the 'everyone' I was talking about."

"I know, but there are people who have your back, JJ. I know you won that medal fairly."

JJ took a deep breath. "Anyway, I'm trying to apologize for biting your head off earlier and trying to explain why. I was stressed about the race, I was upset about all this doping shit, and I shouldn't have taken it out on you. I'm really sorry."

Brandon pressed his lips together and nodded, his face infuriatingly blank. JJ was usually good at reading people, but even after these past few days, he still could never quite tell what Brandon was thinking. But then Brandon said, "I forgive you."

"All right."

"It hurt a little when you said that I don't care about any of this. That's not true. Maybe I'm not demonstrative about it, but I *do* care. If I didn't want to win, I wouldn't be here."

"I know."

Brandon sighed. "Although, you know how on reality TV shows, the contestants are always saying things like 'She's here for the wrong reasons' or 'she doesn't want this as much as I do' or 'he doesn't *really* want to be here'? I always think, if one person is more talented than the other, their motivation shouldn't matter. Like, why does wanting it more make one more worthy of winning? I can *want* to run a marathon in under three hours, but that doesn't mean I can actually do it."

JJ chuckled. Brandon was a trip sometimes. "In other words, if you run the race faster than anybody else, it doesn't matter why."

"Yeah. Running fast isn't a demonstration in morality. But we treat it like it is sometimes. I mean, even when you watch Olympics coverage on TV, they manipulate viewers. Like, this runner has this sad sob story or overcame this tragedy, and I guess the intention is for the viewer to root for that person to win, because it makes this perfect story, but this is the real world. It's not scripted. Sometimes the person who overcame extreme odds to be here loses. Sometimes someone with no tragic backstory is just really good and wins the race."

"That's true."

Brandon held up his hand. "Which, by the way, doesn't mean that this is all stupid or that I think it's meaningless. What you and I do, it's incredibly difficult, and I respect the fact that the athletes at the Olympics continually push the limits of sport. We're not curing cancer, but we're demonstrating what the human body is capable of on the world stage. And we're bringing in athletes from all over the world, demonstrating unity and sportsmanship, if only for these two weeks. That's no small thing."

"Sure."

Brandon sighed. "I think also, even if I *was* only here to analyze the hurdles from an engineering perspective, why does it matter? Why is my Olympic dream any less valid than yours?"

JJ mulled that over for a moment. He found that, weirdly, he understood Brandon's logic. "It isn't. Some of us just go to the over-the-top place with our passions sometimes."

Brandon seemed irritated now. JJ looked him over. He was pressing his lips together, an odd show of some kind of emotion on his face.

"I'm sorry, Brandon. When I was yelling at you earlier, none of it was really about you. It's about me and everything happening right now."

"Okay. Okay." They arrived at the dorm. After they passed through security and were waiting for the elevator, Brandon said, "Franco is still bothering you."

JJ shrugged. "I thought for years that it was a mistake, that there was no way Franco could betray me like that, that he just hadn't known. Except, you know, you have to take that dumb little card to the pharmacy if you want to buy anything with pseudoephedrine, so he must have known, and I was in deep denial. And now every time that I think about it again, it's like he's stabbing me right in the back all over again."

"I'm sorry." Brandon pressed his lips together and nodded thoughtfully for a moment. "I can't imagine what hearing that must have been like."

"And who knows how long he's been cheating at all this. Part of me has suspected he was doping for a while."

"No wonder you want to beat him."

JJ sighed. He tried to tamp down the anger he felt bubbling up at the situation. He didn't want to blow up at Brandon again when he was trying to apologize. "Anyway, I wasn't the only one who got snagged by a low dose of pseudoephedrine, which is why they changed the regulation. If I took the same pills tomorrow, I wouldn't test positive. But you have to understand that with an accusation like that, even if you're acquitted, you're never really innocent. But…." JJ groaned and waved his hand. "I don't want to talk about it anymore. I'm tired of talking about it."

"I'm just trying to understand."

"I know." And JJ did know that Brandon was trying to apply logic to a situation that lacked logic in order to comprehend what JJ had experienced. "I guess Franco was willing to win at any cost."

"No," said Brandon. "I want to understand what you experienced. I want to know why you got angry. I don't care about Franco. I want to understand you."

BRANDON BREATHED in deeply a few times. He did forgive JJ. He understood JJ a little better now. But he still felt like he was missing one piece of the puzzle. He rocked on his heels as they waited for the elevator. There wasn't really anyone around, but still, Brandon waited until they were alone in the elevator to ask, "Am I spending the night with you?"

"If you want to."

"I do."

It surprised Brandon how much. He could probably go back to his room, although Jamal would still be there for the duration; since he'd won the silver medal, he'd decided to stick around for the Closing Ceremony. But even if Jamal had flown home and Brandon had the room to himself, he would want to spend the night with JJ. So since half of his stuff was now in JJ's room anyway, Brandon followed JJ out of the elevator and down the hall to his room.

When they were safely in the room, Brandon grabbed JJ and kissed him, making it slow and trying to be heartfelt, because he really did care for JJ, and it wrecked him inside that JJ was going through all this. JJ had won his race today, had won his first ever gold medal, and JJ still felt like it was tainted.

Brandon was terrible at this type of thing. He wasn't good at pep talks, at helping people feel better. Earlier that year, a distant great-aunt had died, and Brandon's mother had been beside herself over the loss, but Brandon hadn't known how to comfort her. He'd bought flowers. He'd gone with his mother to the funeral. He'd let his mother cry on his shoulder. And the funeral itself had been dreadfully sad—Brandon's great-aunt had clearly touched many people, even if she hadn't had much of a relationship with Brandon—but Brandon hadn't known if he should be feeling things he wasn't.

This was always his struggle. How did others come up with just the right thing to say when someone was struggling? Brandon didn't know how to do that, and it made him feel broken sometimes, like he was a piece of furniture that had been assembled but was short a screw.

But there was something primal about his feelings for JJ. He might not have known how to make JJ feel better about his issues, but everything about JJ made Brandon's pulse race, made his heart pound, made a thrill go through him. Kissing JJ made his skin feel electric, made warmth spread through his chest. Even simply seeing JJ across a room made Brandon's heart race. A soft contentment settled into him as he and JJ kissed each other.

JJ snaked his arms around Brandon's shoulders and returned the kiss, nipping at Brandon's lower lip.

Brandon kind of wondered if he'd maybe made an error here too, in kissing JJ. Because Brandon had meant for this to be comforting, but based on the force with which JJ pushed Brandon against the closed dorm door, JJ seemed to think this was a prelude to sex.

Not that Brandon would object to sex, but....

"Hey, stop. Wait a second."

JJ backed off, his eyes wide. "Did you not come here to—?"

"I assumed we would be having sex, but I...." Brandon let out a breath. "I have to confess something weird."

JJ smirked. "All right." He walked backward into the room and sat on his bed.

Brandon sat beside him but kept a little space between them. "I just wanted to say that I often find myself in situations in which I wonder if I should feel some stronger emotion than I do, and it makes me feel like something inside me isn't working properly. But I *do* care about you. I feel *that* strongly. And it's upsetting to me that you can't celebrate your medal for the achievement it is, that you're still upset and frustrated about everything."

JJ chuckled softly and shook his head. "Thank you. I'm glad you care about me. I care about you too. And I've never met anyone like you. You're so forthright all the time. You never have an ulterior motive. You just say what you think. I'll have to remember that."

"Has that not been your experience with others?"

JJ put a hand on Brandon's thigh, and Brandon had to admit that he liked it there. So he covered JJ's hand with his own.

"I feel like ever since I started winning international races, everyone wants something from me," JJ said. "My parents do, my coaches do. Hell, the companies that want to endorse me definitely do, attaching strings to everything. It's honestly gotten hard to tell when someone is being straight with me and when they are lying. And ever since the thing with Franco and the cold pills, and the way my old coach is likely in on all of it, it's gotten so I don't feel like I can really trust people anymore. I do trust Tamika, and I mostly trust my parents, and now I trust you. But you have to understand what a big thing that is. I don't trust easily."

"I can tell. I'm glad you trust me. I really wouldn't deliberately do anything to hurt you."

"I know. That's why I felt guilty for yelling at you earlier. And I can't even promise I won't yell at you again, because I know I probably will."

"Tamika said it's how you deal with stress."

"Probably not a very productive way to cope, huh?" JJ let out a breath. "We're good now, right? I thought you were telling me with your lips just now that I'm forgiven and we're back on good footing."

"Yes."

JJ smiled. He gave Brandon a quick peck on the lips, but now Brandon wanted him to stay longer, so he hooked his hand around JJ's head and pulled him close. Brandon tasted salt and beer, but it didn't bother him. They had celebrated at the America House. JJ's parents had been very nice. Brandon had felt super awkward about the whole thing because he didn't know how to explain his relationship with JJ, so mostly he'd been quiet and listened to the conversation around him.

JJ pulled away slightly. "You've got *your* final tomorrow, right?"

"Yeah, in the evening."

"I have to run the one-hundred prelims tomorrow."

"Do you feel ready?"

"Girl, I never feel ready."

Brandon couldn't help but smile at that. "Maybe you need some help taking your mind off the race?"

JJ pressed his forehead against Brandon's. "What did you have in mind?"

"Let me show you."

CHAPTER EIGHTEEN

JJ HAD been living on his own in LA for almost three years, in an apartment in West Hollywood that was small but enough. He'd started getting endorsement deals around the time he qualified for his first Olympics and made it known that he'd be pursuing a career as a sprinter. At first it had been small potatoes. A little company in Malibu made pain creams and health remedies with all natural, organic ingredients and wanted JJ to film a commercial for them. An up-and-coming athletic apparel company wanted him to model some windbreakers. Nothing glamorous, which was why he still had the bartending job, although he also kind of thought having a job kept him grounded. Even after the big-name athletic companies had started waving checks in his face, he knew this moment was fleeting and he'd need something to do with himself when his legs stopped working.

What that thing would be still eluded him. He had a bachelor's degree in biology; he probably could have done something with that. He could get a job in an office, which sounded dreadfully boring. He could coach, although he wasn't sure he had the right temperament for it. He envied Brandon and his faith that his life would go in a certain direction, his plan to use his engineering degree to make the world a better place.

Bartending wasn't really a career. Although if JJ won another medal or two, maybe he'd start making the kind of money through endorsements and sponsorships to buy his own bar.

His first showing at the Olympics had been respectable, but he'd finished just out of the medals in the sprint events. Something about losing had really motivated him in training, and once *Sports Illustrated* had called him the gold-medal favorite in their Olympic preview issue, the big guns had been all over him. He'd had to hire an agent to help him sort through everything. The good news was that he could afford to live in West Hollywood for a good long time to come.

But the thing was, between running and bartending, he only really had time for one-night stands with bar patrons.

And yet here was this guy, one who completely understood about training regimens and who had his own other stuff to worry about, who was here in his arms now. And JJ wanted to keep him in his arms for a good long time.

The geography was simple. Brandon lived mere blocks from the USC campus and was a two-minute drive from where JJ trained. It wouldn't be like the time JJ had tried to have a relationship with a guy in Highland Park, which had been just too much driving. JJ had spent more time in his car during that relationship than anywhere else.

LA was kind of a terrible city, but it was home.

And Brandon lived in it too, so they could keep this rolling after they got home, but could they really? Could JJ?

Did it matter right now?

"I'm sorry," he panted.

Brandon had been busy nipping at JJ's collarbone and running his hands over JJ's chest when JJ said that.

"For what?" Brandon asked.

"Can't shut my brain off."

"Huh?"

JJ gently pushed Brandon off to the side and sat up. "I'm thinking too much."

"What about? Your races tomorrow?"

"No. About LA. About us."

Brandon's face went completely blank again, which JJ was starting to recognize as a sign that Brandon was thinking something through. It was like he slipped a mask on so no one could see his inner thought process. "About us in LA?"

"Yeah. I had this cute little fantasy of me popping over to see you between practice and work. You know that Filipino fast food place on Normandie?"

"Yeah."

"I eat a lot of meals there on the way to work because the food is good and they have a drive-through window. But I could, like, bring you takeout and we could eat together and have sex on my nights off."

"Sure."

JJ laughed. "Girl, you could be a little more enthusiastic."

Brandon smiled briefly. "Sorry. But yeah, I'd like to keep seeing you. Are you worried about that?"

"No, it's just what I was thinking about."

"Instead of sex."

"Yeah. Which is why I apologized. What the hell is wrong with me? I liked what you were doing."

"What do you want to do?" Brandon shook his head. "I hate when you ask that question because I never know the answer. But if you could do anything with me right now, what would it be?"

"Oh, I'd fuck you to next Tuesday."

Brandon's face went crimson, but he smiled, so JJ felt confident he'd be into that.

JJ sighed. "But I'm exhausted, honestly. I think that's why even my dick wants to go to sleep."

"Then let's sleep."

"You sure?"

"If we're going to keep seeing each other after the Olympics, we have all the time in the world. We both have to run tomorrow, though, so we should rest."

"You're so sensible."

Brandon lay down on his tiny strip of mattress. "I try."

"I also have to do a dumb interview for TBC in the morning."

"Well, you did win a medal."

"Sure." JJ sighed. "Actually, you know what we could do? We could move these two beds together so that we'd have enough space to properly sleep instead of trying to wedge us both onto this twin bed. There's a clean set of sheets in the closet."

"Okay. Stay put."

Brandon had to kind of roll over JJ to get out of bed, but then he worked fast. He took all of his stuff off the other bed and put it on the little desk in the corner. Then he grabbed the sheets from the closet, made the other bed with the efficiency of a hospital orderly, and then pushed the beds together. The cheap metal frame likely didn't weigh very much, and Brandon hefted it as if it were made of Styrofoam. The bed being here meant that it would take some tricky maneuvering to get into the room because now it partly blocked the doorway, but JJ didn't care, and Brandon didn't seem to either, as he settled on the other mattress.

"These sheets smell like bleach and not like you," Brandon observed.

"You sound disappointed."

"I am."

JJ shifted over to lie closer to Brandon. "This whole week, I've mostly just smelled like sweat all the time."

Brandon shifted a bit and seemed to get comfortable. "Yeah, but I like it."

JJ laughed. "Babe, you are one of my favorite people. I'm sad we didn't meet sooner."

"Me too."

JJ reached over and touched Brandon's face; then he brought their lips together. They kissed slowly, and JJ had the peculiar feeling again that he'd like to hold on to this for a long time.

Then he laughed.

"What?" Brandon asked.

"I never, in a hundred million years, thought that I'd ever fall for a nerdy white boy, and yet…."

"I still can't quite believe sometimes that you want to be with me."

"You're one in a million, I guess. One in a hundred million. But let's not overthink it. I want to be with you, you want to be with me, so let's just enjoy it however long it lasts."

"Sounds good to me."

WHOEVER FURNISHED the dorms in the Olympic Village had put up the flimsiest curtains, so Brandon had woken up with the sun every morning he'd been in Madrid. The window was also trapping the heat from the sun in the room, and Brandon was already sweating despite the gentle hum of the AC.

As he woke up, it sank in that today was his hurdles final. For the first time all week, he was nervous, his gut churning as he rolled onto his back and looked up at the ceiling. He hadn't felt nerves like this before a race in a long time. He supposed it was the higher stakes of being at the Olympics. If he tripped over a hurdle, everyone watching on TV would see it. That was potentially millions of people.

Stranger things had happened. At one of his first World Cup races, nerves had made his body tighten up so much that he hadn't quite made it over the third hurdle. He hooked his foot on it instead and fell on his face, spraining his ankle in the process. He hadn't been able to finish the race; Grady had had to help him off the track.

He'd been very careful about hurdle height in training after that. He'd practiced with the official hurdles on the practice track dozens of times this week, and he'd had no issues in the preliminary heats. But now all he could imagine was hooking a hurdle and falling on his face again.

"You okay?"

Brandon turned and looked at JJ, a little surprised he was there, despite clearly being in JJ's room. "I…." But Brandon couldn't answer the question.

"You look worried. I've never seen that much emotion on your face before."

"Really?"

"You're hard to read. That's why I appreciate that you say what you're thinking most of the time, because I can't really tell what's up with you otherwise. What are you thinking now?"

"That I'm going to fall on my face during the final today."

"I have a hard time picturing that, but that's also a pretty normal thing to feel. By that, I mean, it's not rational, but I think Olympians dating back to Ancient Greece have had the same fear."

"It only takes one mistake. You stumble on your start or you hit a hurdle during the race, and even if you only graze it, that slows you down, and it's over. No medal."

"You've looked amazing all week. Just keep doing whatever it is you've been doing and you'll be fine."

Brandon thought he might throw up.

"Here, I'll tell you what we should do. You need a good luck charm or something."

"I don't like to wear jewelry or anything. It messes with my focus if it's flying around when I'm running."

"I've got more gold nail polish."

Brandon looked at JJ's face and met his gaze. Then he looked down at his patriotic nails, which were chipped enough now that they looked a bit beat up. JJ's nails were gold, and Brandon liked the idea of taking a part of JJ with him to his race.

His body went tingly everywhere. He looked at JJ and knew they had something special together. In the spirit of letting JJ know what he wanted, he leaned over and gave JJ a slow kiss. JJ put his hand on Brandon's cheek and opened his mouth, deepening the kiss, curling their tongues together. When Brandon pulled away, JJ said, "Wow."

Brandon felt that too. He wanted JJ with him on the track, as a supporter, as a friend, as a lover.

Nothing he'd ever experienced before had prepared Brandon for the heady feeling of being with JJ. Was this what falling in love was like? Because if it was, it felt pretty awesome.

"Let's paint my nails," said Brandon.

JJ laughed and touched his lips. He blinked a few times as if he were trying to focus again. "Okay, hang on."

Brandon felt oddly content as he watched JJ walk into the bathroom and emerge with a bottle of nail polish remover and a couple of cotton balls.

Brandon wasn't sure exactly what came over him, but when JJ sat back down, Brandon took the polish remover and the cotton balls and set them on the desk. The two of them sat opposite each other, JJ on the edge of the bed and Brandon in the desk chair, and Brandon took JJ's hand. He looked at their joined hands and marveled at them for a moment. It felt like a profound moment, but a soft one, a simple one, just two people who cared about each other making a connection. And maybe that was all love really was. Brandon didn't have much firsthand experience, at least not like this. He understood sex. He loved his family, most of the time anyway, but that wasn't romantic love. It was nothing like this.

And because he wanted to, Brandon traced his fingers down JJ's strong forearm. He glanced up and saw that JJ stared at him in something like awe. Brandon was not the most intuitive of men, but he understood that JJ was feeling something of this too. So Brandon leaned over and kissed JJ. He slid his hand along JJ's arm. JJ used his other hand to cup Brandon's cheek. Brandon traced his fingers over JJ's shoulders, his back, his neck, his closely cropped hair. JJ's hair was barely there, but it was surprisingly soft.

Brandon hadn't meant to push JJ down on the bed, but he found himself straddling JJ's hips. Because, yeah, he wanted JJ suddenly, fiercely. Part of it was looking for some kind of familiar expression that Brandon could understand and relate to, but part of it was that his feelings for JJ overwhelmed him. Maybe it wasn't love, not yet, but it was definitely something, and he needed JJ to know he felt this way, but he couldn't make his mouth form the words.

JJ didn't seem to mind at all. He shifted and lounged back on the bed, then held Brandon's hips in his hands. JJ's cock was hard and pressing into Brandon's ass, and it felt shocking and amazing.

Brandon didn't want to have sex as much as he wanted to keep kissing JJ, so he bent his body and slid beside JJ. Brandon was wearing only a pair of briefs, and JJ didn't have on much more—only briefs and a T-shirt—but they divested each other of their clothing. JJ had dark stubble across his chest from where his hair was starting to grow back, but Brandon liked the feel of it against him, as if there was something raw, real, not perfect between them.

They kept on kissing and rolling around on the bed. Brandon's instinct was to part his legs and let JJ inside, but not today, not before his race. He told himself they would have amazing sex tonight, after he had his gold medal. But right now he just wanted to make out—albeit when they were both naked—and kiss.

JJ rolled on top of Brandon. "Thought we were painting your nails."

"You distracted me with your hotness." Brandon smiled to show he was kidding, except he wasn't, not really. JJ was smoking hot.

"I do that," said JJ, grinning right back. "You're pretty distracting yourself."

"I didn't exactly to mean to rev us both up like this, but since we're here…."

Brandon wrapped his hand around JJ's cock. It was hard and hot, and Brandon put some pressure into his stroke. JJ groaned and tweaked one of Brandon's nipples, which felt wired right to his dick. Brandon bucked his hips against JJ, and JJ squeezed a hand between them and grabbed Brandon's cock. They stroked each other and writhed on the bed until Brandon felt like he might die from arousal. Brandon arched his back, urged JJ on, and kept stroking JJ's cock. Then he kissed JJ, hard, fast, fierce, and nipped JJ's lower lip. He didn't want to leave any marks, not yet anyway, not when they both had to wear uniforms that showed a lot of skin later that day. But he could kiss JJ as much as he wanted. He could touch JJ anywhere he wanted to. He could slip his hand between JJ's legs and cup his balls, feel their warmth, listen to the sounds JJ made in response.

And he could throw his head back and groan as he came into JJ's hand, the orgasm ripping through him.

JJ followed right behind him, hissing and sighing as he spilled on Brandon's belly.

Brandon's heart pounded and his skin tingled and he wasn't quite ready for it all to be over, so he kissed JJ again. JJ put a hand on Brandon's chest and sighed into Brandon's mouth.

A few minutes later, when both of their bodies resumed their normal rhythm, JJ said, "Look at the mess we made."

"Mmm." Brandon's brain felt all soft and mushy. This was one way to work out his nerves, he supposed.

JJ smeared his spilled cum into Brandon's skin. "An ex of mine called abs like this cum-catchers."

Brandon laughed at the expression. "I guess they did do that."

"Your body is something else. If you retire from hurdles, are you going to be able to find something else to do with it?"

"My gym habit is pretty intense. I can't see stopping cold turkey. And I'll probably still run. Just not competitively like this."

"All the more reason to get your gold medal today. Come on, babe. Let's get your nails ready."

JJ hopped out of bed and put his briefs back on. Then he walked over to the desk and picked up the polish remover.

Brandon sighed. He slipped into the bathroom to clean up but didn't bother to put any clothes back on. If JJ liked his body, he'd give JJ a show.

A few minutes later, as JJ swabbed the old polish off Brandon's nails, Brandon said, "Thank you."

"For?"

"For doing my nails. For being amazing this week. For making me feel things I've never felt before."

JJ met Brandon's gaze. "Yeah? Never felt?"

Brandon squirmed, feeling self-conscious suddenly. "I get that you're a lot more worldly and experienced than I am, at least when it comes to sex and relationships and stuff, but yeah, this is all new to me. I like it, though. I want to keep feeling this way for a long time."

JJ smiled. "Some of this is new for me too. I don't go on a lot of second dates. And though you and I could not be more different, we seem to understand each other, don't we?"

"I think so. Is that weird?"

"Nope. Give me your other hand."

"I want to win a gold medal today. No, I want to break the world record. I want to run this race faster than anyone else ever has. Is that an unreasonable thing to want?"

"Girl. That's what we all want when we walk up to the starting line. You know, Usain Bolt's world record in the one-hundred is 9.58. I ran a hundred meters in 9.56 in practice once, which of course doesn't count because it wasn't in competition, but I think about that sometimes. It's brutal on the body, of course. Pushing yourself beyond what you think you can do. I'm gonna do two coats of the gold, so try not to move your hands too much. This stuff takes a minute to dry."

"Do it."

Brandon was not a fan of the toxic smell of the nail polish, but he enjoyed talking with JJ, and he found JJ's attention on his hands and the slow swipes of the little brush to be fascinating.

He never in a million years would have thought to paint his nails. But now he couldn't imagine racing without it.

CHAPTER NINETEEN

Day 14

JJ STOOD just off set in the TBC studio in the Olympic Broadcast Center, a high-rise building off Retiro Park in Madrid. The car ride between the Olympic Village and this building had been the most of Madrid he'd seen since he arrived. This was often the case when he traveled for races; he'd been all over the world but had only really seen tracks and stadiums, since he rarely gave himself enough time to see the cities themselves. He could practically hear Tamika, who stood beside him now, telling him that this was all his own fault. He could have taken an extra week off from his job and spent time before his races touring Madrid and getting in extra practice.

The fact that he was standing in a studio now was his own fault too, now that he thought about it. *Wake Up, America!* was TBC's popular morning show, and they always had the previous day's American medal winners on the show for brief positive interviews. The USATF rep who had ridden over in the car with JJ and Tamika had said JJ could expect a softball interview mostly about how great he and the American athletic programs were.

A PA signaled to JJ, which was his cue to step onto the set and have a seat on the big white couch in the center of it. The PA walked over and fussed with his collar.

And JJ was suddenly terrified.

He couldn't tell what was causing his premonition that this was all about to go terribly wrong, but he felt ill-prepared. He tried to tell himself that the interview would only be a couple of minutes, and the reporter interviewing him—Nikki Kenmore, one of *Wake Up*'s cohosts—did not exactly have a reputation for being a hard-hitting journalist. The USATF rep had also told JJ he should consider toning down his more… colorful tendencies.

All he had to do here was say he'd worked very hard to win the medal currently hanging around his neck, and it was great to be a gold-medal winner, and go, Team USA!

Nikki Kenmore sat in the chair perpendicular to the sofa. She smiled at JJ and introduced herself. He shook her hand and tried to act normal.

"You look nervous," said Nikki.

"I am a little."

"Calm down. This will be no sweat."

Behind the camera, a guy with a headset said, "And we're on in three… two…."

"Welcome back! I'm here now with sprinter Jason Jones Junior, who yesterday won a gold medal in the two-hundred-meter sprint. How are you, Jason?"

"Please call me JJ. And I'm great." There. That was easy enough. But, ugh. Jason was his father. No one had called him Jason since elementary school.

"I'm sure many of our viewers watched your race yesterday. Let's look at it now."

Nikki turned to look at a monitor, so JJ followed her gaze. And there was the two-hundred-meter final on screen. He hadn't even seen this race and wasn't a fan of watching himself run because his eye immediately picked up on every little thing he did wrong. But he tried to keep his face placid now as he watched this race. He could see the moment when he'd kicked into the next gear, when he'd made some unconscious decision to win this race if it killed him, and it was surreal to see his own legs powering across the finish line.

Nikki asked, "Did you have to really dig into yourself to do that?"

"I did, yeah. I mean, these guys are the best in the world. Any one of the runners in the final could have won the race. I put everything I had into it."

"Amazing. Truly amazing. Now, this is your second Olympics, correct?"

"Yes. I finished just out of the medals four years ago. Well, except in the relay."

"I understand you're running in the four-by-one-hundred-meter relay later this weekend."

"Yes. Two more finals, assuming I make it out of qualifiers. The one-hundred tomorrow and the relay on Sunday."

"You feel ready for those races?"

JJ was wary of falling into some false sense of security. These were easy questions. When would she ambush him?

He got his answer one minute later, when Nikki said, "You've had a rocky road to get here, though, haven't you?"

Shit. JJ braced himself.

"You grew up in South Central."

"I—"

"You must have had a difficult childhood."

"Well, actually, I have a great family, and—"

"And then there was this flag on your record. You won a World Championship a couple of years ago but had your medal taken away."

JJ took a deep breath. He felt anger simmering in his chest and had to tamp it down before it boiled over. He couldn't be anything but the nice, friendly athlete on TV. He said, "I had the sniffles and took some cold pills without realizing they had pseudoephedrine. They have since changed the guidelines for that, so the amount I took wouldn't have tested positive. I've been tested nearly every day since I arrived in Madrid, and everything shows that I'm running without any performance enhancing drugs here."

"I'm happy to hear that. Now let's talk about your manicure. Is it true you do your own nails?" Nikki grabbed JJ's hand. "They look fabulous. I can't get my nails to look this good when I do them myself."

JJ glanced at Nikki's nails, painted a network-approved pale pink. He smiled. "It takes practice, girl." Without doing it on purpose, he'd changed his tone of voice, but at the same time, he was tired. If Nikki Kenmore was going to frame this story in her way, then JJ would get in the last word.

Nikki grinned in a fake way that didn't reach her eyes. "Thank you so much, JJ. And congratulations! And now to Gerry Reid with a check on the weather!"

"We're clear," said the director.

Nikki stood, so JJ mirrored her movement. "Thanks so much," she said. Then she walked off the set.

"That was weird," JJ said as he walked back to Tamika.

She shrugged. "Sorry about that. I had no idea she'd ask about some of that stuff. Every other interview I've seen has just been the standard platitudes about hard work and love of country and all that."

JJ sighed. "Well, when you have the token gay kid from South Central on your show, why not use the opportunity to create a spectacle."

"You did a good job."

"Thanks, I guess. Can we get out of here?" JJ wanted to get to the track. He needed to loosen up for his own races, but almost more than that, he wanted to see Brandon run.

As he walked away, he could only hope Brandon was having a better day.

CHAPTER TWENTY

Transcript from the TBC broadcast of the four-hundred-meter hurdle final

BOOTHE: WE'VE got breaking news from the Olympic Stadium. Apparently a syringe was found in the men's locker room. Authorities are still testing it, and we do not yet have confirmation that the syringe contained any illegal substances. But in light of the increased scrutiny on track athletes at the games, all of the races today were delayed so that authorities can investigate and some of the athletes could undergo additional testing.

GRAYSON: Thanks, Leslie. We're in the booth getting ready for the four-hundred hurdles, which should be starting shortly, about twenty minutes after its original start time. But that's American Kevin Ling out warming up on the track now, so I think we'll be starting shortly.

CASSELLO: What can you tell us about who we'll see?

GRAYSON: I'm still waiting on the lane assignments, but for sure, we've got José Sanchez from the Dominican Republic in this final, as well as Stefan Abramanian from Qatar. We will also be seeing Rami Benjamin from Antigua and Barbuda—he qualified in fourth in his heat. I also expect Amadou DiFranco from Senegal to do well. He was a little slow in prelims, but he's blazing fast when he turns the gas on, which he usually does in finals.

CASSELLO: And the Americans? We've got Ling.

GRAYSON: Yes, Kevin Ling is out of the University of Michigan program. He's not the fastest of these finalists, but he's got great technique. If any of the other runners make mistakes, he has a shot at a medal. We also have Jerome Winthrop. He's a runner from California, an excellent hurdler. And finally there's Brandon Stanton, who won both of his preliminary races and looked fantastic.

CASSELLO: He really did look great. He's got a shot at gold today, yes?

GRAYSON: Yes, definitely. Oh, there he is now. I talked to his coach earlier. You know, Stanton is an engineering student at USC, and his coach, Grady Brown, says Stanton is some kind of math whiz. That he uses math when devising his hurdles strategy.

CASSELLO: It certainly seems to be working. Oh, would you look at that. His nails are painted gold, just like Jason Jones Jr.

GRAYSON: Yes, I asked around about that. Their coaches are married to each other, so they've been training together here in Madrid. Apparently JJ's influence has rubbed off on Stanton.

CASSELLO: Well, JJ won a gold medal last night, so maybe there's something magic in that nail polish….

IT FELT like Brandon's stomach was trying to eat itself. His morning with JJ had calmed him down some, but he was freaking out now, his hands shaking as he adjusted the blocks. He looked up and tried to make eye contact with Grady in the stands, hoping that would ground him. Instead, he was startled to see JJ staring back at him. Grady was there too, but he almost didn't matter if JJ was watching.

Brandon suddenly felt like he'd found the solution to a complicated math problem. It had started somewhere with his mom picking him up after late track practices in high school, added with his aptitude for hurdles, his approach to the event, and Grady's coaching. The first few international races he'd run had been pretty intense because he hadn't actually believed he could compete against the best in the world, but then he actually did. The first time he'd won a World Cup race, he'd probably been more surprised than anyone else. But something he did worked.

Everything he did had led him here.

Edwin Moses's ideal of thirteen steps between hurdles was a key element of whatever equation he was trying to solve now. His mother and brothers sitting somewhere in the stands was part of it too. But what was on the other side of the equal sign? Did all that work equal a gold medal at the Olympics?

Did it equal JJ?

Brandon didn't preoccupy himself much with whether he'd have some kind of happily-ever-after. He'd always assumed he'd stumble into something when the time was right. He'd heard other runners talk about having their spouses looking on from the stands. Was this what that felt like?

It *was* nice knowing JJ was watching him. And it grounded him too. Brandon wanted to win this race now. He could win this race. He was good at the hurdles. He *was* one of the best runners in the world. He wanted to show that to this audience, to Mom, to Mike and Danny, to Grady… to JJ.

He shook out his hands and finished fiddling with his equipment. He put his feet in the blocks and tested them. The fit was right. He pressed his fingers into the track where they belonged. He was startled by the gold nail polish. He'd forgotten it was there, but he liked it. Maybe it wasn't a good luck charm exactly, but JJ was with him.

He did a practice start and felt good popping out of the blocks.

He'd done an extensive warm-up inside at the practice track, and the Team USA physical therapist had helped him stretch out, so he felt good physically. Strong, loose, limber. Now that the nerves were wearing off a little, he felt adrenaline start to kick in. He jumped a few times and shook out his limbs.

"I can do this… I can do this…," he repeated to himself softly.

Perhaps this was the less rational part of racing. Some of it was math. Some of it was ability. And some of it was mental.

"On your marks."

Brandon and the other runners got in their blocks. Brandon had been assigned to Lane 4, right in the middle, by virtue of his finishing the semi in first place.

Brandon couldn't see the runners behind him in the staggered starting blocks. It didn't matter; he'd see them soon enough. He had to run his own race. Brandon put his fingers behind the line and marveled again at the gold nail polish.

"Ready."

Brandon rose up in the blocks. He could do this… he could do this….

At the gun, he pushed off the blocks and into a run. He didn't count steps now because that would slow him down, but he cleared the first hurdle and felt the track under his feet. The spikes in his shoes made the track a little sticky, which kept him from slipping when he jumped and cleared the next hurdle. His feet pounded into the track. He leaped and cleared the third hurdle… then the fourth….

A runner to his right stumbled. The others fell behind as Brandon pushed ahead. Someone on his left caught up, but as they rounded the corner, they fell back again. When Brandon got to the last straightaway, he was in the lead but couldn't tell if it was by a lot or a little. He cleared the last two hurdles, then broke into a run, trying as hard as he could to keep his lead, even though his legs were burning. The pain didn't matter. Nothing mattered except getting to that finish line. He could do this. He could get there first.

He ran over the line with no other runners around him.

Then he looked up at the scoreboard.

Gold: USA Stanton—46.77—OR—WR
Silver: DOM Sanchez—46.92
Bronze: USA Ling—47.03

It took a minute for it to really hit him that he'd won. Not only had he won, but he'd done it in world record time. Only one-hundredth of a second faster than the current record, which had been on the books for nearly thirty years, but still, he'd done something extraordinary.

That was when his legs gave out on him.

He landed on his ass hard. Then he burst into tears.

It wasn't in his nature to cry, but it was like all of a sudden he felt too much, and with no way to process it, his emotions leaked out. Then Kevin Ling helped him up and handed him an American flag. José had a flag for the Dominican Republic in his hand, and he walked over to hug Brandon. They'd all known and competed against each other for as long as Brandon had been running on the international circuit. Brandon didn't make friends easily, but Kevin was jovial and friendly with everyone, and he and José were training buddies. All three of them threw their arms around each other now and held up their flags and posed for photos together. But Brandon barely knew what was even happening, still unable to stop the tears. He looked down at the flag in his hands, at his gold nail polish, and then he looked up at the stands and tried to find JJ again. The Team USA coaching staff sat just a few rows up from track level, and Brandon could see that JJ was screaming and jumping and cheering.

Brandon ran a victory lap with Kevin and José before they were herded back into the stadium to change. In a daze, Brandon slipped into his official Team USA tracksuit. Ten minutes later, some official led the three medal winners over toward the podium to get their medals. Brandon could still barely process what was happening. He looked up at the stands, but JJ wasn't there anymore.

And wasn't it funny that he looked for JJ first and not his family?

The Stantons were all sitting up and to the left of the Team USA section of the stands. Brandon's gaze caught on an American flag waving near where he thought his family was, and he guessed that was his mother, but he couldn't really see anyone's faces. He felt gratified that his family had come all this way to see him run, but his feelings about it all were complicated. He wished he could bask in their unconditional love, but he knew his brothers placed conditions on him. He was acceptable now that he was doing this amazing thing, winning a gold medal for jumping over hurdles faster than any other human ever had in competition—holy cow, that was unbelievable—but would they support him in the same way if his accomplishment was something less relatable? If he designed something that earned a patent or won an award? Would they show up like this when he graduated from USC? When he got married? He wasn't sure.

He let out a sigh, his eyes still stinging from the tears, and tried to focus on the good thing that had just happened. The amazing thing. He was standing atop an Olympic podium to receive a gold medal. He smiled to show how that felt.

It occurred to him to wonder why JJ had left, but a quick glance at the scoreboard showed the one-hundred-meter semifinal was coming up. So that was a little disappointing, but he could talk to JJ about this medal later.

Because here came three women in tan suits holding medals on trays. And the president of the IOC himself—a short German man with silver-framed glasses—picked up each medal and draped it around the neck of first Kevin, then José, and finally Brandon.

It was heavier than he'd expected. He'd held JJ's medal the night before, but it felt different draped around Brandon's neck—when it was something Brandon had worked for and earned. There was more weight to it.

When the flags of the medal winners were raised, Brandon focused on the American one in the middle. He stared at it as the national anthem began to play. He closed his eyes briefly, trying to absorb the moment, to commit how he felt now to memory. He'd done something very few other men had ever done.

Rather than head back to the locker room, Brandon went to the stands to talk to Grady, who immediately folded him into a big bug with a lot of backslapping. "You did great, kid. I'm so proud of you."

The great amount of noise around him made Brandon turn around. A bunch of other US track athletes were in this section and were cheering their heads off… for Brandon, he realized belatedly.

He accepted the congratulations from a lot of people he recognized but couldn't attach names to, and then a hush fell over the stadium as the one-hundred-meter sprint semifinal was announced.

Brandon settled into the seat JJ had just vacated to watch, but he couldn't stop fingering the gold medal around his neck.

Down on the track, JJ looked relaxed. He stretched a little, fiddled with his blocks, and tucked the necklace he wore under his jersey.

Tamika arrived in the stands, sat next to Brandon, and patted his thigh. "Well-deserved win. You looked great out there."

"Thank you."

"Now to watch my guy win."

THE ONE-HUNDRED-METER sprint was the most physically and psychologically demanding race on the track. And it only lasted about ten seconds. It wasn't just running fast. Any guy off the street could run pretty fast. To compete at the elite level required training, of course, but it also required an innate understanding of how the race worked.

The right start was key.

First, a runner had to arrive. Many were intense and focused. Some, like Usain Bolt, goofed around and played to the cameras. Regardless, a runner had to arrive at the track knowing like he knew his own name that he would win the race. Confidence was crucial. JJ sometimes donned the accoutrement of the cocky, the gold shoes and the painted nails, as a way to playact at confidence, reasoning *fake it 'til you make it*. But he also knew he could win the race because he'd done it before, and any faltering could mean the difference between first, second, or finishing out of the medals.

Then one had to get in the blocks. Getting into a crouch allowed the runner to effectively coil himself up and then apply more force to propelling himself forward. Having something solid to push off from was an innovation that allowed runners to hurl themselves forward at a specific angle meant to build speed. Brandon would probably have a lot to say about, like, potential energy or something about physics—JJ hadn't paid close enough attention in class to remember what it was called. What JJ knew was that one had to pop out of those blocks hard and fast in order to launch into the race. JJ had read that at the early modern Olympic Games, runners brought trowels with them to the starting line and dug their own divots in the track from which to push off, since the running blocks everyone used now were not a thing yet.

Modern blocks were, however, completely customizable, from how far apart a runner could set his feet to the angle one's foot was positioned in the block. Some runners were completely anal about their blocks, measuring to the centimeter exactly where everything should be. And JJ knew firsthand that if something was off, it could throw off his whole race.

Once the blocks were set, the runner had to have amazing reflexes, be able to hear that starting gun and react to it faster than the other runners without, literally, jumping the gun. These days one false start could put you out of a race entirely. Reaction time was something Harold Abrahams—of *Chariots of Fire* fame—had spent an enormous amount of time mastering.

Once the runner got out of the blocks, he had to pull himself upright and run as straight vertically as possible to power himself forward the most efficiently. That was Jesse Owens's technique. Once the runner got his body into position, he went into something Tamika called "cruise mode," in which, for a few seconds, was running at constant speed. Many sprinters could cruise as fast as 27 miles per hour. This was the part of the race when JJ's mind generally emptied. Then, about twenty meters from the finish, his brain clicked back on and his body started to slow down. Any given sprinter really only had about eighty or ninety meters of sprint in him, so the last ten to twenty meters were the struggle to maintain form and keep pushing forward. It was the rare runner who could maintain speed or decelerate slower than everyone else, something greats like Carl Lewis could do. But even Carl Lewis couldn't run faster at the end of his races; he just decelerated slower than everyone else.

You couldn't be tense. The trick was to relax as much as possible. Runners had to keep their movements fluid, loose, easy.

Jesse Owens had been part of a class of sprinters who were thin and light and appeared to just float to the finish. Usain Bolt had a bit of that too. In more recent decades, though, sprinters had gotten bulkier, more muscular, and used raw muscle power to increase velocity. Bob Hayes had been the power sprinter who destroyed Jesse Owens's Olympic record in the 1960s. Hayes changed the way sprinters trained and approached the race. And by 1968, the Olympics had a synthetic track, which changed the race again. It was in 1968 that Jim Hines broke the ten-second barrier.

Of course, needing that raw muscle power was what tempted so many sprinters to take steroids and other performance-enhancing drugs.

Either way, now runners like JJ had to have both power and speed. JJ lifted weights and did a little boxing on top of his running drills. He had to condition his whole body to build it for speed. And he thought it was important to acknowledge how the runners who came before him had shaped the sport, especially the black runners. JJ recognized that he was part of a long legacy of gifted black athletes who represented the United States on the track, and he wanted to win for himself, but he wanted to win for Jesse Owens and Bob Hayes and Jim Hines and Carl Lewis too.

And then there was the finish line, looming before every runner on the track, each one hoping to get there first. For ninety-nine meters, every runner gave every bit of strength and speed he had, and in that last meter, when everything hurt, when the runner's muscles were screaming, when it felt he could never take a deep breath again, when there were seven other runners very close to him, he had to give it one last burst of strength to hurl himself over the finish. He had to calculate when or whether it was appropriate to dip his head to maybe edge out the competition. And he had a fraction of a second to make that decision.

All that for less than ten seconds of running. No wonder everyone wanted any advantage they could get.

Could Brandon's mathematics approach actually help? JJ had googled after talking to Brandon about the number of steps. The average sprinter ran the one-hundred meters in forty-five steps. Usain Bolt took forty-one steps, because he was so tall that he had an unfathomable eight-foot stride. So maybe there really was something to Brandon's theory that fewer steps meant a faster race.

JJ tried to remind himself that this was the semifinal, not the main event. He just had to get through it to make the final. No big deal. He could do this.

Except, of course, he knew as well as anyone that anything could happen in ten seconds.

At the signal, he got himself in his blocks. His feet felt good. He carefully placed his fingers behind the line. Then he waited for the gun.

THE GUN sounded and the runners were out of the blocks. The one-hundred-meter sprint was a blazing fast race, but in the semifinal, there were still enough runners who weren't quite competitive that the field was pretty stretched out after the first five seconds. The top five sprinters in this heat were all close together and, from where Brandon sat in the stands, appeared to cross the finish line in a single row, with no clear winner. And because there were five of them clumped together, one of them would not even make the final.

"Who won?" Brandon asked, looking toward the scoreboard, which hadn't posted the results yet.

"Not sure. JJ must have made it, he must have been toward the front, and the top four will advance. He's fine."

Brandon wasn't sure if Tamika was reassuring him or herself.

But they needed reassuring. A finish like that meant that one of the best sprinters in the competition might not make the final. JJ might not make the final.

Brandon held his breath. For JJ's sake, it couldn't end here.

There was a long delay. Officials were on the field looking at tablets that likely had the photo finish on them. The race played on the Jumbotron, but even having a larger picture didn't make it clear who had qualified for the final and who had not. Grady and Tamika had an intense conversation about how something like this should be handled, if the photo finish was enough.

And then, finally, the results posted.

1. JAM Blake—9.68
2. USA Jones—9.69
3. USA Martinez—9.70
4. NAM Frederick—9.72
5. GBR Pritchard—9.73

"Slow heat," said Tamika. "That's about a tenth off the world record pace."

The photo finish image flashed on the Jumbotron, showing that Ajani Blake from Jamaica had finished just a hair ahead of JJ.

"He's gonna be pissed," Tamika said softly.

"You were right, though. It doesn't matter. He made the final. Finishing second will still get him a good lane assignment. I feel bad for Pritchard."

Tamika shook her head. "You're right. But he's always irritable when the results are not what he expected. Fair warning."

Brandon looked back at the track, where JJ and Rafael Martinez were having what looked like an intense conversation before a few officials cleared them off the track so that the second heat could begin.

"Should I talk to him?" Brandon asked.

"I'm sure he'd like to talk to you, just…." Tamika frowned, her gaze tracking JJ as he walked off the track. "But if he's mean, don't take it personally."

"Oh." Brandon filed that away for later, then said goodbye to Grady and Tamika and went into the stadium.

JJ WINCED when the needle hit his arm. He stared intently at a poster that displayed the country codes for every nation competing at the Olympics. He played a game with himself where he tried to guess the country based on the code while a male doctor drew his blood for testing. He got stuck on BDR, which distracted him enough to mentally picture his blood flowing into a tube, so he peeked at the answer and saw it was Burundi. Where even was Burundi?

Then he remembered why he was here. "Did they ever find out what was in that syringe they found in the locker room?" JJ asked, hoping the doctor would know.

"I'm not really supposed to say," said the doctor. He had an American accent.

"Cone of silence."

The doctor didn't look particularly amused. "Do you think this is a game?"

The shift in tone—and of the needle in JJ's arm, which stung—alarmed JJ. "No, of course not. Just…." He sucked in a breath. "I was curious."

"It was an insulin dose, if you must know. I believe one of the hammer throwers is diabetic."

"Oh. That's good. I had hoped none of my fellow runners were stupid enough to leave a steroid syringe lying around."

"I need more blood. Don't move."

JJ wanted to jerk away, but he held still and focused on the poster. But he couldn't help himself and asked, "Why?"

"Why? Because you have a red flag on your file. We need to be thorough."

"Right, but this is the third time I've had blood drawn this week. Surely by now you—"

"Listen, I've been doing this all day and I don't have patience anymore. I know some of the other WADA doctors are nice, but I'm tired, especially of athletes giving me lip." The doctor jerked the needle in JJ's arm, which stung even more.

"Sorry," JJ murmured.

"I've seen dozens of you just today." The doctor attached a second vial to the tube coming out of JJ's arm.

JJ's pulse sped up. He glanced back in time to see the doctor fill the vial and worried he'd throw up. He wanted to run from the room, but he was trapped. And light-headed. He wanted to protest, to fight back against this asshole, but instead he began to panic. If he moved, if he fought, this was all over. If he yelled at the doctor, the guy could have him yanked from competition. JJ had no power here, and he hated that.

The pressure on JJ's arm changed, and he glanced over to see that the doctor was pressing a piece of gauze to his skin. It was over. Thank God.

"Okay, you're done. Don't move yet. Let me grab a Band-Aid."

The doctor slapped a "flesh-colored" bandage on JJ's arm—JJ's skin was about five shades darker than the plastic—and excused him. But JJ felt shaky.

All of this was because of Franco.

He always felt woozy after getting blood drawn, but the rude doctor made everything worse. Once he got to the locker room, he made a beeline for the toilets and promptly vomited up everything he'd eaten that day. He sat on the cold tile floor for a long moment after he flushed and stared in dismay at the toilet. Then he vomited again.

When he felt stable enough, he stood, flushed again, and walked to the sink, where he washed up and splashed cold water on his face. He still felt queasy but thought the vomiting was over. He took a deep breath and felt pretty stable.

And then he got angry.

What part of coming in second made anyone think JJ was cheating?

He groaned to himself. He didn't want to feel this angry. Really, things were fine. All of those drug tests had shown he was clean. He'd already won one gold medal. And he'd advanced to the one-hundred-meter final. He was fine. He was good, even. That doctor had been awful, but it was over. He was still on track to accomplish everything he'd set out to do in Madrid.

So why did his gut churn?

He stopped, took a deep breath, and counted to ten.

When he got to his locker, Brandon was sitting on the bench there, his new gold medal hanging around his neck.

He was staring into space and didn't notice JJ approach, so JJ took a moment to take it all in. Brandon wore the official tracksuit the American Olympians had to wear during medal ceremonies and public appearances. It was navy blue with red raglan sleeves and white trim, with a little bit of a vintage vibe to the shape and coloring. Brandon looked great, his hair a bit disheveled, the tracksuit hugging his body, although the reflection of the bright locker room lights off his glasses obscured his eyes a little.

And he was… *here*. Waiting for JJ. He'd just won a gold medal and should be out partying somewhere, but of course, that wasn't in Brandon's nature. Instead, he was *here* for JJ.

JJ was really falling for this guy. Seeing him cooled the fire in JJ a little. Or ignited a different fire, it would be more accurate to say. He smiled to himself.

Brandon looked up as JJ approached. "Hey, congratulations. I'm really proud of you," JJ said.

"Thank you. I saw you in the stands. I'm glad you were watching."

"Of course."

"I watched your race. It was really exciting. Photo finish and all that."

"It was slow."

"You qualified for the final."

JJ put his combination into the lock on his locker and pulled it open. "I'll need to shave about a tenth of a second off my time if I'm going to win the gold medal. I didn't like my start. Didn't get quite the push off the blocks I wanted."

"I thought you looked good."

"Right."

JJ took a deep breath. He didn't want to yell at Brandon, didn't want to ruin his Olympic moment. Because Brandon had won his race *and* broken a world record that had been on the books for a few decades. Brandon deserved to celebrate. He didn't need JJ's frustrations poured all over him.

JJ cleared his throat. "You have plans now?"

"Dinner with my family. My mother wants to go to this restaurant a few miles from here rather than eat hamburgers at the America House. She wants to try real Spanish food, she said."

"All right."

"I want to invite you, but I don't know if I'm quite ready to tell them all I'm seeing someone. And, well, my family can be a lot."

JJ glanced back at Brandon. He probably meant exactly what he said, and it was an understandable sentiment, especially since JJ had been cagey about their relationship to his own parents. They'd known each other less than a week. An amazing, intense, very good week, but still. And yet the thought still passed through his head that Brandon might not be willing to tell his mother he was seeing a black guy.

JJ sighed and changed out of his uniform. Brandon hadn't said anything like that. JJ shouldn't put words in his mouth.

"Are you okay?" Brandon asked, sounding cautious, as if he wasn't sure he should be asking.

"I'm fine."

"Can I come by when I get back from dinner?"

"Of course. My door's always open to you."

It took some effort, but JJ mentally pushed aside everything he was thinking about so he could focus on Brandon, who definitely didn't need JJ to take out his frustration on him. He smiled and focused on Brandon's face. No more asshole doctors or photo finishes. Just Brandon, the gold medal hanging from his neck, and the awesome potential of the night ahead.

Brandon stood. He closed the distance between himself and JJ, standing close enough to be heard when he whispered, "I wanted to see you before I left for dinner. Maybe I want to do my own celebrating tonight."

God, this guy knew just the thing to say. "Why, Brandon. Are you propositioning me?"

Brandon smiled. "Yeah."

Heat spread through JJ's body. Yeah, he would like to celebrate with Brandon. "All right. Rafa wants to talk to me about something, so maybe I'll have dinner with him."

"Rafa?"

"Rafael Martinez. My sprint teammate. Don't be jealous, girl."

"I'm not. I know who he is. I didn't know that's what he was called."

JJ gave Brandon a quick peck on the lips before he pulled on a clean shirt. "Come by when you get back from dinner, and I'll show you a good time."

The way Brandon's face went flushed was all the information JJ needed about where his head was at. Yeah, this had the potential to be a really good night.

"I better get going," Brandon said, pointing toward the exit. "My family is waiting."

"Seriously, congratulations. That was an amazing race. I'm super proud."

"Thanks." Brandon ducked his head, looking bashful. "I'll see you later, okay?"

JJ watched him go, feeling a little sad for reasons he couldn't put a finger on. He did feel better generally, though. He tried to tell himself that everything was fine. He'd had to do the blood test because all eight of the top qualifiers for the final had been required to do it. JJ wasn't being singled out specifically. Rude doctor notwithstanding, none of this was personal. Even though it felt that way.

CHAPTER TWENTY-ONE

DINNER WITH his family had been… fine for Brandon. Everyone had been enthusiastic—maybe a little too enthusiastic. Danny had shown off Brandon's medal to anyone who got near their table, which Brandon found mortifying. Mike had remained taciturn, mostly speaking in grunts and monosyllables. Brandon was okay with that, although he could tell that Mike was burning to say something that would, in all likelihood, upset Brandon. He could only speculate, though, because everyone remained on their best behavior.

Well, until Danny had asked, "What's with the nail polish?"

"Oh," said Brandon. "Well, I've made friends with Jason Jones Junior. He's that sprinter you guys saw yesterday. He paints his nails before races. It's kind of his trademark. He offered to do mine, and I thought it would be fun. Like a good luck charm."

"Kinda girly, isn't it?" said Mike around the piece of steak in his mouth.

Brandon generally avoided conflict, but he was so tired of his brothers' nonsense that he said, "So?"

"Your race was on television," Danny said, as if that explained everything.

Brandon rubbed his forehead. Both of his brothers had lifted weights and played football as teenagers but were now settling into their softer middle-aged bodies. Brandon didn't judge them for that, but he did judge them for questioning *his* masculinity. Brandon didn't think of himself as feminine at all, although he didn't believe in rigid gender roles either. If he wanted to wear nail polish, why should it matter?

"So a sportscaster comments on my nails. Who cares? I don't."

"Then why do it?" asked Danny.

"For fun."

"People will think you're gay," Danny whisper-hissed.

"I *am* gay. Did you forget that?"

Brandon's mother had intervened then and changed the subject. Nothing remotely controversial was spoken of for the rest of the meal.

Still, Brandon was relieved when he got back to the Olympic Village. He loved his mother, he did, but when she'd told the third random stranger in the restaurant in her broken Spanish that her son had won an Olympic medal, he'd almost crawled under the table.

His family was all back at the hotel now and he was back among other athletes. That felt safer somehow.

Brandon went by his actual assigned room to get a change of clothes and was surprised to find it empty. He went to the little dresser in the corner and started pulling out his clothes, wondering if he should just move in with JJ for the rest of the week. Something told him not to do that quite yet, though. It was only a few days, but it felt like more of a promise than Brandon was willing to make.

He was nearly done repacking his bag when Jamal came in.

"Hey, stranger," said Jamal.

"Hey. I hope you enjoyed your time with the room."

"I did." Jamal grinned. "Shara had to fly home today, though. She hadn't planned to stay for the Closing Ceremony. She has a job back home she had to get to."

Brandon nodded. Because he worked for USC, they had let him have the whole week off, since he was indirectly representing them at the Games. But he knew a lot of the runners like him—those who weren't trying to do this professionally, who didn't have endorsement deals or sponsorship money to help them pay their bills—had other obligations back home to tend to.

"Sorry to hear that," Brandon said.

"So do you have someone you're hooking up with? Is that how you were able to find somewhere to stay the last few nights?"

Brandon intended to lie and say JJ was only a friend, but he couldn't keep the smile off his face when he thought about JJ, and he knew that totally gave him away. "Yeah, kind of. We met here in Madrid, but we've already talked about continuing to see each other when we get back to LA."

Jamal gave Brandon an attaboy-style little punch to the shoulder. "There you go. That's awesome. *And* you won a gold medal today. I saw the broadcast at the America House this afternoon. That's incredible. Congratulations."

"Thank you."

"You gonna spend tonight with this person you're seeing?"

Brandon couldn't remember if Jamal knew he was gay. He decided he didn't know Jamal well enough to come out to him, so he just said, "Yeah, that was my plan. But since we've only been seeing each other for a couple of days and I want to keep it going when we get back, I don't want to do anything as official as to move out of here entirely. Is that silly?"

"Nah, man. If you need the room, it's still here."

"Thanks."

"Don't sweat it. And hey, if you get into some big fight, I won't be mad at the company tonight."

Brandon deduced that Jamal was probably bored without Shara around. A number of the athletes had also already flown home for similar reasons, and those athletes who remained were prepping to compete or otherwise not around. "Do you want me to stay?"

"Definitely not. Go celebrate your gold medal with your boo. I'll see you tomorrow."

"Okay. Thanks."

Since JJ was only one floor down, Brandon jogged down the stairs with his overnight bag a few minutes later. When he knocked, JJ greeted him with a smile. That boded well. Brandon had been thinking about what Tamika had said of JJ likely being pissed after the outcome of the race and how irritable JJ had seemed in the locker room just before Brandon had left for dinner. JJ seemed fine now, though.

"Hi," Brandon said. "How was your evening?"

"Not terrible. Rafa and I ate at the America House, where the American broadcast showed your hurdles race about ten thousand times."

"Oh God."

"No, it was good. I enjoyed watching it every time. You're really good. Also, you make a face when you're focused on clearing the hurdles that is not very different from the face you make right before you come."

Heat flooded Brandon's face. "I didn't need to know that. Now I'll be thinking about that the next time I run."

JJ laughed. "Come on in. How was dinner with your family?"

"Fine. Well, the food was amazing. I had this egg-and-potato thing that was delicious."

"Family, huh."

"I love them, but we don't understand each other. That, and both my brother Danny and my mom kept heaping all this praise on me. It was too much."

"Must be hard to hear how amazing you are over and over."

Brandon sighed. He unzipped his jacket and took it off. "You make it sound silly. I don't love this kind of attention. I felt really awkward the whole time."

"I'm sorry. Come here."

JJ had moved the beds so that they were still pressed together but not blocking the doorway the way they had been before, so it was easy enough to maneuver around the beds and into JJ's arms. JJ folded him into a hug, and Brandon was surprised by how comforting he found it. They sat together on the edge of the bed, and he rested his head on JJ's shoulder.

"Is it ridiculous that I like you so much?" Brandon said. "I don't have a ton of experience with relationships, but I've never felt as happy with someone as I feel with you."

Brandon regretted saying that aloud until he felt JJ's hand on the back of his head. "I don't know if it's ridiculous, but I feel the same way." JJ let out a breath. "I didn't get a chance to shower at the stadium. I must smell ripe."

Brandon inhaled, taking in the musky scent of JJ's sweat. "I like it. It's sexy."

JJ laughed. "All right."

Brandon's skin tingled as JJ continued to hold and stroke him. He didn't want to let go, loved holding JJ and being wrapped up in JJ, but his cock also rose in a conspicuous way, and he wanted to do something about that too.

JJ reached between them. He grabbed something, which Brandon belatedly realized was the gold medal. "You still have this on."

"I like it. Also, I forgot I had it on under my jacket."

JJ laughed. He fingered the medal. "We match now, I guess."

"Let me take it off." Brandon lifted the medal off over his head. "I got a call from the USATF that they want me to be on *Wake Up, America!* tomorrow. I guess all the American medal winners go in for interviews. I've never been on TV before."

"There's not much to it. Wear the official tracksuit and your medal, answer a couple of softball questions, say something inane like 'I'm so proud,' and that's about it."

"Have you done interviews like this before?" Brandon immediately felt stupid for asking. "Duh, I forgot that's where you went when I left for the gym this morning."

JJ laughed. "Yup, I did the song and dance with them today. It wasn't my first time, though. I was on the four-by-one-hundred relay team that won silver four years ago, so they had the four of us sit there and be interviewed about how much we had wanted to win but we just weren't faster than Jamaica. Lucky for me, all those guys retired. The new Jamaican team is very young and less experienced. Beatable, in other words."

Brandon nodded. He wasn't totally sure what to expect and he was nervous he'd say or do something stupid in front of the camera, but the woman from the USATF had assured him that everything was pretaped because of the time difference between Madrid and New York, so anything really dumb could be edited out. That was small consolation.

Brandon stood and placed his medal on the desk and took off the rest of the official track suit until he stood in a white undershirt and his briefs. JJ stood and started to strip too, and was down to his warm-up pants, which were slung low enough on his hips that Brandon could see the V formed by his lower abs and obliques.

Brandon wanted to touch, so he did. He ran his hands over JJ's chest and over his abs and felt as much of that warm skin as he could.

"Mmm, are we eager, babe?"

Brandon didn't want to talk it through. He wanted to feel, to do. He rarely did anything without thinking over every minuscule part of it, but he wanted to just have this. He kissed JJ instead of answering. JJ answered with a curl of his tongue into Brandon's mouth. Brandon moaned against him.

Brandon pushed JJ toward the bed, and they fell back onto it, landing with a bounce and some laughter.

JJ hooked his arms back around Brandon and pulled him close. They rolled together and kissed more.

Brandon could feel JJ's erection pressing against him, and he wanted that, craved it. Actually, what he wanted was to be riding JJ's cock, but expressing that aloud felt like such an odd thing to say. Then he remembered that JJ wanted him to say what he wanted.

Brandon sat up and whipped his undershirt off. JJ ran his hands over Brandon's bare skin. Brandon straddled JJ's hips and said, "Should I tell you what I want?"

"Always. What do you want, babe?"

"I want you to fuck me. I want to ride you just like this."

"Mmm. Perfect." JJ leaned up and kissed Brandon, then pulled him back down so that he was lying on top of JJ. "Condoms and lube are in the drawer."

Brandon felt like his whole body was on fire. They were really going to do this. He wanted it badly, wanted it more than he wanted to eat his next meal. He reached for the drawer in the flimsy little bedside table and managed to snag the edge of it with his fingertip. It slid open easily, so Brandon grabbed the bottle of lube that was there and a couple of condoms, which he realized were mismatched brands. They were probably from the welcome kit all the athletes got.

He hadn't done this in a while. He'd been too busy with school and Olympics training. But in a lot of ways, it was familiar. He knew what to do, had some ideas for what he wanted to do to JJ. But in other ways, this was entirely new. Had he ever been with anyone he cared for as much as JJ? Had he ever been with anyone he'd been wanting for days like this?

Brandon peeled off all of his remaining clothing and then took off the rest of JJ's. He kissed JJ, and JJ immediately put his arms around Brandon and shifted his hips up against Brandon's. Brandon decided he didn't want to waste a lot of time. He grabbed the lube, smeared some on his fingers, and touched the entrance to his body.

JJ stared. Then he blinked and swatted Brandon's hands away. "Let me do that."

Brandon turned around and got in a 69 position. He expected to feel JJ's fingers at his entrance but instead felt JJ's tongue. He moaned, surprised by how good that felt, and then he licked JJ's cock from root to tip. When JJ groaned, his whole body vibrating beneath Brandon, Brandon took JJ's cock in his mouth.

They each doubled down, kissing and licking more aggressively. Brandon wrapped his hand around JJ's cock and continued to suck it as JJ pressed a slippery finger inside Brandon and licked at the base of Brandon's balls. Brandon was so aroused, it was uncomfortable, and he squirmed a bit under JJ's touch. When he couldn't stand it anymore, he tore the wrapper off a condom and rolled it onto JJ's cock. Then he turned around.

"You were serious," JJ said with a bit of a wheeze.

"I'm always serious."

JJ grinned. "I know. I like that about you."

Brandon met JJ's gaze. He felt dangerous suddenly. Powerful. He straddled JJ's hips and grabbed JJ's cock. JJ was at his mercy. And all Brandon wanted was JJ's cock inside him.

Very slowly, he lowered himself onto JJ's cock. It stung a bit, but Brandon liked it, went with it. They'd been postponing this precisely because Brandon hadn't wanted this pain to derail his running in any way. But now he wanted it. He needed it. There was no reason to delay this anymore. And when he was fully seated on JJ, he felt stretched and full and amazing.

"Perfect," he whisper-sighed.

JJ smiled. Then he hooked a hand behind Brandon's head and kissed him.

But Brandon wanted something else to happen here. Not sweet lovemaking but raw sex, sweat and pleasure and orgasms. Brandon sat back up and braced his hands on JJ's chest. Then he moved.

He rode JJ for all he was worth, enjoying the feel of JJ's cock rubbing all the best places inside him, his own arousal rushing through his body. JJ reached for his cock and started to stroke it, which was almost too intense.

"I'm gonna come," Brandon said, entirely too soon, but he couldn't hold back anymore.

"Yeah. Come on my cock."

Brandon bit his lip to keep from calling out too much, but then looked down at JJ, his own face distorted in ecstasy, and he gave up. He groaned and continued riding JJ until everything overwhelmed him, and he came on a long moan, shooting across JJ's chest.

JJ cursed and grabbed at Brandon's hips before surging up. Brandon thought he could feel the moment when JJ came, as if he vibrated inside him. JJ's features went lax and he threw his head back, practically growling as he came.

JJ slipped out sooner than Brandon wanted him to, but Brandon took the opportunity to roll off and lie beside him as he tried to catch his breath.

"Wow," JJ said.

"I didn't expect to come so soon."

"Me neither. I guess we had a lot pent-up need."

Brandon sighed. "I've been wanting that all week."

"Mmm. Brandon?"

"What?"

"Please come get what you want from me anytime."

JJ WAS not at all surprised when Brandon joined him in the shower. He wasn't mad at it either, especially not when Brandon put his arms around JJ from behind and pressed their wet, naked bodies together. JJ felt Brandon grow hard against him, and he thought about asking Brandon to reciprocate the favor from earlier, but he knew better. Nothing could affect his performance in the one-hundred tomorrow. So instead he hooked his hand around Brandon's head, pulled him forward, and gave him a slobbery kiss.

Brandon giggled, which was adorable.

"We do sex pretty well together," JJ said.

"Yeah. I want to do it again."

JJ sighed. "Me too. Although maybe not right this minute."

JJ leaned back into the spray and continued to wash himself, although Brandon didn't seem to want to pull away and kept his arms firmly around JJ. It made getting clean an interesting ballet.

JJ was experiencing some kind of postorgasm down, anxiety about his race the next day seeping in. He didn't say anything because he didn't want to take anything away from Brandon's victory today, and truthfully, he was happy to let Brandon try to distract him with sex. Especially since, before Brandon had sneaked into the shower, JJ had been replaying that day's race.

By random luck of the draw, most of the fastest men were in his semifinal heat, and the analysis JJ had read on the internet afterward indicated that a lot of sports reporters thought that the semifinal was a preview of the final. JJ second-guessed every single step he'd taken, wondering why he hadn't been able to push himself faster than the other runners, stressing over the fact that he'd come in second.

The results of the race had been a fluke; it could have been any of them in first. But that was the issue. If JJ couldn't run faster than the three other top runners in the race, he wouldn't win.

Brandon's hands were everywhere. JJ leaned back against him and tried to push the upcoming race out of his mind. Brandon was hard, his cock pressing into JJ's ass. It wouldn't take much to shift around so that Brandon's cock slid into the space between JJ's thighs, but JJ waited as Brandon trailed kisses from his ear to his shoulder.

This man.

"You keep saying you're awkward," JJ said, "but there is no awkwardness detected here."

"I feel comfortable with you."

JJ closed his eyes. "Thank you. I understand how much that means."

Brandon hummed softly. "I don't feel comfortable with everyone. Very few people, in fact. That's why I'm here with you and not partying with the other Team USA track runners."

"I know." JJ reached back and cupped his hand around Brandon's head again. Brandon squeezed JJ in his arms, which were delightfully strong. JJ ran his hand over one of Brandon's forearms. "I appreciate that you trust me. I'm honored that you do."

JJ was glad he'd earned Brandon's trust, because he trusted Brandon. Brandon had no ulterior motives. JJ knew he wasn't always the most honest person, but he had been with Brandon. He'd been candid, said what he meant, and expected the same in return.

And that was why he admitted, "I'm worried about the race."

"You're amazing, JJ. I know you can win."

"I *can*. I don't know if I will."

"Want me to help take your mind off of it?"

That seemed like just the thing, so JJ parted his legs slightly. Brandon seemed to take the hint—JJ was simultaneously jealous of the men who had come before and seen something worthwhile in Brandon, and grateful to them for giving Brandon experience enough to be good in bed—and kissed JJ at the back of his neck. Then Brandon slipped his cock between JJ's legs. JJ pressed his thighs together.

Brandon slid his cock into the space JJ created. He reached around and wrapped his hand around JJ's cock and pushed them into a sexy synchronization. JJ pressed his hands against the shower wall and ducked his head under the water, which put him into some kind of sensory overload. Brandon's body behind him, the water coursing over him, and Brandon's hand on his cock was a lot, all at once, but it was amazing, delicious, perfect.

Before JJ could even figure out what was happening, and as Brandon's hard cock pressed against his balls, he felt the familiar tingle. How was it that Brandon always made him come so fast? But did it matter? Brandon moaned behind him, then whispered that he was about to come, so JJ surrendered to his body and everything that he was feeling.

And just before the end, the thought passed through his head that he was with a man he trusted, was attracted to, and genuinely cared about—meaning he was with someone he could definitely fall in love with. Before he could contemplate that too much, Brandon pressed his thumb near the head of JJ's cock, and it felt so good that JJ groaned, even with water coursing down his head.

Then the world went blissfully blank for a long moment.

JJ came into Brandon's hand on a moan. The only things keeping him upright were his hands on the wall and Brandon behind him, because his knees gave out as if he'd just run a mile at top speed.

Then Brandon stiffened behind him and came, grunting as he did so.

JJ loved the realness of the two of them naked in the bright lighting of the bathroom, flaws and all, connected intimately. Brandon hugged JJ tightly, keeping JJ's back pressed against Brandon's front. The moment felt… sweet. That wasn't an adjective JJ would have connected with Brandon, but now Brandon was acting really sweet. It squeezed JJ's heart.

"Brandon?"

"Mmm."

"Don't ever let anyone, especially not me, tell you you're awkward or unworthy in some way."

Brandon took a deep breath, and JJ felt it against his back. "Thanks."

"We're going to get all pruney if we stay in this shower much longer."

"Yeah. Let's go to bed."

"You don't have to ask me twice, babe."

CHAPTER TWENTY-TWO

POSTSHOWER, THEY settled into bed, but JJ couldn't fall asleep. Given how much Brandon was moving around, he seemed to be having trouble sleeping too.

JJ mostly ignored Brandon's tossing and turning at first, as his mind wandered toward his race again. Well, mostly the drug test immediately after the race. The rude doctor. Franco's betrayal. That syringe in the locker room had turned out to be a hammer thrower's insulin shot improperly disposed of. One would think someone who'd been dealing with diabetes for a while would know how to properly take care of his paraphernalia, and JJ almost wondered if someone had planted the syringe to arouse suspicion, but he didn't want to sink too far into conspiracy theories.

Coming in second in the semifinal was messing with his mind too. Being named the fastest man alive at the Olympics had been a dream of JJ's since he'd started sprinting. He worried now that he wouldn't get it, and he wouldn't have too many more shots at it, if any, after this.

It was a lot of pressure, like a weight on his shoulders. JJ understood that everyone here was feeling the same way. And some of these athletes had coaches who wanted them to win at any cost. They had their athletes on complex drug programs, used at certain times in the season, weaning off the obvious red flag drugs in time for the athletes to be tested at competitions. Scientists were even working on how to manipulate genes to give people what nature didn't. So it was impossible to know who was doping and who was clean.

What was it that his former coach Marcus had told him once? If everyone was doping, it wasn't cheating.

Well, JJ still thought it was cheating.

But not every athlete agreed with JJ. And if other athletes were competing with enhancements, what did that say about the integrity of the race results?

JJ had to think of the long term, because he couldn't run forever. He didn't think some of his competitors had such a long view of things. They needed the medal now; they'd worry about everything else later. But JJ knew better than to think he'd still be running competitively at forty. If drugs had scary side effects, if they messed with his heart or caused cancer or made him infertile or gave him depression, that would affect the rest of his life.

Brandon tossed and turned for a few more minutes while JJ stewed, stressed about the race, worried about any of a thousand things that might be working against him. Maybe he was competing against athletes who were doping. Maybe he wasn't really fast enough to win the race. Maybe he'd have an off day, maybe he hadn't trained enough, maybe his losing sleep now would doom him tomorrow.

He wanted to win that race more than he wanted anything else in the world.

Brandon rolled over and looked at JJ. "You awake?"

"Can't sleep."

"Thinking about your race?"

"Can't think of anything else."

Brandon propped himself up on an elbow. "What are you thinking about specifically?"

JJ sighed. "You know, in 1988, Carl Lewis tested positive for pseudoephedrine and some other stimulants and was initially banned from the Olympics in Seoul. But he was acquitted and got to compete. I looked into all of this when I had my hearing with the World Athletics. He claimed he was taking cold medicine and drank some tea or something like that. They call it 'inadvertent use.' That was what we pleaded in my case. But for Carl Lewis, even though he went on to win more competitions, there always seemed to be this cloud over him. I saw him do an interview in a documentary about steroids and even *I* thought his story about drinking tea sounded shady."

Brandon nodded slowly. "I know you're worried people think you're guilty of doping. I don't. Your coaches don't. It doesn't matter."

JJ thought of Franco. That one stupid moment, two white pills in the palm of Franco's hand, a choice that would have changed the entire trajectory of JJ's career. "I hate all this, you know? I want to run. I want to be the fastest man alive. I don't want to think about doping. I don't want to think about my opponents. I'm tired of constantly being tested. I'm tired of getting woozy from getting my blood drawn. And I hate that there's a tiny part of me questioning whether putting myself through all this is really worth it."

"It is."

"Says you. You've got your gold medal."

"So do you."

JJ groaned and got out of bed. "But it's not the one I want. And even I know that's a shitty thing to say. But I want the medal in the one-hundred. That's the real prize. And I'm worried I won't get it because of any number of reasons."

"I'm sure you'll be fine."

JJ recognized that Brandon was only trying to help, but JJ had been mulling over all this long enough that he was angry now. Something in him was on fire.

"What if I'm not?" JJ said. "What if I'm not good enough? What if this is my last chance and I don't get it done? Then what?"

Brandon sat up. "Not winning a gold medal doesn't make you a bad person."

And sure, maybe that was the right thing to say, but coming from Brandon, who didn't always understand these things well, it seemed even more robotic—like platitudes without sentiment.

"It makes me a failure," said JJ.

"It doesn't. You've accomplished a lot here already. You're a fantastic sprinter. You have a gold medal. You can't control how well or how poorly the other runners perform, just your own race. So push it as hard as you can, and you'll do well."

"No," JJ said. He shook his head. "That's all bullshit. All of it. That's what you say to another athlete when you're giving a pep talk, and we all know it's bullshit."

"JJ."

"Don't say my name like you're scolding me."

Brandon let out a huff of breath. "You're stressed about the race tomorrow, and I get that. But you finished second in the semis, right? You were only behind by a hundredth of a second. I know you can do this. You know you can do this. What else do you want me to say?"

"You can't know that—there are too many variables." JJ knew also that Brandon was trying to help, but JJ was just so fucking angry at all of it. Not at Brandon, but at everything else. Well, maybe he did resent Brandon a little for having his life sorted out. Brandon knew who he was, what he wanted. JJ wanted to win races. After that, he had no clue. "Do you have something you've wanted for your whole life? Your engineering degree, for example?"

Brandon shrugged. "Not my *whole* life. I want to do something meaningful. Make something useful."

That pulled JJ back for a moment. Brandon had never struck him as someone out for power or glory. He was after a quieter kind of success. He'd apply his incredible capacity to solve complicated math problems to some invention or device the same way he applied it to hurdles, meaning he'd probably create something amazing before anyone even noticed he was working very hard.

And of course, he was modest about it. Brandon was so fucking genuine. JJ could never make him understand.

Still, he tried. "Well, imagine you have a goal. Something you've been working toward for years. What if someone told you that you couldn't have it?"

"That's not what's happening here. You have an opportunity to win tomorrow. The race hasn't been run yet."

"But can't you see? There's so much that goes into every race that is not rational. Who's cheating? Who isn't? Will it be too hot? Will my shoe come undone? So yeah, I'm *stressed* about the race. I want to win it more than I want anything else in life. Can't you understand that?"

"Of course, but you can't change most of that. Still, there are some things you *do* have control of. Focus on those."

JJ let out a disgusted grunt. He knew he was being ridiculous, but he had too much frustration built up and nowhere to put it.

"Dammit, Brandon. What do you know? You can't fix every problem with math."

BRANDON BALKED.

You can't fix every problem with math.

Why was JJ so angry? What had Brandon done wrong here? They'd had what Brandon thought was good sex. He'd tried to cheer JJ up. If JJ was having some kind of crisis of faith, Brandon was not equipped to deal with it. Obviously nothing he'd said so far was what JJ wanted to hear.

Tamika had warned him, but Brandon still felt ill-prepared for this attitude from JJ.

JJ was pacing now, furious at something, probably his fate or the race or general anger at the lot he'd been dealt.

"You're not mad at *me*, though, are you?" Brandon asked.

JJ stared at him for a long time. "Maybe I am a little."

"Why?"

"Because you don't get it. You don't understand what this means to me or what I've had to go through to get here."

"So talk to me. Tell me about it. Don't yell at me."

"I can't make you understand. You've got some screw loose that doesn't allow you to really understand human emotions or something."

Brandon took that blow like a punch to the face. He tried to analyze JJ's body language. He was angry, clearly; his knit eyebrows and the hands on his hips and the way he leaned forward all showed that.

It wasn't exactly a quality Brandon found appealing. JJ had to find a better way to deal with his anger than taking it out on whoever was closest. Maybe JJ was just blowing off steam, but his words hurt.

Brandon might not have understood every nuance of the emotions of people around him, and maybe he spent too much time with his head in books or studying or whatever else, but he still felt emotions. He wasn't a robot. And he'd spent a week falling in love with a man who was now telling him he didn't know anything about emotion. Brandon knew plenty, especially now that JJ was making him feel things he never had before, and he was offended that JJ was dismissing that.

Well, fuck that. Brandon didn't usually curse, but that was the thought that popped into his head. He didn't have to sit here and listen to this. JJ could get a handle on his emotions and find a more productive way to deal with them than yelling at Brandon, who still hadn't done anything wrong.

Brandon got out of bed and found his clothes. He pulled them on.

JJ sat back on the bed. "What are you doing?"

"I'm not going to sit here while you take out your anger on me. It's not fair."

"No, come on, I didn't mean it."

"I know." Brandon stopped shoving his stray things in his bag and looked at JJ. "I know, but some of the things you said were hurtful. You must think at least something in them is true. So why am I even here? If you think I'm some unfeeling robot, why are you even with me?"

"Come on, Brandon. I don't really think that."

"I think you do." Brandon sighed. "You're passionate and emotional and I understand that. It's one of the things I really like about you. But it sucks to be on the other side of it. And honestly? I deserve better. I don't need to stand here while you tell me I can't feel anything, because I feel a lot, and I feel a lot *for you*, but I can't be with you if you're going to act like this." He took a deep breath. "And if you *don't* think these things, that's even worse. Why say them, except to be hurtful? You're stressed about the race. I get that. But I'm done."

Brandon was likely leaving things behind as he grabbed one of his shirts, stuffed it in his bag, zipped it, and threw it over his shoulder. Right now, he didn't care. He could come back for his things later, or… well, things were replaceable. Brandon hadn't decided if he was storming out for now or for good, but he was definitely leaving now. He'd sort out the rest later.

"You feel a lot for me?"

"Yes."

"I… I feel a lot for you too. Please don't go. I'm so sorry."

"You keep saying I can't possibly understand what you're going through, but you forget that I'm also an athlete and I know what the pressure is like. And even if there are other issues I don't have firsthand experience with, you don't respect or trust me enough to explain them to me. You make assumptions and get angry." Brandon slung his bag over his shoulder. He closed his eyes for a moment. He and JJ had gotten along so well all week, and Brandon had thought JJ really *saw* him and understood how he thought and why he acted the way he did. But maybe all of that had been in Brandon's head. Because if JJ thought *this* was acceptable.... "I don't know what this is, if it's nerves or stress or a breakdown or what, but I can't be a part of it."

Brandon stormed out of the room, leaving JJ standing there naked, which meant JJ couldn't chase him into the hallway. Brandon walked halfway toward the elevator before he realized he didn't know if it was safe to go back to his room, since Jamal probably thought he was gone for the night. He sent Jamal a quick *Can I come back to the room?* text. Jamal's immediate response was *Sure.*

So Brandon went back to his room, wondering the whole way if he'd done the right thing or if he should have tried to reach some kind of understanding with JJ.

But JJ had said some things that really hurt Brandon, and they both needed some time away from each other to see if they had anything worth fighting for.

Jamal was sitting up on his bed, watching a movie on his tablet, when Brandon came in. Brandon dropped his bag on his own bed.

"What happened?" asked Jamal.

"We had a fight."

"So you do have a girlfriend here, not just someone you're hooking up with. Not gonna lie, I kind of wondered who you'd been spending nights with."

Brandon sighed. He didn't have the energy to put up any more walls tonight. "I'm gay, Jamal."

Jamal looked startled by that. Brandon wondered for a moment if he'd have to spend the night on the sofa in the lounge at the end of the hall, but Jamal said, "Wow, really?"

"Yeah. So I guess… I mean, I *have* been hooking up with a guy. And we just had a huge fight. And I stormed out because I was mad. And I'm not even sure if I did the right thing. But he… I don't know. It felt for a little while there like we were perfect for each other, but apparently I was wrong."

Jamal reached over and gave Brandon a tentative pat on the shoulder. "I'm so sorry. Do you want to talk about it?"

Brandon didn't, not really. He shrugged.

"I had no idea you were gay. I mean, my gaydar isn't very good on the best days, so I guess I shouldn't have been surprised, but wow. You think you know a guy."

"I don't really date a lot."

"Still. Okay, you don't have to answer this, but now I'm dead curious who you were hooking up with. Someone I know?"

"Probably." Brandon flopped down onto his back. He felt completely miserable. This night should have been his big triumphant celebration. After all, he'd won a gold medal and broke the world record. Instead, his heart was breaking. Then he groaned for even thinking such a stupid cliché.

He glanced over at Jamal who was looking back at him anxiously.

"JJ," Brandon said.

"JJ?"

"Jason Jones Jr."

"Oooh," Jamal laughed. "Holy shit. I mean, I knew he's gay, everyone knows he's gay, I just… I mean, the two of you together, I can't really picture it."

Brandon pressed the heels of his hands onto his eyes.

"I guess that explains the nail polish. I know that's JJ's thing."

Brandon lifted his hands and examined his nails. "Oh. Yeah. JJ painted my nails."

"So you're, like, boyfriends."

"Well. Maybe not anymore."

Brandon closed his eyes and thought the conversation was over, but Jamal shifted around and then said, "What was the fight about? Wait, you don't have to answer that. Sorry, I know we're not close friends really, but I've never seen you this unhappy. Didn't you win a gold medal today?"

"Yeah." Brandon tapped his chest, expecting it to still be hanging there. And, fuck. He'd left it in JJ's room.

But he'd deal with that tomorrow. JJ wouldn't do anything to it. He'd just have to "forget" to wear it to his TV interview.

He cursed mentally.

"Would it make you feel better if I took you to the America House and bought you a drink? It's still open for another hour," Jamal said.

Brandon sighed. "No, that's okay. I appreciate your trying to help. I mean, I don't know, maybe it's all for the best. It was a weird Olympic bubble romance. It had to end sometime."

Jamal was silent for a moment, so Brandon looked over at him. "Let me ask you something. Do you like him?" Jamal finally asked.

That was exactly the problem, wasn't it? Brandon liked JJ a lot, felt like they understood each other even though they were so wildly different, and he'd started imagining what things could be like if they continued dating in LA. He liked the idea of them training together and going on dates and the whole nine yards, but he didn't love that JJ kept circling around to Brandon's key deficiency.

"I do really like him."

"So what's the problem?"

Brandon thought for a moment. "Honestly? I don't really have enough relationship experience to tell when a fight is just a fight and when it's the end of a relationship. But even then, what relationship? JJ barely knew my name before Sunday. I like him… I really like him. I do. But I don't know if this is right."

Jamal nodded. "That is a pickle. But I think… I think sometimes you have to take a chance. You both train at USC, right? So you'll probably run into each other again."

"Yeah."

"I mean, you could see how it goes. I assume he said something that upset you and that's why you are here and not with him."

"Yes."

"Could you forgive him for what he said? I mean, assuming he properly apologized. Groveled, even."

"I… yeah, probably." And he would. He understood why JJ lashed out to a point, but he wasn't going to be a doormat either. So yes, if JJ apologized in a way that seemed sincere, Brandon would forgive him. But JJ would have to agree to some things in return.

Jamal smiled. "You know, my first date with Shara was kind of a disaster. She was a little awkward at first, I kept getting tongue-tied and said something she got kind of offended by. It was kind of awful. But I *really* liked this girl. So I waited a couple of days and then I called her and apologized. Asked for a second date. Thank God she said yes, because things have been awesome ever since. So if you really like JJ, give him another chance. Yeah?"

"*If* he apologizes." Because Brandon wasn't going to walk back into a situation in which JJ didn't take his feelings seriously. JJ had to apologize in a way that showed he understood what he'd done wrong and knew how he was going to fix himself so that he didn't do it again.

"Oh, of course. Make him beg."

Brandon laughed, despite how miserable he still felt. "Thanks. I feel marginally better now."

CHAPTER TWENTY-THREE

Day 15

SOMETHING WAS wrong. It took JJ a few minutes to figure out what that was, but then he saw the other twin bed pushed up against the one he lay in, and Brandon wasn't in it. JJ was alone.

Because Brandon had left. JJ had practically pushed him away.

Why had he said those things? As soon as he'd said Brandon had a screw loose, he'd regretted it. He didn't think Brandon was a robot. Hell, the sex they'd had last night had shown how much passion Brandon had beneath the surface. JJ hadn't known why he'd said the things he had, because he didn't really believe them. He'd been angry and frustrated… and he'd done exactly the thing so many people in his life had told him he shouldn't: take out his anger on whoever was closest. Tamika yelled at him for doing just that all the fucking time.

And now he'd done it to Brandon. And Brandon had left.

Fuck.

JJ was an asshole sometimes, but he hadn't meant to push Brandon away. So why had he done it?

Because he'd panicked. About all of it. About the race, about everyone doping, about his feelings for Brandon, which had grown rather intense in the few short days they'd spent together. Because JJ knew Brandon *saw* him, that despite his self-professed ignorance of human emotion, he probably even knew what JJ had been doing when he'd said those terrible things. But he'd stood up for himself and left, as he should have.

JJ rolled onto his back and stared at the ceiling. He knew he needed better outlets for his frustration. Brandon had been right that JJ probably could have explained what his issue was, that he could have told Brandon about the rude doctor or about vomiting after getting blood drawn or about how it had felt in those harrowing moments while they waited for officials to make a call based on a photograph, knowing one of the top sprinters was about to lose his shot at winning the title of Fastest Man Alive. He could have explained any of those things, but he hadn't. He'd assumed Brandon wouldn't get it, and he'd been angry instead.

JJ didn't trust easily—too many people in this fucking sport had betrayed him. Franco and Marcus were the worst offenders, but he'd grown weary of trying to guess who cheated and who didn't, who was nice while hiding a figurative knife behind his back. He didn't really trust men much either; he realized as he lay on that stupid twin mattress that he basically always assumed everyone he met had some other agenda.

What had made him this untrusting? Not any one thing, he realized. Just a lot of life experience as a black gay man in the United States. He pushed people away as a habit. He'd done the same thing to Brandon. Sweet, sexy Brandon, who was frank and straightforward and had no other agenda except to earn his degree, get a good job, run the hurdles faster than anyone else in the world, and now, be with JJ. Brandon had been here because he wanted to be here with JJ. He didn't want anything from JJ except his affection.

And JJ had pushed him away. One fucking week of them together and JJ had been considering moving back to the old neighborhood to be closer to a man he'd basically shoved out the door last night. To say JJ had regrets was an understatement.

If he had any hope of keeping Brandon, he'd have to apologize. A lot. And he'd have to show Brandon that he knew better than to treat him that way. Make Brandon realize that he'd acted out and pushed Brandon away because of his own issues and not anything Brandon had done. Convince him that he'd work on those issues and, if Brandon took him back, he'd hold on to Brandon and never let go.

But how on earth could he do that?

And, oh yeah, he had to run the one-hundred-meter final today.

He got up and showered. He didn't have to be at the stadium for another couple of hours. He sent Brandon a text:

I am so sorry. I'm an asshole.

JJ paced around the room for a while. He wanted to vomit. He'd really fucked up with Brandon. And now he might lose him, which was a terrible thing to contemplate. Not to mention he'd yelled at Brandon the same day Brandon had won that gold medal.

The medal which… was right there on the little desk in the corner.

That only made JJ feel worse. He was a monster.

He texted again: *So, so sorry. I have your gold medal. I'd like to give it back to you. And also apologize a thousand more times.*

He hit Send but suspected he needed to do more than that. He sat on the bed and started typing furiously with his thumbs.

You have every right to hate me. I don't think you don't have feelings. I know you do. I shouldn't have said that. I don't manage my anger well. It's something I need to work on. But please don't give up on me. Don't give up on us.

He waited around for another half hour, puttering around the room and waiting for Brandon to respond. He shaved, he repainted his nails, he changed clothes twice. When no response arrived, JJ packed his bag and decided to head to the stadium. Maybe he could run laps to work through some of his nervous energy.

BRANDON AND Jamal headed to the stadium as spectators. Brandon had texted Grady on the bus there to ask if he'd be around, and Grady said he'd be hanging out in the stands most of the day and Brandon should join him there. All but one of the athletes Grady coached had already finished their Olympics, so Brandon figured Grady was hanging around in case Tamika, who coached several athletes running that day, needed help.

Brandon's mother called to invite him to do some sightseeing with the family. The thought of spending a whole day with his mom and brothers made him nauseous, so he begged off, explaining that he wanted to watch some of his friends run races that day. His mother seemed so delighted he had friends that she didn't seem offended that he was blowing off family, although she extracted a promise for him to come to Sunday dinner in Pasadena more often in exchange for not going with everyone on a bus tour of Madrid the next day.

That taken care of, Brandon and Jamal went into the stadium via the main entrance and settled into their seats in the Team USA section as one of the long-distance races was starting. Those races didn't really get interesting until the last lap or two, so Brandon looked at his phone. There were five texts from JJ.

"He's groveling," Brandon said, holding up his phone.

"Oh, really?" Jamal raised an eyebrow.

"Part of me kind of feels bad for storming out. Should I apologize?"

"Nope."

"No? Really?"

"Do you think you had a good reason for storming out?"

"Yes."

"Then don't apologize. Is his groveling sufficient?"

Brandon looked back at his phone. The last text said, *I get why you're mad. I shouldn't have taken out my anger on u. I pushed u away bc of my feelings 4u. It was shitty. I really care about u. I want to b with u. I will work on how I deal with stress. Please just give me another chance.*

"It is. He's saying the right things."

"I think you should let him sweat."

Brandon stared at his phone, then at the track. "Well, maybe I shouldn't make him sweat too much. The most important race of his career is happening in a few hours."

Jamal laughed. "All right."

"I mean, he knows he fucked up. He knows why he fucked up without me having to explain it. He still wants to be with me. The… oh."

Another text message came in. *Please just say something. Tell me to fuck off if you want to. I can't stand not knowing.*

Brandon sighed. "I think I've let him sweat long enough."

Grady walked into the section and sat beside Brandon. "Did you break that poor boy's heart right before his big race?"

There was no question about to whom Grady referred.

"Is he a mess?" Jamal asked.

"He's half hysterical right now. Tamika's got him doing drills, though, and he's fast as lightning."

"I think I should probably tell him I forgive him," Brandon said as the stood. "I'll go talk to him."

"Unfortunately, I can't let you do that. There was some kind of security breach yesterday and they're being very strict about who they let into the locker rooms and the practice track. Only athletes still competing allowed. They're checking names off a list. And you're done, unfortunately."

Brandon sat back down hard. "Oh."

"What kind of security breach?" asked Jamal.

Grady shrugged. "I think a reporter? There's been a recurring issue with tabloid reporters accosting athletes while they're trying to train. They had to basically lock down the Aquatics Center because unauthorized people were harassing that diver Tim Swan."

"I heard about that," said Jamal.

"So I should just text him?" Brandon asked. "Because that seems insufficient."

"You kids and your texting. That thing in your hand makes calls, you know."

"Except for the part where we're in Spain. I couldn't afford to pay for an international phone plan while I'm here. I've been using an app that runs on Wi-Fi to text JJ all week."

"There's your answer, I guess," said Grady.

Brandon wanted to see JJ. He thought it would be better to discuss all this in person. Brandon forgave JJ as long as JJ promised to do real work not to be so hostile when they fought. Or, really, as long as JJ didn't really believe that Brandon was a robot, that was enough. Because Brandon might not have been demonstrative with his emotions, but not being able to talk to JJ now was distressing him.

Some guy who clearly knew Jamal walked over and gave Jamal a complicated handshake. Brandon squinted at him and thought he might have been another USC runner, but he couldn't put a name with the face.

"Hey, Andy," Jamal said. "You know Brandon, right?"

Andy squinted at Brandon. "Hurdles, right?"

"Yeah." Brandon felt irritated by the interruption.

"You broke the world record yesterday! I saw that from here in the stands."

"Brandon goes to USC," said Jamal.

"Engineering major," said Brandon, trying to be friendly.

"Get out, really?" Andy laughed and sat on Jamal's other side. He pointed his thumb at his chest. "Econ."

"Cool." Brandon looked back at his phone.

"You'll have to excuse my friend," said Jamal. "He's having some relationship troubles."

"Ah, say no more. Your fingers are clearly itching to send that text. Go ahead."

Brandon let out a breath.

You can't fix every problem with math.

He certainly couldn't math his way out of this one, as JJ might say.

He leaned forward a little so he could use his body to block anyone from reading his text. Then he typed:

I was mad last night because I felt like you didn't take my feelings seriously. That's why I walked out. Because I do feel things. I feel them for you. I want to be with you too. But not if you can't figure out a way to deal with your stress without saying shitty things to me.

He didn't hit Send, though. He sat with that for a moment.

He hit Send but then immediately followed up with: *I hate that we have to have this conversation with text messages and not in person but Grady says they won't allow me into the stadium.*

He bit his lip and waited. The response came almost immediately. *Thank God you responded. I agree, I'd rather talk to you in person. I'd hoped to catch you this morning so I could do that and give you your medal back.*

Brandon had gone to the Olympic Broadcast Center very early that morning without his medal. A few people had asked him about it, so he'd just acted goofy and said he'd forgotten it. The whole interview had been an exercise in awkwardness, as the woman interviewing him asked superficial questions about his college major and the rumor that he used math to strategize. The whole thing had lasted five minutes, but those had been some of the longest minutes of Brandon's life.

But he'd gotten through it, and now he had a half-hysterical possible boyfriend freaking out at the other end of this text conversation.

Brandon glanced at Jamal, who shook his head. "Don't apologize. You're in the right here."

"What makes you think I'm apologizing?"

"That look on your face, like you're about to do something your mother wouldn't approve of."

Brandon barked out a laugh. He'd done a lot of things with JJ his mother wouldn't approve of.

He texted: *I still think we should talk. I'm sorry for ignoring you this morning, but I was angry and didn't know how to respond.*

JJ wrote back: *Y r u responding now?*

I needed you to know before your race that this is not over.

There. That was good. That was what Brandon needed JJ to know. Maybe things between them wouldn't work out, but maybe they would, and he wanted to give them the opportunity to explore that when they got back to LA.

So you're not leaving me, JJ wrote.

I like you, Brandon said. *Love* felt like too strong a word, but he could see himself falling in love with JJ. It was such a novel thing, and he'd never been in love before, but JJ saw things in Brandon that no one else saw, which was why he knew exactly which buttons to push, which lines to cross to drive Brandon away. Of course, Brandon also understood exactly what JJ was up to.

I like u 2, JJ texted back with a line of heart emojis.

Brandon sighed. He wrote, *We should talk when all this is over, but I think we could be good together. I'm not ready to throw that away yet.*

JJ responded: *Me neither. I'm sorry I pushed you away last night. This has all happened so fast. I'm falling for you and it freaks me out. It shouldn't bc u r great.*

Well, there it was. Brandon felt a little flutter in his heart. He wondered if this was what everyone felt when they were on their way to falling in love with someone. He wondered how many people fell for their complete opposite. What did it say about him that all he wanted to do was run into the stadium and down to the practice track and kiss JJ?

And sure, Brandon had doubts, but he didn't feel hesitant about forgiving JJ.

Don't tell me I don't feel anything ever again, and you're forgiven. Because I feel a lot, even if I'm not good at showing it.

Brandon stared at the 3 little dots as JJ typed his response. Then it popped up:

Never. I know there's passion in you. I know.

Brandon closed his eyes and let out a breath. Then he wrote: *Win a gold medal tonight and I'm yours.*

He worried as soon as he hit Send that JJ wouldn't know he was joking, but then JJ responded with a winky emoji followed by, *No pressure, right?* A moment later he added, *All right. For you? Anything.*

Brandon smiled and sat back in his chair.

"I think a whole lifetime passed while you were texting," said Grady.

"You forgave him, didn't you?" said Jamal. "That looked intense."

Andy was busy looking at his own phone and probably didn't really care about Brandon's personal life. Brandon just shrugged. "We've reached an understanding."

"Thank God," said Grady. "I'm going to talk to Tamika about instituting some kind of no-drama-at-the-Olympics policy."

"Good luck with *that*," said Jamal. "The Olympics are *all* drama."

Chapter Twenty-Four

Tamika snapped her fingers in front of JJ's face. "I'm gonna need you to pay attention."

JJ swatted her hand out of the way and went back to typing on his phone. "Do you *want* me to be a big ball of stress, or do you want to let me fix things with Brandon?"

Tamika rolled her eyes. "I feel like I made a critical error introducing you two to each other."

"I thought you wanted us to hook up?"

Tamika shrugged. "Maybe I was matchmaking a little, but I really thought you'd make good training partners more than anything else. And I figured that maybe you'd meet and make googly eyes at each other for a few days and then maybe something would happen when we all got back to LA. I didn't expect things to get this intense, this fast."

JJ rolled his eyes.

"I don't know Brandon that well, really just things Grady has told me, but he seems so… virginal."

"He's not."

"Because of you?"

JJ stopped what he was doing and looked up at Tamika. "Girl, please. I was not responsible for his deflowering."

"But you two have had sex."

JJ hated that this many people were up in his business. Well, he hated that Tamika was nagging him. She had a point, of course, because he had to get ready for his race and also some more relay practice, since the four-by-one-hundred was tomorrow. But he needed some sense of resolution with Brandon before he could do anything. It felt now like they had a truce. JJ was reading between the lines that Brandon was still mad, and he had every right to be, but he'd also said *this is not over*.

JJ raised an eyebrow at Tamika. "You want the gory details? You want me to tell you that he's a big old bottom who was practically begging me to—"

"Nope." Tamika held up her hands. "Sorry for asking."

JJ grinned, the first genuine smile he'd allowed himself all day.

Tamika rolled her eyes. "So, okay, tell me what happened. CliffsNotes version."

JJ leaned against the wall and hit Send on his most recent text to Brandon. "We've been talking and making out and all that good stuff since Sunday, basically, but then we got into a fight last night and I said some things that were unfair."

Tamika pursed her lips and glared at him for a moment. "What was the fight about?"

"Why are you giving me the third degree?"

"I'm trying to figure out how to get you to process this and move on so that you can win your race today. Why did you fight?"

JJ pushed off the wall and started pacing. Brandon had essentially forgiven him and he didn't want to talk about this anymore, but he said, "*Fine*. I was stressed about the race today and I picked a fight with him because of it. But he also only responded to me being stressed with bland platitudes. He was trying to make me feel better, but it rubbed me the wrong way. I know part of that is because he's awkward socially and doesn't always know how to react to someone as passionate as me."

"As hotheaded as you, you mean."

"Well, be that as it may, I overreacted and called him a heartless robot, basically. And he took offense."

Tamika sighed. "Christ, JJ. You never learn."

"What do you mean?"

"That's your MO right there. You feel stress and then just lash out at whoever is closest. How can Brandon, a man you've known less than a week, intuit what you want or need to hear? That poor kid."

"Don't 'poor kid' him. He totally called me on what I was doing. Before he stormed out and left me alone, of course."

Tamika laughed. "Are you kidding?"

"No. He's onto me. Maybe he understands emotion better than he thinks." JJ held up his phone. "He basically told me that he won't take me back unless I promise to find better outlets for my frustration. He doesn't want to be my punching bag. And I don't want to punch him. I just… I don't know. I don't know where to put my anger sometimes."

"On the track." Tamika pointed toward the practice track. "Anytime you feel like yelling at your man when he does not deserve it, go for a run. You're stressed about a race? Go to the gym. Take it out on an actual punching bag—don't turn your boyfriend into a metaphorical one. You yell at me all the time when you're frustrated or upset, and I let you because I thought you were blowing off steam, but if your man finds it hurtful? Then maybe I did you wrong by letting you develop bad habits."

"I yell at you all the time?"

She rolled her eyes. "Well, not *all* the time. But Brandon deserves better."

JJ sighed. "I know."

"Good."

JJ got another text and smiled to himself. Then he held up his phone to Tamika. "He says he'll take me back if I win him a gold medal."

Tamika laughed. "Man, I like that guy. Well, if your future happiness depends on you winning, we better get back to training. Is all this angst resolved enough now that you can do a few more practice races?"

"Yeah, yeah."

"Good, because I was about to confiscate your phone. Actually, just give it to me."

Tamika held out her hand. JJ stared at it and then handed over his phone with some reluctance. She pocketed it. At least if she had it, she could tell him if anything that needed his attention happened.

He knelt and retied his shoes, then stared at the track, assessing how many people were using it and therefore likely to distract him.

"We still have Lane 8 for another forty minutes. I don't think what we have to do is very challenging. Run a hundred meters in less than ten seconds."

JJ laughed and shook his head. "Sure."

"Nine and a half seconds would be fantastic."

"That's faster than the world record. It's probably not humanly possible."

"It's a goal."

JJ let out a breath and walked over to the track. His blocks were already set up because he'd done several very fast practice runs earlier. Tamika clearly didn't intend for him to tire himself out, but she knew him well enough to know that if he got a time he liked in practice runs, he'd be more confident going into the final. And he *had* been running the one-hundred in around 9.7 seconds, which was right where he wanted to be. He was good. But he could be better.

He got his feet in the blocks. Tamika stood in the empty lane beside him and held up her stopwatch. "You ready?"

"Yeah."

"Set. Go!"

CHAPTER TWENTY-FIVE

Transcript from the TBC broadcast of the one-hundred-meter sprint final

GRAYSON: THE heats were pretty slow. I think this will be an exciting race, but we probably won't see the world record broken. I've been hearing from the runners that this track feels a little slow.

CASSELLO: We've also had more disqualifications.

GRAYSON: That's right, Jim. A Canadian sprinter has been disqualified from this final after testing positive for a stimulant. I actually spoke with an official from the World Anti-Doping Agency, who pointed out that stimulants are allowed up to a certain level. So pseudoephedrine, for example, is a stimulant, but the amount in most cold medicine is well below the banned amount. So you'd have to take something like eight pills to get to the banned amount of pseudoephedrine.

I asked American sprinter Jason Jones Jr. about that, because he once had a medal taken away for testing positive for pseudoephedrine after taking a decongestant. He told me he was glad they changed the rules because athletes shouldn't be penalized for unwittingly taking banned substances, and the new limits are more in line with what people might be taking to enhance their performance.

CASSELLO: How is JJ feeling now?

GRAYSON: He says he feels great. I guess we'll find out in a few minutes.

CASSELLO: Who else do you like in this final?

GRAYSON: It's really a race between five runners: JJ, Rafael Martinez from Team USA, Ajani Blake from Jamaica, Ato Frederick from Namibia, and Johnny Pritchard from Great Britain. Pritchard actually came in fifth in his semifinal, but officials bumped him up to the final because he ran the sixth-fastest time in the semifinals. He is replacing the Canadian runner who was DQ'd. He's got a shot at this, though. I think any of these runners have a shot at this. Blake ran the fastest time in semifinals, but JJ and Martinez were right behind him. Let's show that photo finish again.

CASSELLO: Just incredible, how close that was. This will certainly be an exciting race….

THE ONE-HUNDRED-METER sprint was one of the premier events of the Olympics. It had a bit more pomp and circumstance than some of the other events Brandon had watched. There were so many things happening in the stadium at any given time that it was difficult to watch them all. The pole vault final was taking place in the center of the oval of the stadium. The javelin throw final was taking place off to the side, near a part of the stadium that opened into a field with carefully measured semicircles, the location of all of the throwing events. On the track itself, there had been three other finals that day, mostly longer-distance events.

But now, thumpy hip-hop was blaring through the speakers, and the headshots of each of the finalists flashed up on the Jumbotron and everything happening indicated something important was about to go down.

Jamal was munching on popcorn from the bucket he held. He and Brandon had been camped out in the stands all afternoon, and Brandon felt a little gross from sitting and eating all day. He'd mentioned as much to Grady the last time he'd been in his seat, and Grady had laughed and told him to enjoy his day off from training.

Right.

Grady appeared now and settled into the seat next to Brandon after snagging a handful of popcorn out of Jamal's bucket.

"Hey!" said Jamal.

Grady smiled and ate his popcorn. "We're Team JJ, right?" he said between bites.

"Of course," said Brandon.

"Tamika said he looked good in practice. So now he just has to beat the other four fastest men in the world."

"Oh, is that all," said Jamal.

The music changed, and then the announcer said in accented English, "Welcome to the contest that will determine the fastest man alive! The one-hundred-meter sprint!" Then different announcers repeated the message in six other languages. The crowd cheered.

The runners walked out onto the track and to their assigned lanes. Another hip-hop song played while the runners adjusted their blocks. Then they all stood up again and took a step back. One by one, the announcer called each runner's name.

JJ was in Lane 5. Brandon studied him, both on the track and up on the Jumbotron. He was cleanshaven, for a change. He had a gold chain around his neck that sparkled under the stadium lights. His gold running shoes had a bit of an iridescent quality to them. And JJ had, at some point since last night, changed his nail polish from gold to a rainbow of colors, and Brandon wondered what that was supposed to symbolize. The obvious gay pride symbolism was the most logical explanation, but Brandon wondered if there was a hidden message there too.

Did it say something about JJ's priorities?

Brandon couldn't begin to piece it together, but he liked the manicure.

As the announcer called each name, the runner took a step forward and gave the crowd a little wave, although it was clear that each runner was focused on the race. Rafa Martinez barely even looked up but just lifted his hand as he stared at the track, probably mentally running his race. But then the announcer called JJ, and he grinned and waved at the stands. He looked happy and relaxed. Not stressed. Not that Brandon was very good at interpreting these things, but he'd observed enough of JJ's body language in the last week to know that something about his posture now said, *I got this*.

As if the thought had been summoned from very far away, suddenly *that's my man* pride swelled in Brandon's chest.

"He's gonna win," Brandon said.

"Yeah?" said Grady.

Brandon ducked his head and felt his face heat up. “He promised me.”

“You are too cute for words,” said Jamal.

Brandon rolled his eyes and focused on the track.

Tamika joined them. She sat next to Grady and gave him a kiss on the cheek before she said, “He’s gonna win.”

“Brandon just made the same prediction,” said Grady.

“I don’t know what happened, but for the last hour or so, he’s been totally relaxed and ready. Obviously we don’t know how anyone else will run, and I’m worried about Blake in particular, because he was putting in excellent times in practice, but JJ feels ready.”

The runners were told to get to their marks. The runners almost moved in unison, carefully putting their feet in the blocks, pushing back against them and testing them, then placing their fingers right at the starting line. Up on the Jumbotron, Brandon could see JJ’s nails, and he had in fact painted a rainbow that began and ended with red. The color of love.

Brandon shook his head. He had to stop reading things into the situation. Still, he knew JJ cared about him, so he’d revel in that.

“Ready,” said the announcer.

The gun sounded. Fair start. All eight runners moved in a single line for the first twenty meters or so, but then the weaker runners started to fall back. Brandon couldn’t see anyone’s facial expressions, but he could imagine the look of determination on JJ’s face.

The British runner slipped behind at about the fifty-meter mark. Then Ato Frederick from Namibia slipped out of the lead. Rafa surged ahead, but JJ and Blake from Jamaica caught up quickly. Then Rafa slipped behind. At the eighty-meter mark, it was only JJ and Blake. JJ's arms pumped, his legs churned, and Brandon could see the moment, about ten meters from the finish, that JJ decided to give the race everything he had left. He inched ahead of Blake.

Brandon was out of his seat before his brain caught up to what he was doing, and he shouted "Go! JJ! Gooo!" and jumped up and down. Grady, Tamika, Jamal, and everyone else in the Team USA section were on their feet and shouting too.

JJ crossed the line first.

He'd won. He'd *won*!

Brandon looked at the scoreboard as the rest of the field crossed the finish line and confirmed:

Gold: USA Jones—9.61

Silver: JAM Blake—9.66

Bronze: USA Martinez—9.71

Brandon screamed incoherently with excitement and joy.

"He did it!" Brandon said to Grady.

Grady grinned and pulled two American flags from his bag. He took Tamika's hand. "Come with me, kid," he said to Brandon.

Their seats in the stands were about ten meters to the left of the finish line. Brandon followed Grady down to the front of the section, where the railing separated the stands from the field. Brandon looked at the track to find JJ and found him lying on the track, crying.

"Oh no. Is he injured?"

"Nah, I don't think so," said Grady.

"He's done," said Tamika. "He used everything he had in him to get that done."

Rafa walked over and helped JJ up. They hugged each other.

Grady handed one flag to Tamika and unfurled the other. Rafa noticed it and steered JJ in their direction. There were cameras on the field following them and Blake around. JJ seemed oblivious to the cameras, but he perked up a little when he made eye contact with Brandon.

JJ and Rafa walked over to where Grady stood. Grady passed a flag down to Rafa through the slats in the railing. Tamika held out the other one for JJ, but then JJ did something that shocked the hell out of Brandon. He grabbed the lowest railing, which was maybe four feet above the ground, then half jumped, half climbed until he was standing face-to-face with Brandon, the railing between them.

Then JJ hooked his hand around Brandon's head and pulled him in for a big, passionate kiss.

JJ WORRIED he would fall back onto the track, but if he did and broke his back, it would be so worth it.

He kissed Brandon, fully aware that the cameras were probably on him, and knowing he had announced their relationship to the world. It probably would get whoever aired it some hate mail, but he didn't care.

He had a vague recollection of some skier who had given his boyfriend the chastest of pecks before his ski race at the last Winter Olympics, and people made a huge deal out of *that*. There was nothing chaste about JJ's tongue in Brandon's mouth. Would this even air? It would probably be edited out. Who cared, though? Kissing Brandon was better than winning a race.

Besides which, Brandon didn't seem to be objecting.

Grady cleared his throat, so JJ broke the kiss and leaned away without letting go of the railing.

"Do you want the flag, or…?" Grady asked.

JJ grinned. To Brandon, he said, "I won you a gold medal."

"Guess that means I'm yours."

Grady rolled his eyes, but Tamika's face was basically a heart-eyes emoji.

JJ hopped down and landed back on ground level, on his feet. He took the flag from Grady. Then, even though his legs felt like noodles and his heart was still a little fluttery—from the race or from kissing Brandon, JJ wasn't sure—he made himself do a slow victory lap with Rafa and Blake.

"So that's your boyfriend," Rafa said as they jogged around the track.

"That's Brandon. He's the world-record holder in the four-hundred-meter hurdles, and yes, he's my boyfriend."

"I wouldn't have judged him as your type. Maybe it's the big glasses, but he seems… nerdy."

"He is, kind of, but he also has the body of the man who just broke a world record in hurdles. Like, he's got a fucking eight-pack. Hurdles require a lot of core strength."

Rafa laughed. "I guess he's cute if you're into guys. I've got my eye on a sprinter named Kayla. She won the one-hundred silver yesterday. I was trying to outdo her and win gold, but you know, I'm not even mad that she did better. She's amazing."

JJ and Rafa kind of limped around the last of the track. JJ was still a bit breathless, which made it hard to speak, and Rafa seemed equally tapped out. No one in the final had given that race anything less than everything, and Rafa must have been as exhausted as JJ felt.

JJ took a deep breath. He tried to soak everything in. He'd been gunning for this gold medal for his entire sprinting career. The race had happened so fast that he wanted to take a moment to appreciate his accomplishment. He, Jason Jones Jr., was the fastest man alive. He hadn't broken the world record for the one hundred meters, but he'd gotten damn close to it. It still stung that he'd lost that World Championship medal, but this was bigger. This was the *Olympics*. He would cherish this moment as long as he could.

He'd also kissed Brandon on national television. He hadn't put much thought into it; he'd seen Brandon and been drawn to him, as if he'd been stuck in a tractor beam in a sci-fi movie. All he could think about once he saw Brandon standing at that railing was kissing him, so he'd just… done it.

"My parents saw that," JJ remarked as they stepped off the track.

"I assume you're referring to kissing your boyfriend."

"Yeah. I haven't told them I'm seeing anyone."

"Guess they know now."

JJ and Rafa walked back to the railing where Brandon, Tamika, and Grady still stood, along with JJ's parents. JJ wrapped his flag around his shoulders and waved.

"You've met Brandon," JJ said, gesturing at his man.

"We did," said Mom. "We're so proud of you, Jason. But we're gonna talk about this later. You can explain why you didn't say anything."

"Brandon is a really good guy. Don't give him too hard a time."

"Oh, I believe you. I've been chatting with him while you did your lap. My problem is with you for not telling us."

JJ rolled his eyes, but then he laughed. He'd won a gold medal, he'd won Brandon back, and his mother was giving him a hard time about all of it.

He couldn't have been happier.

Epilogue

Four years later
Transcript: one-hundred-meter sprint preliminary heats

GRAYSON: As a hard sports journalist, I am always reluctant to get into too much gossip. But I feel like any discussions of Jason Jones Jr. must explain what happened four years ago.

BOOTHE: I don't think it's really gossip if it happened on tape.

GRAYSON: [*laughs*] All right. Well, JJ was the Olympic champion in this event four years ago. Let's see that race again.

BOOTHE: It was tight right until the end. Then he *just* managed to get ahead of Ajani Blake from Jamaica.

GRAYSON: After the race, JJ jumped into the stands and kissed his boyfriend, hurdler Brandon Stanton.

BOOTHE: Probably some viewers at home were scandalized, but I thought it was really cute. Did you know they eloped about a month after the Olympics? I asked JJ about that a few months ago, and he said that they basically got up one morning and decided there was no reason *not* to get married. And since neither of them wanted a big ceremony, they went down to city hall. It's practical and romantic at the same time.

GRAYSON: What is Stanton up to these days? He's not competing here, right?

BOOTHE: He retired from international competition about a year after the Olympics because he got a job working for an electronics company. JJ still trains at USC, though, and they live in LA.

GRAYSON: What do you think of JJ's chances in this race?

BOOTHE: He's looked great in competition all year, so I'd say pretty good. He finished first at the US Olympic Trials. But he's turning thirty soon and has said this is probably his last Olympics. Let's hope he goes out on top as defending Olympic champion, right?

GRAYSON: I agree, I think he does have a solid chance of winning.

BOOTHE: I spoke with his coach a little while ago, and she says he's relaxed and ready.

GRAYSON: Well, here he is, warming up. You'll see he's got his nails painted, which is his signature. Gold, of course. What other color would they be?

BOOTHE: Oh, but look, his wedding ring finger is painted red.

GRAYSON: There's Brandon Stanton in the stands with JJ's parents. They look a little anxious.

BOOTHE: Well, sure. JJ wants to defend his title as the Fastest Man Alive. It's one of the most difficult

Olympic events, and he wants to try to win it for a second time. No pressure….

JJ WAS pacing beside the practice track about a half hour before the final when Tamika ran over and said, “Hey, I have a surprise.”

“No surprises.”

“You’ll like this.” She led JJ down a short hallway—this stadium had a lot of little hallways and corridors—and JJ soon understood what she wanted him to see.

Brandon stood there.

JJ smiled. He hadn’t seen Brandon all day. JJ had, in fact, moved into Brandon’s hotel because, after three nights in the athlete dorms without his husband, JJ felt out of sorts. Brandon grounded JJ, helped keep him from getting too irrational, and just generally made JJ feel like a whole person.

JJ jogged to close the distance between them and threw his arms around Brandon. “I’m so happy to see you.”

Brandon laughed. “You saw me a few hours ago.”

“I know, but this is all so intense.”

“By the way,” said Tamika, “I got him in here with Grady’s coach pass.”

“Call me Grady,” said Brandon.

“That’s weird,” said JJ.

“Or kiss me. That works too.”

JJ grinned and kissed the hell out of Brandon. Just being in Brandon’s arms helped him calm down.

Brandon had no business being inside the stadium like this, given that he didn’t even compete as a runner anymore. He had a job in the design department at a huge electronics company helping create cutting-edge technology. Brandon still ran, though, mostly long distances or on the treadmill in their basement gym, and only for recreation.

"So are you going to win me another gold medal or what?" Brandon asked.

"Of course."

Brandon smiled. "I love you."

"I love you more."

"So did you plan this or…?"

Tamika laughed. "I texted Brandon an hour ago when you started freaking out. I thought seeing him might help you."

JJ hugged Brandon again. Brandon kissed the top of his head. They'd probably done the steps of their relationship out of order, and in retrospect, it was probably irrational to get married six weeks after they'd met, but JJ wouldn't have changed anything. In the years since, Brandon had grown more affectionate in public, had gotten better at reading JJ's moods, and had generally become the best partner JJ could have asked for. JJ didn't want to let go now, though he did reluctantly.

"We should probably get Brandon out of here before anyone notices he's not a middle-aged black man," Tamika said, gesturing toward the coach pass Brandon wore around his neck. "I think the guard on duty was a little nearsighted."

"That doesn't speak well of the security here," said JJ.

"You mad about it?" Tamika asked.

"Nope!" JJ kissed Brandon again. "All right, babe. Cheer for me."

"I will."

"Good luck out there," said Tamika.

"Girl, please."

Tamika rolled her eyes and led Brandon away.

JJ glanced at a clock and realized he had to head toward the track anyway. He reflected as he walked that Brandon would love him no matter what, but he wanted to win that medal, partly for himself to prove he could still run really fast, but partly for Brandon, just because. JJ hadn't wanted Brandon to be the main breadwinner in their little family—the two of them plus their dog, a female collie mix JJ had named Flo-Jo—so he'd been working as a manager at the same gay bar where he'd once tended bar, which also gave him more flexible hours so that he could actually see his husband. He had enough money socked away now that he had developed a little fantasy of opening a sports bar and making running it his post-Olympics career. Brandon supported the idea, even though he also pointed out that JJ was surprisingly good as an assistant coach for some of the freshmen on the USC track team. So that had some potential as a future career too.

JJ didn't know exactly what he wanted to do yet. And that was okay. He didn't have to have it all planned out. A little spontaneity could be a good thing.

Arriving back home from Madrid had been a wild experience. That first month, they'd hardly seen each other because JJ worked nights and Brandon spent most days at school or at his job. But they'd talked, and JJ had decided to see a therapist to work through some of his issues. And then sometime that October, they'd had a rare night together and Brandon had said, "I hate that I never see you. I sometimes think it would be better if we lived in the same house so that I can at least see you when we go to bed at night."

And JJ had said, "Maybe we should get married."

It had been such an odd, spur-of-the-moment thing. JJ had almost laughed it off as if he was kidding, but he realized he wasn't. He could see their whole future together. They could buy a house together, set up a home gym, train together, sleep together, get a dog together.

"Are you joking?" Brandon had asked.

"No," said JJ. "I love you. I love you more than I ever thought possible. I want to be with you forever. I don't need more time to decide."

"I love you too, but it just seems so fast."

JJ had reached across the kitchen table in Brandon's apartment, where they'd been eating dinner, and took Brandon's hand. "Babe. Forget about what other people may think. What do you want?"

Brandon's smile came slowly, but then he said, "I want to marry you."

They went to city hall a week later.

It took almost another month to find the right house, a little ranch in Silver Lake near the reservoir, but it was perfect.

JJ's mother had thrown a fit when she found out they'd gotten married without the big splashy wedding she'd wanted for her son, so as a way to make it up to her, he let her throw them a big housewarming after they moved into the new place. JJ had little interest in a big wedding, and Brandon cared even less, so the simple city hall ceremony was everything they'd needed. Everyone said they'd rushed into it, but here they were, almost four years later, and JJ had never been happier.

He touched his wedding ring and twisted it around his finger. Brandon had picked it out for him shortly after the wedding, because they really hadn't done anything logically or in order. It was a simple gold band, but inside it had been engraved with *Madrid, 9.61*,

JJ's time in the one-hundred meters, because Brandon claimed that was the moment Brandon knew he loved JJ, even if he hadn't said so until they'd been home in LA for a week. Brandon's world record time had been engraved inside his own matching band.

Could JJ beat 9.61 now? He'd know in a matter of minutes.

When the time came, JJ walked out to the track. He looked up and found Brandon and his parents in the stands.

He knew he had a shot at winning this race. He'd gotten a poor lane assignment after finishing fifth in the semifinals, but he could still run this race around 9.65 if he really pushed for it, and he definitely would do that here. But it was a long shot. A swan song, maybe.

"On your marks."

That was JJ's cue. With one last glance at Brandon, he got in the blocks.

"Ready."

JJ looked down at his hands, at his wedding ring, and he knew that no matter what, everything would work out the way it was supposed to.

The gun sounded. And JJ took off.

KATE McMURRAY
HERE COMES
the FLOOD
BOOK
ONE
ELITE ATHLETES

Available Now

An Elite Athletes Novel

Two years ago, swimmer Isaac Flood hit rock bottom. His alcoholism caught up with him, landing him in jail with a DUI. After facing his demons in rehab, he's ready to get back in the pool. He stuns everyone at the US Olympic Trials, and now he's back at his fourth Olympics with something to prove.

Diver Tim Swan made headlines for snatching a surprise gold medal four years ago, and then making a viral coming-out video with his actor boyfriend, the subject of splashy tabloid headlines. Now his relationship is over and Tim just wants to focus on winning gold again, but reporters in Madrid threaten to overshadow Tim's skill on the platform.

When Isaac and Tim meet, they recognize each other as kindred spirits—they are both dodging media pressure while devoting their lives to the sports they love. As they get to know each other—and try to one-up each other with their respective medal counts—they realize they're becoming more than friends. But will the relationship burn bright for just sixteen days, or can it last past the Closing Ceremony?

www.dreamspinnerpress.com

PROLOGUE

Two years ago

Olympian Gets DUI

RALEIGH, NC, July 18—Retired Olympic swimming phenom Isaac Flood was arrested Thursday for driving under the influence after a night out at Mercury, a dance club in Raleigh. Police pulled Flood over after swerving across a yellow line. He had a blood alcohol count of 0.15, just under twice the legal limit.

Flood is one of the most decorated Olympians of all time, winning a total of nine medals in three Olympic Games. He retired two years ago, after his last Olympics, and has since cultivated a reputation as a party boy….

Olympic Diver Comes Out in Video

BOULDER, CO, August 2—Olympic gold medalist Timothy Swan announced he was gay in a video he posted on his website last night. In the video, Swan, 22, stated he's dating Patterson Wood, an actor on teen soap *Oak Hills*. "I've never been in love like this before," Swan proclaims on the video, with Wood sitting beside him….

January, this year

"WHAT THE hell was that?"

Adam stared down at Isaac as he treaded water. Isaac found Adam's stare unnerving. He was tempted to dunk his head back under to avoid it.

Instead, he grabbed the edge of the pool and kicked his legs out. "What the hell was what?"

"Your flip turns. You're doing this weird thing with your kick. I think it's slowing you down."

"Oh." Isaac tried to mentally replay what he'd done. He didn't think he'd changed his kick.

"I don't know how I never noticed it before. Have you been doing it this whole time? Jesus. Okay. So, when you flip, straighten out your legs right away to push off. None of that fluttery stuff."

"I'm doing fluttery stuff?"

Adam sighed. "Think about it this time instead of going on autopilot." He took a step back from the pool. "Do it slow so you can think it through. Don't worry about your time. I'm gonna watch on the camera, okay?" He picked up his tablet from where he'd left it on a chair near the side of the pool.

"Okay."

At the ripe old age of twenty-nine, after being out of competitive swimming for three years, Isaac's body didn't function the way it used to. In a lot of ways, swimming felt like habit, as easy as walking. But in others, it was entirely new. He couldn't just hop in a pool and swim speedy laps the way he used to. So Isaac swam slowly, mindful of his strokes. He got to the end and did the flip turn, and thought about where his legs were as he came out of it. He returned to Adam and lifted his head out of the water. "Did I fix it?" he asked.

"Yeah, that was better. But let's try it again. Get out."

Isaac pushed himself out of the pool and got back up on the block, knowing what came next. Adam said, "Do it at speed now. Same thing. Straight legs. No fluttering."

Isaac waited for Adam to get his stopwatch ready. When Adam blew his whistle, Isaac launched himself off the block. He put everything into his strokes, thought about the flip turn, came back. He grabbed the edge of the pool and looked up at Adam expectantly.

"You shaved six-tenths off your one-hundred-meter time. Do it again."

Isaac climbed out of the pool.

An hour later, once Isaac's limbs had turned completely to jelly, he was headed toward the locker room when a guy in a polo shirt snagged him. The insignia on the breast of his shirt indicated he worked for the U.S. Anti-Doping Agency.

Drug test. Great.

Not that Isaac had anything to hide. His heart rate spiked just the same.

"Test his BAC too," Adam said.

Isaac gaped at him. "Coach."

"It's for your own good."

Isaac frowned. Did Adam not trust him? "I've been sober for eleven months and eighteen days."

Adam patted Isaac's shoulder. "I know. We're going to prove it."

The anti-doping guy held up his case full of testing equipment and pointed toward the locker room. Isaac let out a sigh and followed him, resigned. This was his life now, an endless series of tests to prove that he'd dried out and gotten his shit together. No one would ever believe or trust him on that score again, which he supposed he deserved.

Luke Rogers—another swimmer Adam coached, one Isaac considered his chief competition for a spot on the Olympic team—stood near the entrance to the locker room, looking at his phone. "You see this bull-shit?" he asked.

"What bullshit?" Isaac said, scrubbing his hair with a towel, still annoyed about the test.

"That gay diver, Timmy Swan? Apparently he and the actor from that CW show got engaged."

"And I care because…?"

Luke shrugged. "I don't know. In case you thought you were the only aquatics athlete who could snag gos-sipy headlines."

"Apparently not."

"Jealous?"

"Not even a little." He pointed at the anti-doping guy. "Come on. Let's get this over with."

TIM SLID into the shimmery silk robe. It felt strange on his skin, not like the old terry cloth robe he wore at home. "Are you sure about this?"

"Of course, babe," said Pat, who wore a pair of pajama pants made from the same fabric.

Tim didn't know how to articulate how deeply uncomfortable this whole production made him. He'd never been a big fan of having his picture taken, let alone in these ridiculous clothes. And he didn't like that everyone on set was staring at him, and the whole boudoir theme made it feel like they were inviting the entire world into their bedroom. On top of that, he was missing practice—crucial with the Olympic Trials just a few months away—in order to do this dumb photo shoot.

"It's romantic!" Pat insisted.

Tim sighed. He didn't think there was anything romantic about a froufrou photo shoot for an LGBT magazine. He tugged on the cuffs of the robe. "I feel so naked."

"Really, Timmy? There are literally hundreds of photos of you on the internet wearing nothing but a tiny Speedo. You're more covered up now than you are when you compete."

Tim wanted to make an argument about context, but he knew it would be futile. "Fine. Let's get this over with."

They were on a set dressed to look like a bedroom, and everything was gray. The photographer had insisted all the gray made the bright green color of their silky pajamas pop.

"This is good visibility for us," Pat insisted, positioning himself on the bed. He motioned for Tim to sit next to him.

Tim crossed his arms over his chest. "Who cares? Whether or not people know my name won't affect my chances of winning a gold medal. It won't help me do three and a half somersaults off the platform."

Pat rolled his eyes. "Don't be a pill. Come here."

It all felt like a mistake. Just a week ago Pat had come to him with a ring box containing two platinum bands, and Tim had felt so overwhelmed by the gesture that he'd said yes. Every time he looked at the ring on his hand now, though, all he felt was uncertainty. Tim was only twenty-four. Pat was his first boyfriend. He loved Pat, but it felt like this was happening too fast. He needed more time to live his life, to work on his diving, and he wanted to do that outside of the spotlight. Marriage felt like a period at the end of a sentence Tim wasn't ready to finish—a sentence in giant type on a billboard on a major highway that everyone saw on their way to work. And now Pat wanted to do this splashy photo shoot, showing off their love to the world, but Tim only wanted to vomit.

Still, he slid onto the bed next to Pat and let Pat hug him from behind. He closed his eyes, savoring Pat's touch, his big hands, his warm skin.

Then he saw the flash from behind his eyelids.

"That's beautiful," said the photographer.

Tim barely managed to stop himself from running away.

June, two months before the Olympics

Transcript from TBC broadcast of USA Swimming Olympic Trials

DAVIS: I'LL tell you, Jim, I never expected to see Isaac Flood again, at least not in a pool.

O'TOOLE: I agree, and yet here we are. For the last eighteen months, Flood has been working with coach Adam Vreeland at the Southeast Aquatic Center in North Carolina. He's coming out of retirement, but I gotta say, he looks better than ever. His strokes are cleaner, he's in great shape. I think he's got a solid shot at making this team.

DAVIS: All right. Well, here we are at the start of the 400-meter freestyle final. There's Flood in Lane Three.

O'TOOLE: And they're off. Flood is off to a little bit of a slow start. There's Reggie Stevens in Lane Eight. He's always fast out of the gate. And then in Lane Four, right next to Flood, is Luke Rogers. Luke is the favorite to win this event at the Olympics. He's the reigning world champion and has been swimming at world-record pace all season. There, Rogers is pulling ahead. Here they are at the turn. And… Rogers is ahead with Stevens right at his tail. But look at Flood!

DAVIS: This is really a remarkable race.

O'TOOLE: Hard to say how it will shake out. These guys aren't going to put their all into it until the end. But oh, Flood is pulling ahead of Rogers. I don't believe it!

DAVIS: Fourth turn. If you see the line, you can see that Flood and Rogers are both moving ahead of the world record set by Rogers last year. I don't believe it. How great does Flood look?

O'TOOLE: It's a remarkable story. I don't believe it either.

DAVIS: Does this change the makeup of Team USA?

O'TOOLE: I think it might. I didn't think Flood had a chance, but now.... Last turn! And here's Rogers. And Flood. They're neck and neck in the last stretch. Who knew Flood could do this anymore? Rogers is in the lead, but oh my God, Flood is gaining on him again! And it's.... Flood wins the race! I don't believe it!

DAVIS: Well, there you have it. Isaac Flood is headed to his fourth Olympics. And he looks thrilled....

Transcript from the TBC broadcast of USA Diving Olympic Trials

GREGORIUS: Timothy Swan will perform a back three-and-a-half pike, an incredibly difficult dive.

MICHAELS: He's made quite a few headlines lately.

GREGORIUS: True, but not for his diving.

MICHAELS: Still, he's one of the most beautiful divers in the world. He's been doing well in international competition, but there's a lot of competition, especially from the Chinese and Mexican divers.

GREGORIUS: Do you think he can repeat his gold medal from four years ago?

MICHAELS: Not sure. He really came out of nowhere to win that gold medal. No one expected him to even be in the running. He just had a great day. It remains to be seen if lightning can strike twice. But he's my favorite of the American divers to do well in Madrid.

GREGORIUS: And he's a favorite of the tabloids too.

MICHAELS: A very public breakup will do that.

GREGORIUS: Not to mention he's one of the few out gay Olympians. That's gotta be tough for him.

MICHAELS: Let's watch him dive. And… beautiful! Just beautiful.

GREGORIUS: I only hope he can keep his personal life out of the news going into the Olympics. I'd hate to see that affect his performance. Otherwise, he's guaranteed a spot on the team….

DON'T MISS THE REST OF THE SERIES!

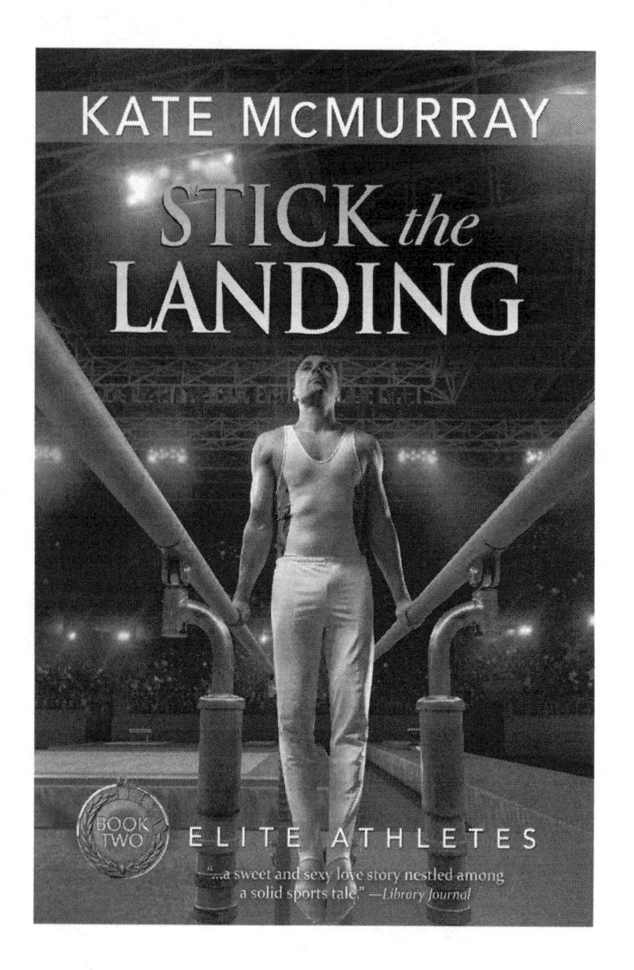

An Elite Athletes Novel

Jake Mirakovitch might be the best gymnast in the world, but there's one big problem: he chokes in international competition. The least successful of a family of world-class gymnasts, he has struggled to shake off nerves in the past. This time he's determined to bring home the gold no matter what.

Retired figure skater Topher Caldwell wants a job as a commentator for the American network that covers the Olympics, and at the Summer Olympics in Madrid, he has a chance to prove himself with a few live features. He can't afford to stumble.

Olympic victories eluded Topher, so he knows about tripping when it really counts. When he interviews Jake, the two bond over the weight of all that pressure. The flamboyant reporter attracts the kind of attention Jake—stuck in a glass closet—doesn't want, but Jake can't stay away. Topher doesn't want to jeopardize his potential new job, and fooling around with a high-profile athlete seems like a surefire way to do just that. Yet Topher can't stay away either….

www.dreamspinnerpress.com

KATE MCMURRAY writes smart romantic fiction. She likes creating stories that are brainy, funny, and, of course, sexy with regular-guy characters and urban sensibilities. She advocates for romance stories by and for everyone. When she's not writing, she edits textbooks, watches baseball, plays violin, crafts things out of yarn, and wears a lot of cute dresses. She's active in Romance Writers of America, serving for two years on the board of Rainbow Romance Writers, the LGBT romance chapter, and three—including two as president—on the board of the New York City chapter. She lives in Brooklyn, NY, with two cats and too many books.

Website: www.katemcmurray.com

Twitter: @katemcmwriter

Facebook: www.facebook.com/katemcmurraywriter